KING TOMMY

"a small dog with a big heart"

A NOVEL BASED ON A TRUE STORY

MONIQUE GOLDA NERMAN

to Zinh

KING TOMMY PRESS

Published in 2017

King Tommy Press
United Kingdom

Cover photo:
Dogma Pet Portraits. www.dogmapetportraits.com
Inside cover photos:
Farlap Photography, Devon
Monique G Nerman
Betti Colombo
Anupama Vinayak
Jan Palmer

Design Sue Snell

Printed and bound in Great Britain by Short Run Press Limited

ISBN: 978-1-5272-0292-4
www.kingtommy.org

In loving memory of my sister Marina
1962-2003

AUTHOR'S NOTE

King Tommy is the true story about the first Indian dog to ever achieve the Therapy Dog status in America. It is also the story of my sister and my dad who shortly after her death committed suicide.

At some point we have to surrender and accept the facts and not punish ourselves for the things we didn't do or could have done.

To help someone who is in deep emotional pain is difficult, sometimes impossible.

To live with the not knowing of what you could have done to save someone can destroy you. Too many days and night are spent going through events in your head without being able to change its outcome. At some point you have to make peace, in a responsible way, in a way that allows you to move on. This is the journey that interests me and this is the story I wanted to write about.

Even though most events in the book are real, I didn't have enough information about the first year of King Tommy's life so I decided to introduce a few fictional characters. I also chose to move a few continents around for my family's story, all for the flow of the story.

I have always had a strong belief in the "powers from above" and that life is to be lived to the fullest.

This novel is a tribute to my most beloved friend King Tommy and to the adventure that life is.

Totnes, Devon, January 2017
Monique G Nerman

THE BIRTH OF A KING

Francisco d' Souza, the youngest priest ever appointed to the oldest church in Mapusa is late. He has managed to get away for a quick hair cut before his first procession in this important market town starts. But Girish, the local barber, has other ideas. This young priest will have the most fashionable hairstyle in India, inspired by the latest trends in Bollywood. Girish has made it his mission Fransisco will look fabulous for his first big ceremony.

Hindu, Catholic or Muslim, it doesn't matter. A celebration is a celebration.

It's taken more than an hour and a lot of hair spray to get it right. Francisco starts to grow impatient, running through the sermon in his head to keep calm and while looking out of the window of the barber shop he sees the first drops of rain coming.

Girish laughs and points at the rain with his scissors. "She is here, she is finally here, Francisco! Monsoon has finally arrived! Now we will need more hair spray! You will look so handsome!"

Life in the small Indian state of Goa is dictated by the two seasons: the dry season and monsoon, the rainy season.

The dry season, with its cool nights, clear skies and strong sun attract tourists from all over the world. The beaches of Anjuna, Palolem and Mandrem will be crowded with people suntanning and dancing to loud music, nomads selling fruit and trinkets on the beach and bull tamers performing at the markets, showing off their animals for a rupee or two. Foreigners riding on their scooters early in the morning heading to yoga classes to stretch their sins and bodies or to hang out at cafés and discuss trivialities of life over Indian chai tea.

While the dry season lingers on, the fields will eventually turn from emerald green to dust, longing for monsoon to arrive again. The rain that everyone hoped would disappear during the previous months is by the end of the dry season a silent wish for most locals, as they shake off the dust from their saris and coconut scented hair. And when monsoon arrives in May, the tourists will be long gone and so will the nomads with their bulls and souvenirs to sell.

Francisco cannot wait any longer, he really has to go. Forgetting about time he has let himself go in the past tense of his memories. The end of season party on the beach wearing Western clothes, not his usual black robe. Dancing all night to the latest House music. It had been so much fun and no one had recognized him, the young priest from Mapusa. Clapping hands and jumping up and down with beautiful Russian and English girls. But most of all feeling the lord inside of him, shouting out with joy with all the other people on the dance floor. God really is a DJ, he smiles to himself, remembering an old hit. His eyes stare at the rain and then at his watch. Fransisco promises to drop in tomorrow to pay Girish and runs out on the street. So many people are already heading towards his church. He excuses himself as he pushes through the crowds.

This is a big celebration and everyone is dressed up, bringing gifts and prayer books to pay respects to Saint Thomas, the Apostle that brought Christianity to India.

So when the crowds hear the thunder from far away their disappointment is all too apparent. Francisco covers his hair with his bible as he takes the last few steps into the church.

Mapusa is the second largest town in Goa, compared to other towns in crowded India it's very small, but in this little state it carries a lot of importance. The Mapusa market, the bus station, the Tivim train station where travellers arrive from Mumbai, Hampi and Kerala ready for some fun or serious business. And unbeknown to outsiders it also has its share of Hindu temples and Catholic churches.

The wooden statue of Saint Thomas is being adorned with flowers inside the church and dressed with a beautiful ruby red and star clad robe. Dusted and polished it will shine with all its splendour for the faithful ones tonight.

The statue, borrowed from Old Goa for this night only is handled with the out-most care. Silence prevails as it gets prepared for the procession to come. As Francisco quickly changes into his blue robe for the procession he admires his church. White washed, with century old sculpted ornaments, simple interior decorations in wood and colourful glass mosaics.

Under the tall ceiling the helpers are sweating in the humid air. They swear silently at the distant thunder and the mosquitoes distracting them.

The men carefully place the statue of Saint Thomas on a carriage and as they all take their places to start rolling the Saint out to the crowds and start the procession, they look for their priest. They can hear him swear at the rain as he runs from his office tying a jute belt around his robe. He calls on the men and gathers them in front of him. Asks them to join him in prayer as he readjusts his hair one last time.

He blesses them and thanks them, and they all pray in unison for the rain to stop for this one evening only, thank Saint Thomas for coming to India, turning them into good Catholics and for a peaceful and prosperous year ahead. Incense is lit and placed next to the statue. And so they begin their procession and Francisco, on his first appointment as the new priest of this large congregation, leads the carriage and Saint Thomas out to the crowds.

As the faithful along the street start singing, cheering and clapping, a small, skinny and very pregnant dog tries to make her way through the streets of Mapusa.

She runs towards the crowd, as if an invisible path is drawn straight through the procession.

She runs under the cart carrying Saint Thomas, and with impeccable timing she speeds between the wheels of the cart and the legs of the helpers, coming out on the other side as Francisco momentarily stops to greet an old lady and bless her. He looks down on the dog and shushes it away with his bible scaring her away from the crowd way into the centre of the town.

She stops at the cinema where last year's hit is still playing. It stars Shahrukh Khan, the superstar of Bollywood, it's been playing for a few months now, three shows a day. All those beautiful love songs and dance routines taking the Mapusa residents far away from their simple lives to a world of castles, kings and kidnapped princesses for a few hours where they can dream themselves away to a life of riches and adventures.

Men standing outside chewing beetle nut during the interval of the film hiss at her and yell "Chelo Chelo", "Go away, get lost!" at the dog as she tries to rest under the roof of the cinema. A betel nut lands on the dog's head and again she gets scared, runs away as the men laugh.

She doesn't know this place, runs aimlessly looking for any place that will be safe to hide. She heads towards the market but where spices, exotic fruits and bright coloured fabric are sold during the day, it is now overtaken by homeless people and street dogs chasing intruders off their territory. A band of rats will happily eat any leftovers no one wants.

She can't risk the market; it isn't safe for her. What she needs is a place to rest, to hide. But not here.

If it hadn't been for the building developers who kicked her pack out of their safe and happy home far away from here she wouldn't be lost and lonely in this place full of houses, cars and humans.

Mapusa may be a small town but for a country dog it is vast, noisy and complicated.

The dog's name is Sutara, and she is an Indian Native Dog.

A dog created by God, as ancient as India's culture and made for survival and freedom. The original dog, some humans said.

Their big pointed ears that stand straight up, curled tail, long legs and the slender body is their trade mark, and man has never interfered in the ancestry. The survival of the fittest has created them and for centuries they lived side by side with the humans without being owned by anyone. They're not mongrels, they're pure and divine, and throughout India their looks are different, depending on the climate. The red haired Indian Native dogs from Orissa look like wolves, big red wolves with white faces and thick coats. Southern dogs, like Sutara, are short haired, slender and graceful.

But with the growing human population and the cities getting bigger, the Indian Native Dog has gotten in the way, losing its territories in the villages, fighting for food along with the humans and sometimes ending up living in cities sleeping on the streets and getting killed by cars or mean humans with their sticks and poison. The big city life and its squalor is not a life intended for this proud, country loving breed.

Sutara is smaller than the average Indian Native Dog; but she has a beautiful tan colour without any markings and very long legs. Big pointed ears standing straight up and green eyes. Those beautiful rare green eyes, which once shone with happiness, are now distressed and fearful.

The statue of Saint Thomas is now completely wet, his robe drenched and the men dragging the cart are slipping on the ground, struggling to pull the heavy carriage and the even heavier saint. Francisco feels sorry for them and helps them push the cart. He doesn't care anymore about his hair or his sermon, he just wants to be over with this fiasco of a procession. He decides to get everyone in to the church, yells at them to turn back and follow him back to safety under the roof of the old church.

The rain pours down harder, the thunder making itself heard over their heads deafen the singing and clapping of the crowd. All young men help to get the statue back into the church and as all the followers push each other to get inside, away from the rain, Sutara's desperate search for shelter leads her back towards the procession. Kicked around by the participants, Sutara manages to get into the church as well and hides in a corner. Francisco is livid, all this commotion and shouting, it's not how it was intended to be. His hair is a mess and now a dog is in the church as well. He needs to take control. He sees that dog is pregnant, and now he doesn't know what to do, you can't be mean to a pregnant dog. That would be a sin. But he has to get her out fast. The church is overcrowded and as the people are slowly calming down ready to continue the celebration he takes off his jute belt and chases her out through the back door. He turns around and finally they are all quiet, waiting for him to start.

He opens up his arms and he is ready.

"Dear friends, family, brothers and sisters. In the name of love and Jesus Christ we are all united tonight."

As Francisco starts a sermon that will upset the older members and get him into trouble in all of Mapusa for a long time Sutara sneaks into a side street that leads her to the poorer Hindu neighbourhood where things are almost dormant.

The thunder scares her but as the lightning occasionally lights up the street, it helps her to look for shelter.

A few dogs already live there and each one of them has a territory to protect, not allowing any other dog near it. They chase her even further until she reaches the end of the neighbourhood. Another flash of light lights up the street and steers her to a house with no fence and no dogs.

It must be the poorest house on the whole street, but it doesn't really matter to Sutara.

She sneaks into the property to have a look under the steps leading up to a porch with badly aligned planks. This will have to would do, a good hiding place for now. There's a small yard around the house, full of plastic bags and garbage. It seems like there's no electricity and the house barely stands – only a matter of time before the tin roof will break in two, leaving one side of the house held only by supporting pillars that will fall apart any day.

Sutara knows this isn't what she would want for her offspring, but it really is time and she can't keep going anymore. Her breathing slows down, her eyes continuously looking for any dangers.

She lays down. All she wants is to close her eyes and rest before she goes into labour. Disappear back to the place she used to call home and raise the puppies in a traditional way.

Sutara was born outside a small village of local coconut farmers, behind the buffalo field where a friendly pack of dogs lived in harmony with the humans, offering protection in exchange for rice, curry and the occasional piece of chicken. They would hunt rats, mice and frogs but never touch the buffaloes or the chickens. The humans would occasionally give them rice and chicken broth to make sure they would guard their homes from a distance.

As she grew up and left to find her own way in life, she had been allowed to join another group of dogs that roamed a big area not far from another small village.

They would sleep under the trees, roll themselves in mud to protect themselves from the mosquito bites in monsoon and keep their distance from the humans. Sutara had turned into an excellent hunter, and she needed nothing from the humans. Sometimes the other dogs looked for food in the villages, some of them became friendly with the humans, and some of them got hurt having rocks thrown at them or beaten with a stick. But Sutara had never been close to any human, she never became a goat herder or a guard dog, she had always been shy and loved the freedom that she had. The pack had lived there for years, mostly in harmony and happiness until one day a building developer from Mysore realized that tourists, both Indian and Western, wanted more from Goa than beaches and parties. He wanted to build "An Oasis of Zen" – a big hotel in the countryside, far away from the beaches, with air conditioned bungalows, swimming pools, and luxurious Indian dining.

"Where the best of the West meets the feast of the East!" it said on a big sign outside the village.

Bulldozers invaded Sutara's territory and the whole pack were chased off – some of the dogs had been poisoned; some beaten to death, but Sutara had managed to escape.

She ended up alone, roaming the streets, not finding a new pack that would allow her in. She had wandered far. Having lost her bearings and not knowing where she was she had ended up in Anjuna, known for once having been the Mecca of the hippie tribe that would hitch-hike from Istanbul to India. They had lived on the beaches of Anjuna, naked and happy, just hanging out. But that was then. In the last few decades it had become famous for offering the sense of freedom Westerners longed for while riding fast on their rented scooters, learning about spirituality and dancing at night under the moon.

Sutara stood by the road and the loud techno music terrified her. The music came all the way from a field up on a hill with multi coloured lights and humans jumping up and down, running around and clapping their hands. She stood there, blinded by the lights, deafened by the music, shivering with fear until a motorbike with a big blond human almost hit her and drove into the ditch. Sutara ran behind a bush and stared at the human getting up from the ditch, all bloody and screaming "This is AWESOME, man! I have just seen NIRVANA, dude!!! I am so god damn HIGH!!!"

She sneaked off and continued her search for a new place to live. Following the main road and sometimes venturing into small paths. Soon enough she ended up in Mapusa and got lost in the maze of streets in the city.

. . .

Hunger made her walk slower, sadness made her walk slower, and her pregnant state made her walk even slower.

At least now she has found a hiding place. If only her pack of dogs were here to protect her from all this evil in the world.

As the hours pass and the rain keeps pouring down, the noise of a man yelling can be heard from inside the house. He makes the thin walls shake. A woman is answering back and thumps can be heard. As time passes the woman's voice succumbs to crying, then praying.

It isn't Konkani, the Goan language, it is Marathi, the language from those who come from Maharasthra, the state north of Goa. Where Mumbai, the capital of the state spreads out and where big businesses and extreme poverty live side by side.

Sutara turns around and around trying to find a better way to lie down to make herself comfortable. She doesn't like being so close to humans. But here she is, far away from the rice fields and the coconut trees that her previous puppies had been born under.

Far away from the gentle breeze and the peace of the land.

She is in pain and the contractions start. There isn't any point trying to dig a hole, as the rain continues to pour in under the porch, through the wooden planks like a stream ending right in her hiding place.

She is shivering, lying down. She closes her eyes, feeling the life inside of her pushing and wanting out. Why, she wonders, why do they want to leave her womb and be born in this squalor? She tries to hold back, and wishes that they would all be born dead, so they wouldn't have to witness this horrible place. Her eyes open as she hears steps, sees a human walking towards the house. The old man stops outside the house and listens to the shouting and crying coming from inside. Sutara looks at him, maybe this human has seen her? But the old man swears at the people in the house fighting with each other and turns around, walks away, wet from the rain and disappointed of his apparent fear of being able to tell them to be quiet. She studies his slow pace and low shoulders walking back to his tiny house across the street.

Sutara is cold and wet; then finally, as the thunder passes and the lightning stops, allowing complete darkness and silence to prevail, the first puppy starts making its way into the world.

It's a girl, red and white. Then number two, a brown and white boy. Oh no, she thinks, not another one.

Another boy, with Sutara's tan colour and a brown patch on the back. He looks so peaceful she almost thinks he is dead. Wishes he was dead.

She looks closely at him, but he is breathing, he is alive. She sighs and starts licking the puppies, cleaning them and then curls up around them so that they can keep warm and get their first meal in this new world outside of her.

She is exhausted, but she can't fall asleep yet. It's cold and wet; the ground they lie on is a pool of wet mud.

Her only joy at this moment is that they are a small litter. Food will be hard to find, and if they all survive the night, it will be easier to keep them under control in this foreign place she knows nothing about.

She looks at them. Even if they are all so small and blind, she can tell that the third one is the one that will look very much like Sutara.

He is still only a tiny little piece of life, but Sutara knows, he will be a perfect specimen of the proud and free dogs of India.

But how will she move them and to where? This muddy ground will take lives; she is sure of it.

• • •

Sutara has just fallen asleep when she hears the front door of the house open.

She breathes softer, and looks up, seeing through the planks up to the porch.

A young woman comes out, quietly, as if she is a ghost. Her thin body is shivering and just below her eye there is a big fresh bruise.

Her black hair that was once shiny and smelling of coconut is now a tangled mess.

She is wearing a cheap sari that has faded from bright blue to grey. Once it had gold flowers printed on it, but now it is full of holes. Just like her soul. Grey and empty.

Garati's eyes have a layer of surrendering about them. Her

marriage to Tajim is making her the loneliest person in the world and when she breathes she struggles to know why she really has to breathe hope into her empty life.

A few years have passed since their wedding and Tajim drinks a lot, more than when the matchmaker had chosen him for her. He had been a perfect match. The astrologer had promised many children, a beautiful house and a blessed future in a small town in the South of India far away from Mumbai, where she had grown up. After a few months of bliss here in Mapusa, he started getting violent with his young beautiful bride, and the baby she was expecting died when he had hit her. Who could have foreseen this? Garati thinks, why couldn't the astrologer have seen this? Her parents had paid him so much money to be sure that the youngest daughter would get a better life away from Mumbai. It was all so perfect, her name, the Virtuous matched with Respect, Tajim's name. He was a bit older than her, and he bragged about his wealth and he seemed kind. Her parents were pleased and couldn't wait to marry off Garati.

Her family is far away and they haven't seen her in a long time. She misses them, and wishes she had the courage to leave, go all the four miles to the train station in Tivim, buy a ticket and take the train back to Mumbai.

In the beginning she loved going to the market, buying beautiful things, produce that was so tasty and cheaper than in Mumbai, live a better life.

It wasn't a bad catch, for a girl from her caste and family.

But then Tajim's good heart and intentions disappeared and Garati found herself stuck in the rickety house that he had lied about. When he had travelled up to Mumbai to meet her he had shown her family photos of a big house that he claimed was his. He had also shown photos of a big tourist shop in the market that he also claimed was his. He said that the occasional smell of alcohol was from his kidney problems. After a quick and small wedding, he had taken his young bride to Mapusa and she had barely unpacked her bags when he opened his bottle of Feni, the local Indian liquor made from cashew, and started drinking. In the privacy of their home he turned violent. He did have a job in a tourist shop, but soon after their wedding he got fired. The shop keeper didn't like his smelling of alcohol. Tajim didn't care, as long as he could drink and keep his job he would just answer back to the owner and say "I am a good sales person, you can't survive without me." Was that really true? the shop owner had been thinking for a while, he knew Tajim had taken a young wife, so he was trying to be patient with him. His patience came to an end when Tajim started shouting at a tourist who wanted to bargain and he hit the big German man in the head with a blinking statue of an Indian God. The German tourist had taken a nice grip around Tajim's wrist and thrown him on the ground. The other shop vendors had been laughing and the owner of the shop had given the tourist any souvenir he wanted as long as he didn't call the police. Tajim was fired and feeling ridiculed by the tall German he made sure he got back at him by breaking his wife's arm that same night.

Now and again Tajim sells cigarettes and Feni on a street corner, when he is not too drunk to be able to walk or speak, which is most days.

Garati survives and struggles on. She wonders if this is how it will be the rest of her life.

As she wipes her face to soothe the bruise with a dirty wet towel, she hears a noise. She thinks it's the rats, she is so fed up with this filthy house. The rats, as big as dogs, running in the house, in the yard, everywhere.

But it's something bigger than a rat, she can barely hear it breathing, and something moving, but not like a rat. And then a little noise, like a peep.

She looks around. Nothing. Then she looks below her and realizes that this someone or something is below her, hidden in the empty space below the steps.

She hears a quiet growl, and a licking noise.

Garati walks quietly down the steps and kneels to have a look and Sutara growls louder.

Garati smiles, she can see the whites of her eyes. From where the dog is hiding it must be a dog that just had puppies.

The rain doesn't bother her, it soothes her, makes her mind clear.

She can see Sutara lying in the mud, shivering, skinny and afraid.

Garati is curious, how many puppies could there be? What do they look like?

She smiles, gets up and goes to the back of the garden, rummages through the garbage lying around and finds an old wooden plank.

Brings it to the dog, reaches in under the porch and puts it on the ground for Sutara. Then grabs an old cloth and puts it on the wooden plank along with a dirty towel. Anything for the dogs to have a dry place. Sutara moves her puppies to the piece of wood. Tramples on the cloth and the towel, lies down on it and feels relief from the mud and the rain.

Garati smiles again and looks up to the sky. The rain gets caught in her eyelashes, she loves the way it hits her face and soothes her pain. She clutches on to her Ganesh pendant that hangs from a cheap necklace and says a prayer.

Her Ganesh, the Indian Elephant God who protects the poor and removes obstacles. Ganesh who brings luck and is kind.

She says good night to the dogs and walks quietly back into the house.

A LONELY HEART LOST AT SEA

"Karma", a ninety foot sailing yacht is making her way across the Caribbean Sea.

She is impressive, a masterpiece of a yacht that attracts attention wherever she goes. Countless are the ports where by passers have stopped and admired this expensive toy, snapping a photo of her wondering what their lives would have been like had they followed their dreams. It takes a whole lot of crew for this delivery to Mexico and as they head away from the pirate ridden coast of Haiti the wind picks up.

The crew are on night watch, one of them keeps his eye on the radar and the other one stares out into the distance, for the sign of life they are waiting for.

A container ship out at sea is heading in a straight line, a navigation route; "Karma's" route is set so that they will sail very close to each other without colliding, each on a separate linear route. Lauren has seen it before, how in a few minutes a ship that seemed very far away turned up right next to them, in a perfect line that made the two ships pass each other with only a couple of hundred yards' distance between them. The navigation lines of life, she thinks, and smiles. Once off course it all blows up in your face.

Heading forward to the bow she holds on to the railing while the waves wash over her. Her eyes looking far out into the darkness, in search for a light, a sign of life from that approaching ship.

The other watch person is shouting at her, it's too dangerous to be at the bow with the waves hitting the yacht like that. "Lauren, put that God damn life jacket on!" But she has no fear and nothing to lose; she is a sinking ship with no reason to stay afloat. When your internal compass breaks down years pass diligently disintegrating your sense of direction. You disappear from the face of the earth, flying below radar into a journey that will never take you back to who you once were.

Footprints of a face and a voice that will look familiar but never listen or speak in a similar manner again.

The yacht is sailing at top speed, asking the oncoming storm for more.

She makes her way back to the cockpit, her co-crew waving at her. "Eighteen knots! Can you believe it? Oh look, Nineteen knots!!!! This is amazing!!!!"

She checks the radar and sees the blinking red dot – and then she can see it: the big container ship pass her yacht on the starboard side, as predicted, only a few hundred yards away.

It's all so perfect, as if life is showing her that there is a way to make things work again, that lightness does exist. The sailing yacht races on, on that perfect straight line at top speed. She can hear herself breathe with suspense, excitement and something inside of her makes itself heard again.

JOIE DE VIVRE

It was all about being bigger than life itself.
Not her, but what life should be about.
It used to be like that. Do anything you want, no limits, no rules.
Life, that is.
A celebration to all the Gods and spirits and everything in between.
In this new life, the life that was not about living, but about dying slowly from inside, drenched by a sense of guilt hanging over each and every single breath, this event was somehow unexpected. It had happened in such a subtle way, refined, as if not to scare her.
Lauren who went on a whim to Asia on her own, young and curious she had sneaked into a dance hall during a harvest festival in a remote part of Laos. The incredibly loud and high pitched voice of a Luk Thung song, the Thai country music, with equally ear splitting electronic instruments playing from the Karaoke machine had her amused. The hall was full of people, mostly farmers and many were drunk. They noticed her and started to laugh at her freckles, pulled her into the hall and had her sing one of the songs with one of the local women. And then she danced and laughed. She couldn't speak Lao, they couldn't speak English. Who cares, life comes together everywhere. In Luang Prabang she had walked barefoot on the century old parquet floor of the Royal Palace. She had fallen in love with Asia that moment, the soles of her feet in direct contact with history. Buddhist temples everywhere

with the most intricate pieces of art and sculptures. Reds, gold and white, taking her mind away from everything she knew and the battered old sneakers she used to wear.

Back on a plane to California, wearing flip flops, her life would not be the same, ever again. Five years later she had a degree, determination and hard earned cash working part time jobs, she was back on a plane. This time to the city of Angels, the one on the other side of the world called Bangkok, not the one she had just left.

Jet lagged and curious, wandering in small alley ways full of children and people shouting at each other, bargaining, gambling, decorating ghost houses outside their homes. Lost and tired she followed a street dog that seemed to know his way around, taking her to where she needed to be. The Reclining Buddha. The most famous of all Buddhas.

She bought chicken from a street vendor, fed the dog and walked into the temple.

Shoes off, soles of her feet on the cold marble floor. How giant he was, and how beautiful his black eyes were. Looking at her as if holding the key to all the wisdom life had to offer, but with a vague smile implying you had to give something to get something. This giant Buddha lying down covered in gold, all of 100 feet long. The soles of his feet were made of pearl and the temple where he lived was dark red with paintings and decorations that were centuries old. His robe sculpted with movements of the sea and his neck long and regal. So many people coming to look at him, yet what a quiet place it was, everyone barefoot silently walking around him, occasionally kneeling or taking a snapshot.

Incense, Buddhist Monks in orange robes, chanting, then silence, hands in prayer pose. Sitting down on the floor in front of the Buddha.

On her right an old man with closed eyes, beads in his hands, meditating, on her left a woman painting her toe nails. The Buddhist way.

Motorbike taxis at top speed against traffic. Ten lanes, all jammed with honking cars, Tuk-tuks, the colourful Thai rickshaws and buses spewing out diesel fumes.

The motorbike taxi driver impatiently honking and then shouting "Hold on!" in Thai, full throttle towards a suicide mission at top speed in between the ten lanes, turning right in front of oncoming traffic, then under a bridge, approaching the Formula one moment.

The driver smiles: "Mai Pen Rai!" "It's OK, no problem!" and honks his way into a slalom between the lanes in one-way traffic.
The wrong way.
Bring it on life!
And a year later Lauren was back on another flight again to California, this time with a clear path in front of her.

• • •

"Karma" is moving slowly forward, past the Cayman Islands towards the Yucatan peninsula.
The wind has died down and it will be a long and hot day waiting for the wind to pick up speed.
As dawn turns into noon, Lauren can't keep calm. The memories are coming back making her feel restless. The wonderful memories of what it was like to be alive. Not dead, not like she had been for the last few years. If the memories of the good days came back, then the memories of the bad days, of what had turned her into a living ghost, would come back too. By the time they arrived in Mexico, she needed to make a choice. She didn't want to, but hiding here at the front burning up under the sun, pretending to be fixing something at the bow didn't really work for that long.
Something pinched inside herself. She sighs and looks ahead.
Dead calm.

• • •

The sun is shining in Mapusa, the storm that lasted almost seven days has passed and for the last two weeks the heat and the sun rays have been drying up the land and life is starting to return to normal in town. The children are out playing, and the street vendors are selling again; the mothers are outside washing and drying their clothes. The humidity still lies in the air and another storm and more rain will come, but not today.
Garati is in the back of the house; in her simple kitchen she is preparing food, rice, dahl and chapatis, the plain flat bread. The other day her neighbour gave her a piece of chicken; she is preparing it and puts it into a bowl with the rice. Tajim is sleeping, snoring. She hides the bowl in a cloth and sneaks out of the house.

Sutara is under the steps, wags her tail at Garati, who puts the bowl of chicken and rice next to her.

As Sutara eats, Garati looks at the puppies.

Their eyes have opened and they squint, trying to focus, or open them wide, trying to see what's around them. One of them has very special eyes, not only does he try to make eye contact with this new added sense of having a vision, it looks as if he keeps looking at her with his gold coloured eyes. He crawls and tries to stand up, takes a few wobbly steps, falls and then rolls on his stomach, looks towards Garati like he is smiling.

She thinks of what to call him, but she is afraid, in her world life and death always walk hand in hand. Better wait.

Sutara allows Garati to pick him up. She holds him close to her, caresses him and smells him. Looks into his eyes and sings in a soft low voice to him. When she holds him she feels calm.

From inside the house her husband starts yelling. Garati puts the puppy back next to his mother and hurries back into the kitchen. The neighbourhood kids sneak up to Sutara, who growls at them. Garati quickly steps outside and shouts at the kids.

They run off laughing. Garati goes back to Sutara and the puppies, to make sure everything is fine with them. Mister Badhu looks out of his house, a few doors down from Garati's house. He is the one who brought her the piece of chicken for the dog. There are enough dogs in the neighbourhood as it is, no one needs more puppies around here, but he saw how Garati snuck out in the middle of night to help the dog, and he notices how happy the dogs make her, so he tries to help.

It gives him something to be cheerful about, in his old days he doesn't have many things that make him smile. He and his wife should be enjoying a happy life at their children's homes but life has worked against them.

His son is in Dubai and never sends money as he promises. How they worked to pay for an education for him. And for what? Leave them here in this poverty all alone? He looks at Garati who has sneaked out of the house again, doting over the dog, so gentle and loving, all that fussing around for a dog. He goes up to her and greets her, Garati smiles back and thanks him for his kindness.

Oh Shiva and Laxmi, praise your names, to do so little to make someone so happy. Mister Badhu wishes that Garati was his own daughter. Such a gentle soul, but what a shame her husband is such a horrible man.

The whole neighbourhood is afraid of that evil drunk, who beats his wife and shouts at the children. If he only could tell Garati that it doesn't have to be like this, that she deserves better.

From inside Garati's house he can hear Tajim shouting at Garati again. She rushes back inside and brings Tajim his food. He yells at her, tells her that her food tastes bad, that she cooks like a Dalit, an untouchable person, and that he expects better food from her.

Well then, Mister Badhu thinks, get a proper job and help your wife. Sutara looks at Mister Badhu. He looks back her and smiles. You take care of Garati, and I will keep feeding you chicken.

Sutara has dug a big hole in the ground under the porch for the puppies. It's a good hiding place and they are safe there when she goes hunting at night. They are old enough now to leave alone for a little while now and then.

She leaves the puppies in the hiding place and goes out on the street to stretch her legs a little bit and have a look at what is going on in the street but as she trots away she turns back to look at her puppies noticing the tan one with the strange gold coloured eyes standing up to look at her.

Sutara has had several litters but no puppy had been as beautiful as her golden eyed son.

She worries about him. Will he be able to survive? He is different from all the other puppies she's had. Always so understanding with this human, the woman seemed important to him, even at this young age. From the first day he opened his eyes, he was already making eye contact, using his eyes like the humans do. She hadn't taught him that.

She knew the dangers of being too close to the humans So many dogs kept by humans were tied to a short chain under the hot sun or the rain without any food or water. They were the living ghosts, who were waiting to die. Who would never be alive, just have a heart that was beating and a soul that was dead. How those dogs would howl of fear and howl of craziness, for each day that went by their howling became more harrowing and in the end faded into a silent mumble of insanity.

Others, beaten up for no reason, left by the road to die or even poisoned, like her own pack.

She was lucky she had never stayed close to humans; afraid they would hurt her or catch her, she had never fallen for their tricks of offering food.

This human had been kind to her and had saved her puppies, but still, Sutara would keep watch in case the human changed her mind.

CHANGES

Sometimes changes come easy. All you have to do is call the Salvation Army in Santa Ana, tell them you have a whole house full of furniture and clothes and it's all theirs if they pick it up by Friday. Notarize all paperwork; sign everything off to your oldest friend. No forwarding address and no new phone number. All you need to take with you is cash, a toothbrush and your passport. Damaged goods travel lightly.

A one-way ticket out of LAX and off you go. Leave the ashes in a box at the funeral home, who cares, it's paid for.

And from then on everything has to be loud, fast and deafening so the war inside your head can't be heard. Wild parties, wild men, lots of them mixed with a whole lot of tequila and chicken buses along Mexican cliff sides.

Drinking and dancing for that pain in the chest that no one can heal. A force majeure of erasing the person you once were and desecrating all you considered holy and treasured.

And don't stop, keep moving, make sure no one gets too close.

Screw God, screw art. Screw describing what life could be if you chose light instead of darkness. Because you're there now, in that place of darkness, that place where you're at war with your whole life and all you can do now is turn up the volume and dance.

• • •

After a year of travelling from beach to beach and from party to party she had gotten tired and was broke. Landed on an island in the Eastern Caribbean. Felt lost, too organized, too clean, too friendly. Not like the other islands in this part of the world. A lot of British people would invite her over for Pimms, whatever that was. They would want to know where she lived. Nowhere. What she did. Nothing. Where her family was. In a box at the funeral home. No, she couldn't say that, so she said "Away". Where was she from? Orange County. How come her face was covered in freckles? The Scottish postman! And they all laughed. Pimms was actually a really nice fruity cocktail and the ex-pats took a liking to her.

One of them needed help to clean a sailing yacht. Scrub it, wash it, and polish it. She stayed on, the money was good and the captain figured out she had a sense of detail and no fear. He trained her to become a deck hand and Lauren noticed how her hands became damaged from pulling the ropes, from the salt and the work. It was all part of the plan. Hands full of muscles and small scars can't use small brushes and paint. Perfect. The job was tiring, tedious, made her brain stop thinking so much about not thinking. She didn't have to try so hard erasing her memory, it happened all by itself just by learning. And she thought if she got washed away in a storm and drowned she wouldn't have to keep working at dying slowly. Sadly, her balance was perfect, so that plan failed just like everything else in her life.

• • •

It had been going on for a long time now. Turn up and get some job delivering yachts for a while. Sober up, wash your hair and put on some clean clothes. Call the agency and get on a boat. Off you went. And off you left.

Across the Atlantic or Caribbean, to the Azores, or Mustique. In full sail, crossing seas, with no questions asked. Live it up and leave and on and on it went. Until "Karma".

She had returned to Saint Martin after a few months in Costa Rica. The parties on the beach were a blast and then she went into the jungle. In one of her many drunken moments, she had decided to walk alone into any old jungle and die there, either bitten by a snake or starve to death. After two days she had walked straight into a lodge, realizing she never had wondered that far into the jungle and the smell of freshly made food served to the guests made her change her mind. She dug up her dollars and paid for a room. It seemed as if whatever she was trying to do, to end her life or just rot away, there was always something at the other end to keep going no matter how hard she tried to erase herself. It was getting old. But what else was there? Lauren booked her ticket back to the Caribbean island holding a Mai Tai in one hand and covering her ear with the other one. Trying to have a conversation with a travel agent in a day time disco had its disadvantages.

She landed, checked into a cheap motel and went straight to "The Red Piano". Rum and coke and an overweight pianist playing Barry Manilow on the red grand piano in the middle of the bar, hence the name of what once had been the fanciest establishment of the island. She loved the tackiness of the place, the worn out décor giving it a sleazy but fun look, and the piano, as if the eighties had never left the place.

He was at the bar with some other guys and he had looked at her, sitting on her own by the red piano as she sang along to "Mandy" with a face so full of freckles you couldn't really make out what origin it had. Wearing a flowery shirt and some worn out jeans, typical ex-pat, he thought, definitely not a tourist. A dark tan and blonde hair that badly needed some trimming. A diver? Sailor? A wife? She didn't look like a sailor, she had fine hands with some scars on them and a strong body, but she did have that look of someone who was looking at the world from the outside, not living in it; and there it was, hiding it all with a smile and a laugh to the pianist hitting a bad note. Looking into her glass and then catching him looking at her. Looking back at him without embarrassment, without shyness. Beautiful eyes, beautiful everything, like a scruffy unpolished diamond.

He had been there on a holiday with his friends. They were all behaving like frat boys, just too old for it, and kept toasting to his return to the big company after a year of absence.

"Hey, bro, we got you back man! Adam, come here, let me give you a big hug, bro!" Unheard of in his field, but he had to do it, leave everything to gain something. In what seemed to be a celebration of reconnecting he went up to her and she smiled at him. He invited her to join his group, reluctantly she had yes. There had been something in his look; it was that look of kindness and sincerity that didn't fit in with the rest of his friends. As the night went on his friends bragged about his accomplishments and about his crazy mind. To prove a point, he had resigned from his job as some corporate hotshot. He had lost control, he said. He needed to know who he was. He went to El Salvador and joined a co-operative of poor farmers. "Best thing I ever did". In six months he organized their co-op into a profitable business, and in return the farmers laughed with him as he had to learn to work with his hands in the field. "My hands that once could only tap on computers and point at people were now digging the earth and loading trays on carts. Can you believe that?" Yes, she could and she looked at her hands, wondering if they remembered anything about her former life.

When his time was up the farmers bought him a fancy Ranchero hat, a white cow-boy hat. "It's my most treasured belonging. I'm Adam, by the way."

"So you're the new Oscar Romero of Silicon Valley now?" She said and it startled him. The smirk, the defence, but he also knew that anyone who knew about Oscar Romero was someone who had a soft heart.

"Yes, I am starting the Liberation Theology software company as we speak."

"No Nobel peace prize for poor Oscar. So, seriously, you think you can just go back and everything will be the same?"

No, it never is. He would start a program where the company he worked for donated money for education and have internships for the working poor. Mentoring, sponsoring. There it was again. Options and helping others.

"Well, I am sure you will look very handsome in your suit and tie in your office on Wall Street. You should probably get a haircut and a manicure before you show up for work on Monday." She had said drily and he had laughed at her.

Their conversations took unexpected turns and went to places Lauren loved, to let thoughts and ideas develop as you go along and piece them together throughout the night. She had paused, decided to open her eyes again and look properly and listen to this man who had found his way in life. It was a long time ago, the intention of seeing, of liking, instead of using and not caring. He had not asked her where she was from and he had not asked her about her past. He had gotten to know her by talking about the Met, and how her eyes lit up when describing Van Gogh, or that painting by Rousseau with the lion. And she listened to him when he told her about how he discovered the world through the simple life of the farmers or by going to the church in San Salvador where Romero had been killed. Central America and violence. And on they talked until he built up the courage to touch her freckles, something he had wanted to do all night, and then he had touched her lips with his fingertips. And before he had kissed her, something he had wanted to do all night as well, he really had wanted to hug her and just take her into his life and take her with him, there and then, but mostly just hold her for a really long time. But she didn't really seem the hugging type and she seemed to have so many protective layers, it wasn't caution, it was something else he couldn't figure out. So he just touched her carefully and reached closer to her and kissed her.

At the touch of his lips and staying with it the feeling of belonging with another person again made itself clear and present. That closeness to someone else that only happens a few times in our lifetime, she had left and walked away.

He had touched something in her that was for no one to go near. The living dead don't like to be awakened, and they are comfortable in their place of regret and anger and the fear of causing more harm. Better shut it down, better stay in the land of nothing. Better move on and pretend that nothing can ever change.

As the sun was coming up she sat in her room waiting for the crew agency's office to open so that she could ask to be put on the first boat out of the island.

And off she sailed. "Karma", a magnificent sailing yacht worth a fortune, was off to Mexico, a long delivery taking her far away from Saint Martin and whatever his name was.

As they left the island and started heading out to sea, dolphins danced and jumped in front of the boat, the sea was so clear and she sat on the bow and looked at the perfect timing of the dolphins. From way below the surface, swimming fast in front of the yacht, they jumped up in front of her, to dive down underwater again, surfing along the yacht with a baby dolphin in the front protected by the school.

She looked at them with joy, but when one of the dolphins jumped high enough to touch her toes, the tears came unannounced.

THE STORM THAT KILLS

The occasional rain comes and goes, but the sun has been kind to Sutara in the last few weeks. The puppies are growing and Sutara looks at them all with pride. The little red and white girl is big, and tells her brothers off all the time. The brown boy is very shy and stays close to his mother all the time. Then there is the golden eyed puppy, who is getting more handsome by the day. He walks tall and proud, and looks at the world with interest. Anything that goes on in front of the house fascinates him. Whether it's the children playing or Garati doting on him. It's as if he takes notes on the world, to be able to create his own version of what the world needs from him as he grows up.

All of them are very attentive to their mother, and it's only at night when Tajim is far away that Sutara can leave them in their hiding place to go out hunting and roaming the streets.

The original hole she had dug for them a while ago has become bigger, as the puppies have grown. She has also dug it quite deep, so that they are all well-hidden when she leaves them on their own. Lately she has been able to go further away at night, stay out longer and hunt with a few neighbourhood dogs. Knowing the puppies are safe in the hiding hole, she has been able to get to know the area better, so that one day, when it's time to leave, they will know which way to go.

Sutara is on the outskirts of the Hindu neighbourhood, outside a shack someone has left a big piece of chicken. She has just picked it up and sneaked away with it when she hears the sound of thunder. Things change quickly in monsoon, and as she looks up to the sky and sees the first lightning she starts running back towards the house. The storm that drowns is approaching fast, navigating slowly and thoroughly towards Mapusa.

It starts raining hard and almost as if out of spite, it stops above Garati's house and decides to hit it with its strongest downpour. Sutara runs as fast as she can, worried about her puppies.

She tries to remember the short cuts that will make her journey back quicker.

The hiding hole that Sutara has dug to hide her puppies during the night is now turning into a death trap.

The rain has made the hiding place fill up with water. The puppies have been trying to crawl out, just to fall back in again, not strong enough yet to hold on to the edge. If one of them manages to hold on, the other one crawls on top of him, panicking and barely breathing, the puppies trample and push each other further down into the water and mud again until they run out of strength. They can hear their mother arrive and they can hear her start digging, thinking it will let the water out, but instead the hole gets filled with more water, more mud. Sutara tries lifting them up, but they keep falling back down into the hole, deeper and deeper. Their little nostrils are getting blocked with mud and rain and life will be soon sucked out of them. In the end they start sinking and she can't see them anymore.

Sutara runs up to the door, barks, scratches on the door, howls. Garati opens the door, smiles at Sutara. "No Dog! You cannot come inside. You have to go back to your babies!" She closes the door, Sutara barks, scratches harder. Jumps on the door.

Garati opens the door again, Sutara runs to the puppies.

Garati can see the state of desperation in the dog's eyes and follows her down the steps, Sutara pulls Garati's sari, leading her to the puppies.

Garati doesn't understand, she kneels down and shouts at Sutara when she licks her face and then barks and barks. Garati still can't see. Sutara runs into her hiding place and starts digging again, whining and crying.

Garati gasps, kicks the wooden planks so that she can lean in and
see the hole full of water and mud.

She puts her hand in the hole. Gets one puppy out, then another
one. Sutara wags her tail in excitement and barks as if telling her
"Find him, please find him."

She digs deeper with her hands, and then finds him. He is not moving.
Garati yells at him to wake up, she yells at Ganesh, asking the God
for help, but no one seems to hear her. She picks up the puppies
and takes them up to the porch.

Sutara is right next to her as Garati gets a towel. Sutara is pushing
the puppies with her nose, trying to make them move. Garati
wraps the puppies in the towel to dry them then opens their
mouths, blows air into their nostrils, massages the hearts, the bodies.
Opens their mouths to get mud out, to see if there is any sign of life.
Sutara is quiet, whimpers.

Garati keeps blowing air into the nostrils for life to return to
Sutara's offspring.

She thinks about the baby she lost and what she could have done
to prevent it from dying in her womb. She works frenetically with
the puppies. She can't let Sutara down, or herself, not this time
and not again. It is the golden eyed puppy who starts to breathe
on his own. He starts coughing and wheezing, spitting out mud
and water. She runs into her house to get another towel and wraps
him in and holds him close to her chest to keep him warm.

With the other hand she wraps the other puppies in the used towel
and silently says a prayer while she closes their eyes. She holds
them to Sutara, so she can say good bye. Sutara keeps licking them
and pushing them with her nose, but Garati tells her to stop.

"They are dead, Dog Mother, they are dead."

She lets Sutara lick the golden eyed puppy dry, and then lies him
down on the ground next to her.

That night Sutara and the puppy stay on the porch. Garati takes
the two dead puppies, walks out in the storm and buries them in
a ditch. She returns and stays with Sutara all night, making sure
that the golden eyed puppy stays alive.

As the first sunlight comes up Garati wakes up, she has been sleeping
holding the puppy in her arms so that Sutara can get some rest.

Sutara is curled up next to her, her head resting on Garati's lap.

Garati strokes her head. "I am so sorry Dog. But we must think
about this little one now. He is all we have left."

For the first time in her life, Sutara allows a human to touch her, to let a two legged animal become her friend.

Garati gets up gets a shovel and fills the hiding hole with dirt. She gets a coconut and puts it in the hole so that no more death can happen.

She tells Sutara to leave the porch and carries the puppy back to the hiding place.

Tajim staggers back to the house as Garati cleans up, removing the towels and sweeping off all the mud and sadness.

Tajim barely makes it up the four steps to the porch where he grunts and lies down, and falls asleep snoring loudly.

Sutara keeps her golden eyed son next to her. He has stopped coughing, but he is weak and not eating properly.

She needs to make him strong quickly. The human has to help her with food now, she cannot leave him alone again.

• • •

And as that same grief stricken sun is rising half way across the world, Mexico and the shores of the Yucatan peninsula become visible.

It's a flat landscape, mangroves and beaches, as far as their eyes can see. "Karma" is approaching the coast line.

Lighthouses giving signals of red and green, it's almost day light and the turquoise waters are clear and magnificent. All the crew is up on deck, taking in the view of this sunrise. From far away they can make out the silhouette of Tulum, the ancient Mayan ruin that lies just above the sea.

Lauren is standing with the rest of the crew looking at the sunrise. They are all silent, admiring the coast line and the red sun turning slowly into daylight.

It's the last day, all that is left to do is find the marina, clean up the yacht and that's it. As they sail into the marina, the Mexicans on the dock stand gathered in admiration of the big sailing yacht and try to help the crew by shouting, pointing and waving, especially at the female crew members.

All clear. It's 10 am and the lines are tied, engines off, champagne uncorked, time to celebrate.

Lauren goes into her cabin and starts packing.

She takes her bag and with a glass of champagne walks off the dock, out of the marina, following a dirt path to nowhere.

Standing alongside the road, she waits for a bus, her passport ready to be used again.

* * *

The birthday of Lord Ganesh is in full swing. It's the most important festival for the Hindus of Goa. In the centre of the town people are gathering to go to the river and place clay statues of Ganesh in the river for prosperity and good fortune for the coming year. Young men and children are throwing fire crackers and on the main square a big set of fireworks are waiting to be launched later on in the day.

Sutara and the golden eyed puppy are on the street outside the house. The puppy is playing with a rag, Sutara protecting her only offspring. Overprotecting would be a better word.

Doting, following, curled up close to him at all times. Tajim is walking up the street on his way home. He is drunk, as usual and walks with unsteady feet, yelling at a neighbour, and continues towards the gate. He has firecrackers, lights them and throws them at houses, at by-passers, at anything.

Sutara can see him, smell him. Smell the firecrackers.

She goes to her son, pushes him into their hiding place, and stands in front of it, creating a shield between them.

Tajim stands there, staring at Sutara. Lights up a firecracker and throws it at her. Sutara jumps away from the firecracker, sneaks up to Tajim, growls at him.

Tajim laughs, walks in to the house.

He stumbles on the porch and then calls Garati.

He keeps calling her, not by her first name, and not the way a loving Tajim should call his wife. From inside you can hear him calling her "You whore! You stole all my money, all the cigarettes got drenched in the rain and that is your fault! All of Mapusa hates you and you should watch yourself showing your face around!"

On it goes, followed by thumping, by cries and by things breaking in the house.

Then it all goes quiet.

Garati walks out of the house, blood on her shirt, her eye is sore and her lip is broken. She goes to the back of the house and hides; she wants to be alone in her desperation.

The golden eyed puppy follows her. Observing her when she cries. Without hesitation he walks up to her and stands right next to her. Not wanting attention or affection, he just stands next to her and looks straight into her eyes, in a calm and comforting way.

Garati puts her hand on his back. He doesn't move, doesn't wag his tail.

With Garati's hand on his back he looks away and closes his eyes. He is focusing on Garati's hand, he can feel her pulse slowing down, her hand getting heavier, accepting his comfort, aimed at Garati and only her.

Garati stops crying and starts feeling better, as if the puppy's attention makes her forget how cruel life can be.

They are in the back of the house, alone, in silence.

The golden eyed puppy opens his eyes again, looking into Garati's soul. It's as if he is smiling at her, telling her everything is going to be better.

Garati dries her tears, smiles at him and tells him things in her language that he doesn't yet understand.

She kisses his forehead, and stands up.

There's a small plastic cover hidden in the back of the house, and Garati removes it to look at her Ganesh made of clay. She has been hiding it from Tajim and can't wait until she can bring it to the river and immerse it with all the other people and eat good Prasadam, the sweets and food that are offered after the ceremony. She knows that she should be in the temple worshipping right now but she is afraid to leave the house for too long, so she makes her own temple in the back yard. The puppy sits with Garati as she is praying in front of the clay statue of the elephant faced God.

Sutara has been watching them from a distance. She sees Tajim, on the porch. She runs quickly to her son, and forces him to run back under the porch with her.

Tajim is standing there, staring at her and her puppy.

It will be time to leave soon, before bad things happen.

Whatever her son is doing to the woman to make her happy she doesn't care, they have to leave and she has to take her golden eyed son away from this house. Only a couple more weeks, maybe more, to make sure he is healthy and strong enough. She has been too soft on him; he is already at that age when he should be moving into the world on his own but she hasn't been teaching him the important things in life. She has to start now, before they leave.

He has put on weight and looks stronger, but it's taking too long, everything is taking too long, Sutara sighs, and prays that they will be safe here for a little while longer.

Garati hides the clay statue away back under the plastic cover. She washes herself, changes her clothes and feels stronger.

As she soaks the bloodied shirt she knows that she has to change, to be stronger, and to protect the golden eyed puppy. Tajim comes out of the house, he sees Sutara standing there, again. Wherever he looks there's that dog and that ugly puppy that his wife is so obsessed about. He has seen how his wife has given them chicken, but him, oh no, only dal and rice, curry and vegetables. She has been doting on that disgusting dog and he is sick of it. He is teaching her to be a good wife, to obey him and make him happy, but no, oh no, it's just that stupid dog. His wife will learn, if not the nice way then the right way. When Garati goes out to the street to get some Prasadam from the neighbour he goes to have a look under the plastic cover and breaks the clay deity into pieces.

FAMILY TREE

It came and went like wave formations. Three waves, then a break, and then again. A long painful waiting game for that tsunami that would eventually break down the few remaining streams of hope. Lauren watched the waves and the blips, the ebb and flow of the breathing being hooked up to the monitor. End of life. The doctors wouldn't say, and Lauren refused to believe it when visiting a body that was technically dead but for the sake of a possible miracle kept alive by machines. She would sit next to her big sister, Heather, and think back at TV shows with families who could talk to each other and have fun together, share secrets and solve problems together. Did they really exist beyond the silver screen? And she would look at Heather, pray for her, for things to change when the monitors would give the go-ahead and everything would be fine.

Beautiful Heather. Or at least she had been once upon a time. Tall and blonde, a typical California girl. She looked like a model and told people that's what she was. Heather had an attitude that would make people back off, but never forget her. Spoiled, loud and fun, she knew no limits. She had never learned them. Border-line, a word that was used to classify someone who was lost, overly sensitive with emotional roller coasters. To Lauren it meant having gone from too much love to none at all, it also meant finding solace in addiction. Borderline, not like Madonna's song, but just a meaningless word to justify the pain done to a soul.

Had it really been the diagnosed illness or the addiction, or just the way you become when you've had too much freedom when the only love you know is taken away from you? When you sit in silence in front of bleeping monitors you've got time to think.

Heather was ten years older than Lauren, and so tall that little, freckle-faced Lauren could hide behind her. And she did. Heather had a high-school sweetheart named Scott who was always by her side. Heather and Scott would take Lauren along with them, stuffing her in the back seat of Scott's Mustang. He had bought the car for Heather, borrowing money from his parents. It was metallic blue, just like Heather wanted. They would head off to a party to get high and drunk. With no mother around and a father who was never that present, it was easy for the two sisters to disappear, to be free to do whatever they wanted. Lauren would hang out with Heather and Scott amidst the dope fumes and lines of coke. When there was no pop to drink, someone would hand Lauren a glass of wine or vodka, saying, "The kid needs a drink." When school let out and her classmates went off to play sports or do homework, Lauren got in the back of the Mustang and off they would go, to Los Angeles, San Diego, Palm Springs. Heather hated their neighbourhood and their entire county. "Orange County sucks," she would say, laughing, and tell Scott to get on to the 405 and hit the road.

They had friends everywhere, and they stayed anywhere they pleased. Lauren might fall asleep on the Persian rug in someone's home in Beverly Hills, or wake up in a waterbed in Melrose, picked up the basics about photography by attending a photo shoot that Heather modelled in. At another party she sat on a rapper's lap all night. He called her Little Sista, and told her that her freckles were her true colours. Heather took Lauren to his studio when he recorded his first hit. She clapped her hands with the other musicians and the rapper pulled her blonde hair as he rapped. As a favour to Heather he had Lauren's name in the credits as "freckly hand clapper".

Heather was everything Lauren wasn't and worshipped the ground her sister walked on until the day the ground gave way under her feet. They were at a party in Manhattan Beach. Scott had been gone for a few days and Heather was heartbroken and terrified. She couldn't find him or reach him. When he finally got in touch with her, he told her he was getting out and getting clean. She was either in or out, but he was going to college and he was going to get straight. He'd had enough and wanted to do something real with his life, not just depend on invites all the time. And he had told her what no one had ever told her before, that she could be something or someone that mattered. Heather was crying, shivering and the host told her to get inside, calm down but instead she tried to jump off the balcony. Lauren held on to her and begged her not to, only to be kicked in the face. Heather went into a rage at her stupid, ugly little freckle-faced sister telling her what not to do. She kicked Lauren again, harder this time, and made another attempt to jump, only to be pulled back onto the balcony by someone else who told her that everything was going to be fine. Heather knew it wasn't, so she jumped.

It was only ten feet off the ground, but it was enough of a fall to do some damage that would never heal. Heather's head was hurting, her leg was hurting and her arm was hurting. But nothing hurt as much as being left alone once again. Lauren ran down to help her big sister, but Heather pushed her away and left the party with a limp and a bleeding head, telling Lauren to wait there, that she would be back. Heather never came back, and the host of the party ended up driving Lauren home the next day.

After Heather disappeared, their father showed up at the house. He looked gloomy, and there was a layer of sadness and defeat over his eyes. He seemed disturbed and distant, but it wasn't over the fact that Heather was out there somewhere, alone and injured, but rather over life in general. He cursed the state of the house yet again and brought in a cleaner. "Your sister is supposed to help you with your homework. Look at this. C's and D's? You're the smart one, how can this happen? Your great-grandfather travelled all the way from Switzerland, poor and hungry, and arrived in this country without a penny! He started up his business. And look at what he made of himself! A businessman, a successful man. I am still paying for this house and you two are making a mess out of it!"

And then he poured himself a scotch and turned on the TV. End of conversation. Another scotch. Lauren learned to decipher his slurs, and as an adult she could understand any drunk she met in her life in what seemed to be an incomprehensible conversation.

Whenever her father came to the house, he would only stay in the living room, never go upstairs, and sleep in a hotel.

Lauren saw him as a stranger, a man that showed up from time to time. She didn't really know where he went or what he did. But he had lived here once, and there had been a family at some point, or why else would she be here?

• • •

Bleeping monitors in front of her, a body that once was wild and free. But no way to fix things while they were happening. Not like in the TV shows with all those clever families.

With her dad a comment about a car or an actress on a TV show could mean something completely different. It was Lauren's task to decipher her father's messages through a remote control. One night, a specific comment made about a volunteer rescuing rhinos in Africa set Lauren off. Her dad had made some comments on how the Rhino was happier in a park in South Africa than living free, and he had looked at her with a strange smile. Alarm bells went off inside of Lauren, but she had nowhere to run to, nowhere to hide. A few days later Lauren was put on a plane with her dad next to her. They landed and this woman met them at the terminal. She had a daughter too, the same age as Lauren, and she had a puppy. "Your dad gave it to me."

Every day Lauren asked about Heather, and every day she was told to do her homework, which she didn't. She wrote to Heather every week, and the letters were never answered. Finally, she gave up and retreated to an imaginary world that took her far away from where she was, became obsessed with maps and foreign lands, places where life was sweet and full of joy. Her dad and his new family, another TV-show that seemed to work really well for everyone except for Lauren. If Heather could only get as far as the neighbouring counties, then Lauren was set on going much farther. At 18, she was allowed to return home. No one drove her to the airport, her dad was away and the new family was breaking up. Not that Lauren cared; she couldn't wait to get on that plane back to California.

Scott stood there, waiting for her at LAX with his Mustang and took her to a beach club to celebrate her eighteenth birthday. Loud music and dancing but this time without drugs and without confusion. And without Heather. She was the little sister he'd never had and that bond had remained. Whatever Scott could never do for Heather he made up for it by helping Lauren and he made a promise to her that evening that he would always be there for her. He dropped Lauren off at the house.

It was with a completely different set of eyes she opened the front door and took a few hesitant steps into the living room.

It smelled of sadness. An empty glass of Scotch was left on a table. She noticed for the first time nothing had changed since she was a little girl. It was as though the house had fallen into a catatonic state and didn't want to be woken up.

Now it was clear, as she opened the doors of all the rooms in the big house, that time had clearly stopped at some point, and that she had grown up in this time warp.

She went to her old room, looked under the bed and found an old school bag. It was yellow and worn out. She remembered her first day of school, and then the person that had chosen the bag for her. A woman with brown hair and a frail body that smelled of hospital. She looked inside the bag and found a school report and a note to the parents. Lauren carried the bag with her as she walked around the house. She didn't know what to look for, but something had triggered her memory. It was the first day of school. It hadn't been that woman who had taken Lauren to school, it had been Heather. But then they had driven to a hospital and Lauren had shown off the school bag and all the new books and pens to the woman lying in the bed. She could barely smile or talk, and Lauren had been scared. It had been the smell, a thick smell of medicine, and whenever the woman opened her mouth to try to speak, or to breathe, it revealed a yellow, fungus-like infection on her tongue.

Lauren had stared. The woman had freckles too, and wore a head scarf. Then the woman in the scarf was gone, and no one ever talked about her again. Lauren couldn't remember her voice, or what she had been like. She couldn't remember her ever having been in this house. But she must have been?

Lauren went into what once had been her parents' bedroom. A large poster of Bob Marley had replaced an expensive painting that used to hang above the bed. Heather, Lauren sighed. She opened the wardrobe and looked through the pile of old clothes, for something she knew should still be there. Under some old shoe boxes, in a small plastic bag, she found the head scarf. Clinging to it were some brown hairs, hairs that had fallen off during the woman's illness.

Lauren stared at the strands of hair in the Hermes scarf and it suddenly came back to her. Her dad coming home one day, sitting on the bed with this scarf, staring at it for days in the solitude of his bedroom. Lauren folded the scarf and put it back in the plastic bag, making sure it went back under the shoe box at the bottom of the wardrobe. She closed the door to the only memory she had of a mother.

She walked outside, leaving the doors open to let some air in, and went to the garage, hoping to find old boxes, old memories, but there were none. She returned to the house and went upstairs to the guest room. Opened the closet door and found nothing. Then she looked under the bed, and found the photo albums. There was her family. Her mother in fancy dresses and at garden parties, with Heather at her side. Earlier photos taken on her parents' honeymoon, her father looking so happy and handsome with his blond hair and strong body. Photos taken in Europe, in Switzerland, in some old village. It must have been the village his family came from. Her mother in a wooden boat on a lake somewhere, with an Italian flag in the background. Her father, sober and loving, holding his wife's hand. The happy couple moving into their house, this house, and a moving truck.

Heather as a baby, with her parents holding her and kissing her. Her dad in a car with Heather on his lap. The proudest dad in the world. Heather dressed up for school, for tennis lessons, for pony rides and her first day at camp. The woman crying, waving goodbye to Heather. More photos of another trip to Switzerland. Heather older, around fourteen, in a beautiful flowered dress, holding the hand of a little freckle-faced girl, dressed similarly to Heather. In the background, the famous water fountain on Lake Geneva. Another photo of the two sisters, in front of the entrance to Disneyland. And then a family photo in a restaurant by a beach, with the woman in the Hermes scarf, holding Lauren in her lap, hugging her tightly. And then it ended. All that was left were empty album pages and dust.

Lauren put the albums away. In her sleep, her dreams took her to the safety of travels to foreign lands.

• • •

That memory of a man sitting on his bed holding a Hermes scarf and then disappearing for good, did that really happen? It did, she remembers it because it was the day when everything changed. Going through the photos again her memory became clearer, of a man she didn't know, a loving man who sang to her and read her bed time stories and of Heather being happiest girl in the world. Then it all changed. Overnight the man became pale, as if his love and commitment stayed with the scarf. He had walked out of the bedroom and never been the same again. Heather had been seventeen, he had given her a check, to cash in and buy food and pay a lady that would drop in a few hours every week to help them clean and cook. And then he left.

Heather had stood there alone with her grief and her mother gone. Lauren watched how Heather took that first step out of the house on her own and then it didn't take long before Scott became her only anchor and the Mustang her vessel.

The next time her dad showed up his smell had changed. From always wearing expensive eau de toilette that would fill up a whole room and charm ladies he would now have a different smell. He showed up one day at the house, with a rental and an angry look on his face. Lauren hadn't recognized him and when she did she didn't care. She barely knew who this man was anymore and when he took her with him to live with his new family she had never once looked him in the eyes. A puppy for his new perfect step daughter?

She remembered how one time on one of his visits he was shouting at Heather. "I can't look at you." It had been the only time Lauren had ever seen her tough big sister go quiet, like it hit her hard. In times of grief and despair, no one knows what things really mean. What he meant had been "I can't look at you because you look exactly like your mother." Heather took it all in and shut it down deep in that vault of anger and loneliness only Lauren knew she possessed and walked out into the night not to be seen for another week.

Once her father had left Heather was back and things went back to normal. Back in the Mustang, taking Lauren on the road trip of her life and protecting her from the mean kids at school who bullied her for her freckles.

"Remember, those freckles are a map of the world, little girl, so it's your destiny to go and find out about that world. And those losers, they don't have a world; they don't have anything that you have. Remember that, little thing. Now, get in, we have places to go. One day, you will have your own places to go to and it will be a great path you will walk on,"
And she did travel when she got older. The more Lauren travelled the more she believed that Heather could be saved. She had seen it, the magic, the miracle, the hope of life in the most desperate places.

• • •

 Lauren was eighteen and two weeks old and hadn't seen her older sister since the fall from the balcony. Three years had passed and she finally stood there, in front of her house, waiting with excitement to see her big sister again.
It took a few weeks to track her down. She lived in LA with her friends, whatever that meant. When she finally found out the exact address Lauren knocked on the door to an apartment in Victor Heights and Heather opened the door. They looked at each other and Heather said "Now it's your turn to deal with Dad, he won't send me anymore checks, you have to talk him, man." Her skin was pale, her eyes were dull and she wasn't beautiful anymore. Lauren took a step forward to give her a hug and Heather quickly took a step back to grab her bag telling her: "You've got money? Of course you've got money, dad's leaving everything to you, isn't he? Let's go out. Let's have fun, like the old days!"
Lauren followed her, Heather walking quickly, frantic. "No, not here, I owe them, let's go there, that's a good place. You paying right?" Heather with her hollow eyes. She never finished her food, complaining about her teeth, about her dad, about life. Lauren tried to stay in her conversation as something in her changed. Instead of being angry of disappointed with her she clung on, because the sadness that overwhelmed Lauren was so deep, and she couldn't understand how things could be so bad and how things could go so wrong.
She gave her money and her new number, but just like before, Heather never called.

• • •

Alone over Christmas in the big house and Scott in Santa Barbara for the holidays. On Boxing Day, she got in the car and drove up to LA, to find Heather. She was outside, sitting on a lounge chair. She barely recognized Lauren and in silence they sat next to each other. Lauren handed her a present. Heather opened it slowly. "Thanks little Sis, what a nice painting, did you do it?" Lauren nodded. "One day you'll be famous and I can sell it and make lots of money." Lauren smiles. "I signed it, made it for you. Made a studio at home. The living room is one big workshop! I'm going to art school in the fall." Lauren replied reaching for Heather's hand, and her sister took her hand away, as if on reflex. "Both of us are on a journey, little sister. It's your time to shine now. "Lauren so wanted to tell her that she was the talented one. That it was supposed to be Heather who went to college, who got a degree and married that hot guy. That it was always Heather who was the intelligent one. Not her. Not that Lauren ever knew what talent Heather possessed except partying and telling Scott where to take them. But it didn't matter. It was Heather that counted, not her. "You wanna come home for a while?" Heather smiled at Lauren and looked away from her and closed her eyes.

·   ·   ·

As the years passed the visits became tedious, hopeless, boring. But Lauren would never fail Heather. Even when moving away she still drove down twice a month to see her, to try and help her. Bringing leaflets, invitations, hope and ideas on how to get Heather to become a whole person again. She so wanted her to be happy and not lose this battle she had never asked to fight. Lauren had a good life in Santa Barbara, not too close, not too far away. Scott was happily married and Lauren rented a small cabin not far from Scott's house. Lauren wanted everything small and easy. All she needed to do was to lock the door and leave, go travelling whenever she needed to which was more often than not. She had been working on a theme for years, finding that inner perfect stillness and paint it with excitement, as if every brush stroke could get Heather's attention and wake her up, give her hope. Liking a solitary life and having Scott nearby to help her get a name she had become a bit of a celebrity up in Santa Barbara, with her freckles, her mismatched clothes and scruffy blonde hair. Some people called her "Uber cool" and invited her to all the parties, where she showed up wearing flip flops. She had exhibitions and was making money. But what mattered to her was to have her phone with her at all times waiting for that emergency call to go off and rescue Heather somewhere. She'd done it all: Emergency rooms, malls and friend's houses. But at some point it all started to take off for Lauren. Finally, after ten years of work, a celebrity had bought one of her paintings, a beautiful phtalo blue "ocean of hope", as it was called. She didn't want to sell it as she had made it for Heather, but Scott convinced her to do it and then the newspapers started writing about her. The rap star who once had her on his lap called and bought a few pieces. He had invited her to New York to meet some buyers when the call came. They were all having dinner at Balthazar's when she excused herself, she had to leave. There was an emergency, she really had to go.

• • •

Tubes, machines, bleeping sounds and monitors, again sitting here next to her, with her closed eyes and the feeling of sitting next to a dead body kept alive by science and doctors. She found it hard touching her, because she knew Heather didn't like it, so she would talk to her, every day, tell her what a beautiful person she was, how everything would be better once she got well again. Tell her about her travels and of the people she met, the places she saw, and the magic in life what would save her and make everything right one day. Make Heather wake up and want to be that person again. The person Lauren had been painting for so many years, in that place of finding life instead of leaving life behind.

Days became a week and another week and Lauren was the middle-man, trying to protect her big sister by having to make decisions about things she knew very little of. Wear sterile protection, a mask and gloves, a hairnet. Listen to the tubes forcing Heather to breathe, stare at the feeding tubes. Back again the next day, to go through once more the not doing enough, not being there enough leading it all to this.

It was starting to sink in, there wasn't going to be a future for Heather, just a final week or two and the magic and Gods that make everything right, where had they gone?

On what was to be the last week she would just sit next to her in silence and look at her, her eyes, her hair, sometimes tell a joke about when they used to be younger and life used to be easy riding a Mustang and go where ever they pleased.

"Heather, did you hear the rain?"

The organs were giving up, every day a different one played up but Lauren didn't care. She started talking again to Heather, telling her that everything would be fine, that she was going to make it, that life would be different from now on. No more suffering. But Heather remained silent.

The final call came at early in the morning. Her dad had finally showed up. She woke him up and they drove to the hospital. Then were told to wait.

A bleeding in a place doctors couldn't reach. Cardiac arrest. And there you are in front of her, and she looks peaceful, as if she finally has found the way home.

All the hurt Heather accumulated throughout her life was finally gone. Silence and no tubes, no machines. No more noises to inflict more pain.

Lauren takes her hand and holds it for a long time.

• • •

They hadn't said a word on the way home, they were not looking at each other, not a tear from any of them.

Lauren drove up to the house and got out, leaving her dad alone in the car.

She took her keys out, unlocked the door, put her bag on the floor and sat down with her hands on her lap.

He came in and looked at her, trying for words that he couldn't really phrase.

"She called me. About six months ago. The doctor said that if she didn't get clean immediately, she would die within a year. It was the pills, you know.

I picked her up, took her home, tried to help her. We went to the hospital together, meetings. And then she left again. She couldn't do it."

"She called you? Why not me?"

"She called me sometimes, you know."

"Why didn't you call me?"

It had been Heather who had known about his secret, how he had called her the times sadness had turned to desperation. It had started after the girl with a puppy, after Lauren had left and moved away.

There had been attempts, last minute calls and negotiations where Heather had talked him out of it. Sometimes it had worked, sometimes she'd had to call 911 and send someone else to talk to him or to save him against his will. Lauren had never known. To her he was a slob, a foreigner in her life, a stranger who couldn't care less. An alcoholic. He had liked it that way, had been easier to hide the truth from her that way. Sometimes failure and sadness looks better in disguise.

"I couldn't afford you losing all you'd worked for. It was your life! And there you were, in New York! In Chelsea! With all those famous people buying your art! I couldn't have her interfere. You had managed to move on. You had your life."

"And Heather? What about her? Why didn't she tell me, or call me? I could have tried, you know, to find alternatives, to try again. My talent is pretty useless, if it means letting someone die. What a horrible thing to have, a talent that allows people to die."

"It's not like that – "

"She could have been alive today."

"Don't you understand that it wouldn't have made any difference? But you.... you were the brave one, no matter what. Heather, she was ..."

"Heather has been hurting since she was seventeen and we never did enough for her. You just left her there all alone, just like that. Like something that was not necessary anymore."

"It was never like that....Heather... "

"Say it."

And Lauren went silent. He went silent and closed his eyes. The TV show that Lauren had wondered about for so many years was finally in her own living room now, it just sounded different.

"You don't have worry about my talent anymore. I am done with talent. I am done with everything. What about Heather and what she could have become? Did you ever think about that? What her life might have been? All you cared about was that you could get away."

"I loved your mother so much. And I loved Heather too, so much."

"Well, love didn't save someone today."

Lauren looked at her dad, this stranger that had sat down on the couch with his hands nervously looking for the remote. His eyes not looking at hers and a darkness around him that scared her. Tears. With the remote safely in his hands he turned on the TV, some mind numbing channel that created harmony in the room, eliminated the silence between them. She took a breath, reached out to him to touch his hand, but at that same moment he reached for something in his pocket and she took her hand back. A small container with pills in it. Lauren walked out of the house, got in the car, drove off and didn't stop until she was far away. She checked into a motel. Turned on the TV and sat alone in that room for two days.

• • •

Lauren's dad looked at his youngest daughter walk out of the house, walk through the garden and get in the car, drive off and not look back.

He leaned back, closed his eyes and tiredness kicked in. Like so many times before he held on to his pills wondering when the right time would be to take them and finish it all off. He had tried before but never succeeded but today it felt like the one time he would do it right. There was no one to call and no need any more to keep pretending.

He had failed with everything and hoped that he could do this one thing right.

I AM THE KING OF THE WORLD

"It's all happening, man! It's all happening! The spirit of Shiva and all the Tantric forces running through my veins! I am feeling it!" Standing way up, at the top of the hills of Ubud, Jerome lifts his arms above the rice fields, the water in them like mirrors reflecting the sun's rays. He also stands tall above the traditional village famous for its Balinese art and eclectic group of foreigners who live there. High up where he looked down at the resorts with their bamboo bungalows and swimming pools and above the jungle and all the people of Bali, the Hindu island of Indonesia. Its fairy tale stories full of magic, with beautiful women dancing temple dances in their colourful dresses, where religion dominates every aspect of life, where the hills and the green colours of the island blind you with its beauty. Jerome breathes in and as he breathes out he lets out a roar, like the newly appointed Tarzan of the island, and then smiles, laughs.

Everyone else involved in the upcoming festival is working hard to get the tent ready, preparing food and decorating the festival area for the opening.

But not Jerome. Jerome is focusing on, well, Jerome.

He has been chosen to perform the opening ceremony for the "The Awakening Festival", a world famous event that attracts yogis from all over the world.

All those years of hard work, teaching Yoga, year in and year out, and now this. Talk about standing on top of the world. His voice, his teaching, him and only all of him, here at this festival! Jerome and Sky, his teaching partner, had proposed a dance ritual with Shamanic influences and mantra meditation – and Ganges, the director of the festival, who once in a life far away from here and now was baptised Renato, had loved the idea. So radical and fresh. This would be a great opening, something people would really talk about.

They would all see and be so impressed. And then from here, Jerome thought, America would be the next step.

He would change his name too, like Ganges did. Go to America and blow everyone's mind away. The dream is here ready to turn into a fabulous reality. Finally.

He sits down in the Lotus position, taki

ng in all this positive energy.

Finally, he was almost chanting. Fi-na-lly. "Oh so beautiful it is here, so incredibly beautiful. The most beautiful place in the world." He is thinking as he hears his name, and knows she has come to look for him.

"Jerome, you should come and help. It is an important part of the ritual"

"I am preparing myself for tomorrow night, the energy of this valley has such a dominant force to it. That's what I am doing now. Absorbing it. Channelling it"

"And what about this night?"

"Mayuko, you know, this is maybe not the right thing."

"Jerome, the tent will be blessed tonight by the Balinese Spirit Man, can you imagine any purer place to be than under that blessed roof? Save a little channelling for me, pretty please!"

Mayuko, the wife of Ganges, looks at Jerome, teasing him with a kiss on his neck as Jerome tries to meditate. "We shall be blessed under the tent Mayuko-san, I promise you it will be the night of nights." As she leaves him alone on the top of the hill he keeps chanting, softly, and smiles again.

Below down in the valley, the participants and organizers of the festival are erecting the main tent. In a few hours the Balinese Spirit Man will arrive and perform the purification ritual. Ganges walks around the grounds, proud with the way things look and quite pleased with this year's line-up. He is taking a risk this time, with all the new workshops, it makes him nervous and worried about money and the reputation of the festival. What Ganges at this very moment really needs is to calm his nerves with is his beloved Genoese focaccia. Sometimes he misses it so badly he flies to Singapore just for one day, just to hurry from the airport down to Orchard Street and walks the five blocks to the "Bar e Calcio", a small Italian café just to have his beloved focaccia. With a fresh copy of the La Gazzetta dello Sport, his favourite sports newspaper, and the freshly baked focaccia specially made for him and fresh out of the oven on his arrival, he eats so much of it he is ready to burst. Barely able to walk he then drags himself back to the airport with the last flight going back to Bali and feels whole again. "Santo cielo, I should have asked the boys to fly some focaccia over, that's what I should have done."

New faces, new teachers and new workshops. Will it work? He is especially looking forward to see what Sky will bring to the Festival. Talk about alternative – now she is doing Reiki on a chair – oh please, Lord Buddha, why can't people just teach Yoga anymore? "Those were the days" he thinks, "when we would just gather in a park or on a beach, with shabby old clothes and just do yoga. How everything changes. Maybe I am getting old." He smiles as he looks at Sky, she has been so helpful all day and he instantly loved her warm energy and her childlike friendliness. Her teaching partner however, that Jerome, not so sure. His touchy feely attitude to all the girls, standing so close to them he can touch their breasts with his chest and the way he walks around like a testosterone filled monkey. Jerome's talk about love here and love there and the "aching frustration that needs to be let out: let the sixth chakra blossom". Ganges just wants to throw up. And that stupid over practiced Indian and American accent, trying to sound like a guru on steroids.

Oh well, as long as they pull off the opening night. This Sky however, with that beautiful black hair and an enthusiasm that never seems to fade, he likes her and her unusual teaching style and how she adds cosmic ways into it. So Goa, so now. As Ganges stands next to Sky he can smell her hair and her skin has a scent of an ayurvedic oil he really likes, what was it called again? Sky talks to him, explains her vision to him. She is on a "war against the tenseness in the spine." she claims, and Ganges nods, looks around, wondering where his wife could be.

Sky tells Ganges about the Gurus and teachers she has been studying with, all those workshops in Europe and India she has attended.

Ganges smiles at her and says "Where there is peace and meditation, there is neither anxiety nor doubt".

Sky laughs "Om Shanti! How true! Is that Osho or Davinda Sinti? Oh, wait, no, I know. It's Ama!"

"No, it's Saint Francis of Assisi. 12th hundred century."

Ganges tells her "Shanti Om" and walks through the grounds towards the festival tent, standing there, ready to be blessed. He knows that it will be a good, no, a great festival this year. He is sure of it. "Oh Bali, beloved Bali. My home and destiny, my beehive of happiness." he hums along as the Spirit Man arrives with his entourage of young Balinese women.

Ganges calls all the teachers and volunteers, inviting them to form a circle in the tent.

The Spirit Man walks with a cane and limps to the middle of the tent. He slowly hums a soft song in ancient Balinese and the rest of the group stands with their eyes closed, holding their hands. Mayuko is late, she sneaks into the tent, and takes her place next to her husband with an apologetic smile.

Only Jerome is missing.

The young women are lighting incense and spreading flowers all over the floor of the tent.

From corner to corner the Spirit Man walks, with his eyes closed and holding on to one of the young Balinese girls for support. Praying and singing, walking around the group with his incense and blessing all the teachers. He moves quietly and one can barely hear him. He then moves to the middle of the tent letting the incense form patterns of smoke. Sky is mesmerized by this quiet man, by the lack of dramatics and the quietness of the ritual. It's as if everyone is absorbed into this tranquillity and state of mind that is bigger than themselves.

All-Divine. That's what she will call this. An all-divine state of mind.

The ceremony finishes with everyone sitting on the floor and the Balinese women throwing flowers all over the teachers.

Ganges gets up, thanks the Spirit Man and ushers everyone out.

As the last person gets out of the tent, it stands empty, purified and ready for a week of intense yoga and music. No one is to enter until the opening tomorrow evening.

● ● ●

During the night Ganges cannot sleep, his beautiful young wife is not next to him, she must be out having fun with the other teachers and her friends. He goes through the running order one more time of the events, of the budget, of tickets sold. His mind needs to rest but it keeps drifting off to his beautiful tent. He walks out of his Balinese house, where his collection of philosophy books and the LP's with his favourite Italian music is his most valued treasure and walks up the path to the tent. It's quiet, everyone seems to be asleep. He tip toes towards the tent, not wanting to be found out. He stands there, in the darkness, looking at the tent, admiring it. Ganges loves it and finally manages to think about the upcoming festival without worrying too much. He knows no one can be in it until the opening ceremony, but he can't help himself, he just wants to have a look at it, just by himself. He has planned this event for a whole year and he wants a little glimpse of the beauty of it all before it all begins.

He looks around; making sure no one is around and then sneaks in quietly.

As he takes his first step into the tent, he hears noise from inside. Confused, he slowly pulls the curtains that leads into the big open yoga platform. With the new moon as a faint spotlight he witnesses his wife and that moron Jerome naked on the yoga stage doing some pretty advanced Tantra lovemaking.

Mayuko with Jerome.

In his purified tent. His labour of love. This cannot be.

From far away, all the way up on the hills of Ubud, the sounds of a man yelling and shouting can be heard. Vague foreign words such as "Brutto bastardo! Io ti ammazzo adesso, hai rovinato tutto, coglione!" and "You are a fake, you long haired monkey faced loser, get out and never show your face on this island again – or I'll have you castrated!"

Sobs of a man crying and begging, soft words of "I am following my faith offering myself as a servant to The Divine" A thump. A woman's voice screaming. Blood and tears.

A whole community wakes up, restless voices, upset dialogues, someone packing his carefully chosen wardrobe in the middle of the night and the noise of little wheels attached to a cheap suitcase against the gravel as it leaves the grounds of the festival.

Someone with that same suitcase and wheels dragging it along the road to Ubud looking for somewhere to stay in the middle of the night. Paying for the room, dragging the suitcase up a small bamboo staircase and then standing by the window waiting for his friend to show up. Hours turn into days and she never shows up.

Jerome sits on his bed looking out of the window. No America. No fame and glory. No Sky.

He stretches his beautiful body. As a young boy he had been selected to become a gymnast, in what was then Eastern Germany. He was of Olympic material.

He trained and trained, stretched and stretched. Eating in a canteen where cockroaches ran around, going to the Academy on cold winter days, along Karl Marx Strasse in Berlin dreaming of seeing the world. He did see the Soviet Union world. He competed and won the junior championships in Odessa; the Bulgarian Friendship games and the Rumanian Communist Games.

Then the final selection for the Olympics came. He had just won the National Championships and he was ready. But his head was getting too big. At the official selection training camp, all the participants were interviewed. The jurors greeted him and he smiled with all the confidence he had. They asked him about his motive, about his goals. Jerome explained his technical achievements and on a personal note, he added: "I can't wait to see the real world! And then we take America! Oh, wonderful America!" The room turned uncomfortably silent. He was told he must have been misinformed. America wasn't the real world; America was the enemy. Jerome started stammering, sweating profusely, conscious of the biggest mistake he will ever make. Excusing himself for getting carried away asking for forgiveness and trying to take his words back he was asked to leave the room. The jury closed the door and Jerome stood outside, left alone in the cold with his dreams and ambitions.

Branded as a traitor to his country, he was asked to pack his bags and leave. End of a short but brilliant career.

His punishment was worse than going to jail, at least for an athlete who had never spent much time behind a desk. Typing school. All day long he had to sit and listen to how to type, how to file, how to be a good party member. He spent hours on end in front of an old typing machine, in front of a bunch of useless papers, asked to find the mistakes in the accounts. Jerome wanted to die. His back was killing him from the lack of exercise, his mind was rotting. After three years of waking up every day to this tedious monotony, he thought it couldn't get worse. But it did. They told him to show up for work the next day at the surage treatment offices in Berlin. Typing and counting. His back so stiff he could barely sit straight. So ashamed of what had become of him, he could barely look up at people when being spoken to. Days turned into years, and Jerome was contemplating either ending his life or try to escape to the West. If he got shot while jumping the wall at least he didn't have to commit suicide. So he couldn't really fail. Twenty years old and already at the stage of life where everything is only a grey fog of sadness. But then history helped him along the way.

The wall came down and his curtain of depression finally fell.

That famous night when it all happened he stood there with all the other East Germans of Berlin staring at the event in disbelief. Spotlights, loud music, people with hammers knocking down the wall. Someone yelled at him from the wall, told him to join them. He realized that it was all over, that he would be free. He got up on that wall, danced with the West, in front of all the television cameras, partying all night. The next day he packed his bags and left for West Berlin not once looking back, ready for a taste of the new world.

Thanks to his clerical past he got a job managing a building that had a yoga school in the basement. It was full of beautiful women and yoga was something he had never heard of. They never paid their rent on time. As a way to make him go gently with the overdue rent Jerome was invited to come and join the yoga classes for free. He could feel, while doing the yoga poses, that his back was feeling better. He was talented and understood movement. The women swarmed around this tall East German man with the bad back and an uncanny way of getting back into shape. They offered to train him to become a yoga teacher, and Jerome, once again, left his job and never looked back. He devoured this new knowledge brought to his life with the same appetite he tasted western women, western music, western clothes and foreign food and drinks. He travelled to Rome, to London and to Paris. He learned so much about Hinduism, Ghandi, India and Buddhism. He loved this new world full of colours and with such diverse

Gods. Finally, after a few years he bought a one-way ticket to New Delhi.

Expecting India to be as cosy and welcoming as the yoga school in Berlin, he sat in the rickshaw on his way into the enormous city appalled by the chaos, the heat, the smog, the traffic and the crowds. He freaked out – all the tales he had listened to, the gold, the temples, the inner peace and the holiness of the Indians – where was it? He got absorbed into the culture shock, struggled to walk on the streets, being trampled on by Holy Cows chewing plastic bags and street dogs barking at him, men following him offering great deals on hashish, fake emeralds and fortune tellers. Beggars on the street pulled at his clothes as he tried to figure out where he was. In the madness of New Delhi, he managed to find his way to the train station and head down towards Kerala on a third class ticket. Startled and overwhelmed he found his carriage and seat on the over-crowded train. He was on the verge of a claustrophobic attack as one of the passengers put her two kids on his lap. He sat next to a big family that giggled at his long hair and tight jeans. The children took turns screaming and pulling his hair as the wife cooked food in the train compartment. The smell of mutton was heavy, and despite the windows being open, it laid itself like thick fog for the whole trip. He was offered food from the family, and couldn't refuse such a kind act from a Muslim family that obviously wasn't wealthy. The spices in the mutton curry made him sick and he spent the most of the two-day train ride in a toilet that hadn't been cleaned in a decade.

He counted the minutes until the train would arrive in Cochin, and as his guts made a sound that would have scared off any thief at night, the train stopped for several hours for reasons unknown. No one seemed to care except for Jerome. The Muslim family prayed on their prayer mats and ate more mutton. Vendors and beggars got on and off the train. Jerome was hyperventilating, panicking, wondering when the night mare would be over. No one knew where they were, no one knew when the train would get to Cochin. Someone told him that maybe it was his bad karma that had created the delay. Jerome was ready to punch the guy.

Then the train started moving again, slowly, and slowly it approached Cochin with a twelve-hour delay. Jerome staggered off the train, got pushed by a porter and fell to his knees on the

platform. He couldn't move anymore. He closed his eyes, feeling lost and tired. A guard came up to him, "No begging here". "I am not begging; I just need to rest. I can't take this anymore."
The guard grabbed him by his shirt and helped him up. "Wait Madam. I will bring you some chai tea." Oh yes, his long beautiful blond hair. Thank you India. The guard came back as promised with the best tasting chai in the whole world and led Jerome to the Ladies waiting area. He held Jerome as he helped him sit down on a wooden bench and as the guard looked at his hairy arms and big hands, he realized his mistake. Jerome could never imagine any tea would taste this heavenly. It was a milk tea with spices and a lot of sugar. He drank it slowly, and for each sip he managed to recover his strength. He looked at the other women in the waiting room, as they all whispered and giggled at him and the guard. He smiled at the women, leaned his head on the guard and fell asleep.

• • •

Ashram time. Meditation and strict vows of chastity and selfless work. From the temple of Ama, the hugging Goddess, to the Sivananda yoga school and various other ashrams Jerome found his faith in India again. His deep faith for Hinduism grew, it all made sense to him, the order of the universe, the law of Karma and the strict rules of Yoga, the whole eight limbs of it. And he also understood that the strictness of the faith also had space for the laughter and love from the hugging goddess Ama. You could travel in Hinduism with your mind on so many different levels, as many as the reincarnations of your past and future. He loved the beautiful temples and the vegetarian Indian food. His stomach got used to the spices and soon he would be able to eat from any food stall and impress the Indians with his tolerance for any curry served in front of him. He went to Mysore, the city of Ashtanga yoga, and it was like landing in paradise. Beautiful women from all over the world united in this place of yoga and Jerome's proud posture, long hair and athletic body was as attractive as the Taj Mahal to many female travellers. He spent most of his yogic energy in the bedroom, and rarely got up on time for the early morning yoga lessons. His strict vows and chastity flew out of the window, it was time for fun again.

And then it was time for a different taste of India. Goa. He was starting to run out of money and he was tired of travelling. "Templed out", as the travellers would say.

Beach bars and sun tanning, all night parties and a changing community. The old hippie scene that had given Goa its fame and glory was going through a face lift. People were opening yoga schools, health food places, fasting clinics and all different types of workshops he had never heard of.

He got a job as a yoga teacher and quickly figured out what students liked to hear and learn. His English got better and better, no thanks to various American beauties that passed through his life. One day he met Sky, who had landed in Goa after training in England with this new yoga style and needed help to get established. Jerome's teaching method was starting to get a bit old. People wanted more, they wanted yoga to be their therapy, to unblock their inhibitions, to make them happy. Sky could bring new visions in and Jerome cultivate the yoga traditions. They started teaching together and they became quickly popular.

Sky was fun, she would make people dance and do funny sounds to some ancient yoga pose, she would make people laugh and call everyone Goddesses, and everyone wanted to sign up for all their classes. Jerome was good looking, great at adjusting students when they were learning new poses, at showing how to do a perfect downward dog and led the classes whilst letting Sky have her new ideas pop in and out of the class.

They had been a team for almost a decade, and throughout the years Jerome rarely left Asia. His childhood dream of America had made itself heard again in the last few years as Sky was planning to get them workshops in other countries, and Bali would have been their ticket to Los Angeles. And now it stood there laughing right back at him. Jerome yelled back at his dream to go and get lost, waving goodbye once again to America.

He took a taxi to the airport and went back to Goa to start all over again.

• • •

It's either go to the left, down towards Belize and Guatemala on a bus or go right and to the airport. She throws a coin in the air and lets it land on the ground. Airport. Sipping her champagne, she stands there, by the dusty road, waiting. On the bus she finishes the drink and when she arrives to the airport she goes to the nearest bar and orders another round of champagne. They pour it in the glass she is carrying and then she goes to the board announcing the departing flights.

Stands there, with her champagne and looks at the destinations.

Cancun offers a multitude of destinations, all she has to do is to pick one and go.

She buys her ticket, gets on the plane and falls asleep all the way to Lima. It's a bumpy landing and as the brakes of the plane makes a screeching noise she looks out of the window, not remembering where she is. All that she knows is that the feeling of restlessness is growing; it's just that she doesn't know what to do next so she does what she knows best. Gets further away, gets on another flight. Lands in Cusco, way up in the Andes. It's been three years now and it can't go on like this, the restlessness inside keeps telling her.

She gets a room at a guest house and then walks up a hill and stands there staring out. No more sea, just solid mountains and a bunch of llamas staring at her with their big long ears and their fluffy woollen coat waiting for the right moment to spit at her in the face. She is trying to figure out what made her come here. Her internal compass keeps failing her, knowing it's somewhere else she should be.

One of the llamas look into Lauren's eyes, walks up to her and spits right in her face. Not a fan of llamas from now on. Not fluffy and cute.

The llama smiles and walks away. Lauren shouts at the llama, and a few tourists standing not far away have been taking photos, laughing.

Keep moving, keep going until you find the right place.

Train station, another ticket, another destination.

The train is about to leave and she runs on the platform and makes it just in time.

There is something wrong here. She looks at the ticket, and the train. This can't be right. How can a country change this much in fifteen years?

Where were the chickens running around on the train? The broken windows and the unusable toilets? Where were all the olive skinned women in their striped shawls and bowler hats, speaking Quetchua, selling tamales, the local corn snack?

Why was everyone sitting on a seat each? What happened to overcrowded trains and the Mormons trying to give you their bibles and impress you with their white shirts and Wal-Mart ties? Air-con? Numbered seats? The train conductor is sober and speaks English, wears a clean uniform and has polished nails.

It had been such a blast, that's why she decided to come back. Fifteen years ago the train conductor had been drunk and fell asleep on Lauren's lap, making the locals laugh when she had drawn a Hitler moustache on the sleepy train conductor and written "Para alquilar"- "For rent" on his forehead. Another traveller on the train had taken photos and the local people thought it was hilarious. The drunken conductor eventually woke up, still smelling of cheap alcohol and staggered around shouting at the passengers as they all laughed at him. One of the local ladies, who had managed to get a goat on the train, looked at her and said "Tu tienes muchas ganas de vivir". "You have a strong desire to live."

Lauren sighs. She had. She is breathing slower now, as the shiny brand new train where chickens and goats are not welcome makes its way alongside the river Urubamba towards the once hidden site of Machu Pichu without any stops or delays.

Final destination Aguas Calientes. She tries to locate familiar faces or people in the little village by the river.

As she checks into an overpriced guest house she thinks about the photos on that train ride. She puts her bag down on the hard mattress and a cockroach runs across the room. What was her name, the girl she had met on the train? And where were those photos? Lauren thinks.

It's almost sunset and she goes up to where the hot springs used to be, or at least where she remembered them to be.

For each step up she sees the face of that person clearer inside her head.

Oh, not another upgraded effort to modernize the world. A fancy entrance with another set of uniforms and clean floors. It used to be free back then, OK so not that clean and without changing rooms but it feels as if the charm of the place has been replaced with a nice fat entrance fee. She changes her clothes and gets into the pool. Aguas Calientes means hot springs, and here she was again, on the top of the Andes in a bubbling pool as the sun says farewell.

She leans back and closes her eyes. Everyone has left and she is the only one left in the bubbling pool.

Again she tries to remember her name.

She opened her eyes again, looked up to the sky. That's it, Sky. How stupid.

Sky who wanted to become a Yoga teacher, who always talked about the Universe. "Ask the Universe for money, honey!" What had happened to her?

The silhouette of the Andes against the royal blue sky was fascinating, those round shaped peaks in a dark shade of emerald. The stars so visible and shiny this high up in the world. So much closer to the sky and the stars, making you believe that prayers and wishes would actually be heard.

 Sky, who had been teaching in a school for homeless kids in Nicaragua. What had happened to her dreams? She had moved to India, but was she still there?

"I am so in the wrong place." She sighs, gets up and wonders what time the next train leaves to take her out of here. This is the past, let's move on, as Heather would have said and again she is on the phone to a travel agent to book another flight. She recognizes the phone box and another memory sneaks back. A phone call from Aguas Calientes to Heather, her voice, happy and determined for a change. She had joined a weekly group that would help her with her recovery, she had liked them and all was great. Lauren telling her the usual adventures, this time it was her and Sky walking along the rail way track on their way to Machu Pichu and when they were in a tunnel they were sure they were being attacked by rebels. They ran and yelled for help. Turns out it had only been rats chasing them in the tunnel. Hearing Heather laugh, Lauren smiles, what a rare treat.

TEQUILA BOOM BOOM

Get off the plane, check into a cheap motel, go to a bar.
It's only noon, but things in Cancun start early.
Strawberry Margarita. What now. Where now.
Change, you say, just change, but you're back where you started.
Exactly here, at this bar exactly three years ago, when you first
left. Change.
The crushed ice with the tequila and synthetic strawberries soothes
the mind.
It was on the plane ride back to Cancun that things started escalating.
Choices and change all sound good on paper, but when you stand
there and don't know how and where to start, the old ways and
the old memories want you to stay back, they want you in that
comfortable bubble, in the dark where the lack of momentum
keeps you numb and in control.
It's the having to deal with it, to lay down your arms and surrender
to the stages of grief that will set you free. You have to go through
the defeat, the acceptance. Or you can keep pretending. Up to you.
But at some point you have to start looking at the bigger picture.
You have to dig deep and answer the questions and eventually accept
that you can't be responsible for everyone's destiny. You have to
try to do your best, and live with the fact that maybe not everyone
will make the choice you consider being the right one.

The dark side of death is that the pain needs to control you, to let you disappear into the state of grief. You have to stay there, and wonder alongside the dead ones in their parallel journey of passing on. You, here on planet earth, in that cloud of non-existence. In that middle land where everything is unimportant and where you feel like you wander through life like nothing exists or matters. Them, alongside you watching you from above, guiding you through the ritual of grief.

You try and try, and you lose yourself, because addiction is a selfish friend, and suicide is a private pact a person makes with himself.

But when you get struck by an overdose and a suicide a few days apart, the guilt doubles up and pain cannot be managed without mental morphine. You have to shut the system down until you are ready to confront yourself with the grief that doesn't require questions or blame.

You are not dead inside, it's just time out, if that's what you choose. Stop running and start over and be kinder to yourself. Yeah right, Lauren laughs, self-help amateur hour at its best and takes another soothing sip.

•   •   •

It all comes together at last, at the biggest night club in Cancun called "El Universo Mundial", to the tunes of the latest Latin hit, the reggaeton sensation "Boom Boom te vuelvo Loca!"

With a couple of guys on holiday from Mexico City she is on the dance floor dancing with her arms up, hips moving and hands clapping to the rhythm. Painted on the ceiling is a map of the world and psychedelic coloured spotlights go from right to left and round and round all over the world. Lauren is looking at the spotlights as she dances. Then all the spotlights go to one place and stop, illuminating Mother India. Flashing in pink, green and red. India is calling Lauren. The East is calling her. Ghandi, here we come! Get that spinning wheel running again! She yells out to the Mexicans, who can't hear her for the music, but they understand it's important, and anything important needs another Margarita. They all toast and celebrate, excited about the American woman's new found mission. Whatever it is, it has to be good.

She salutes this new adventure to come and passes out on a couch in the night club like any other American tourist would do at four am.

CASUALTY

Garati is at the market in Mapusa. It's a beautiful sunny day and she is so happy. The golden eyed puppy is growing and for each day he looks stronger and more beautiful. He looks after Garati, makes sure that she is not too sad, he always runs to her when he sees her with his ears folded back and his whole body shaking from the tail wagging at full speed. She smiles to herself as she thinks about him, and sees a nice piece of chicken that she will buy for him.

 She sees this bright red pillow, and thinks how nice it would be for Sutara to have something to lie on. Garati chooses the pillow with care. To make sure it's comfortable and the fabric strong enough to resist the outdoor and the dust. A couple of tourists are standing next to her, looking at the pillows and fabrics the stall has to sell. Garati thinks how nice it would be to have a stall here and make pillows and blankets for the tourists. Learn to speak English so that she could talk to the tourists and ask them about their lives. She loves coming to the market to look at them and how different they are from her. But when she smiles at them, and they smile back at her, she thinks maybe they are not that different. How she would like to know what the food is like in their markets, if their food stalls are like here, and what they do to with their lives. Garati pays for the pillow and returns to her own reality, thinks about how much these dogs have changed her life. They depend on her, she has saved them.

But most of all, they have seen that she is a good person. They can see right through her, they don't make fun of her, like some of her neighbours, or think of her being stupid because she is illiterate. The dogs understand who she is and they thanked her and cherished her for her efforts. She feels protected by them.

With them there she is not afraid to go home. It's a nice feeling to feel protected by the ones you love.

• • •

Sutara and her son are sitting on the steps of the house, enjoying the late afternoon sun. A motorbike drives by and the puppy and Sutara chase it, then trot happily back to the house. They sit down on the steps again.

The local kids walk by. The puppy gets up again and runs up to them, playfully barking at them and playing with them.

Sutara has a plan, in the next few days they will leave and her son will have to find his own way, eventually. She will help him find a good territory, maybe closer to the beaches where the tourists are, there is more food there, but also bigger packs of dogs to be aware of, but she will teach him how to behave with them, to find a small pack of dogs where he will find his place and new territory. She wants her son to be a country dog, to find happiness in nature, not on this street full of humans. They must leave this place. Sutara is thankful to Garati, and she is first human that she has ever gotten to know.

But their life is somewhere else and they have to leave before the puppy gets too attached.

She enjoys watching the kids play with her son, and he is playing with them, not letting them get too close, but running around them and letting the kids chase him.

Loud music is being played inside the house.

Tajim is singing to the tunes of "Om Shanti Om", his words are slurring and he is shouting out the words. Om Shanti Om, the purest words are being turned into a vulgar angry ranting. He is in the kitchen; a big pot is on the fire, with water in it just about ready to boil.

He keeps shouting as if talking to himself, but then takes the radio and throws it out of the window. He swears and an empty bottle of Feni is being chucked out of the house too. Followed by the kind of laughter only a person with a mean spirited heart has.

Tajim takes the big pot of boiling water out with him. It's very heavy, and he tries to be careful not to spill any of it on him and walks with the big pot down the steps and slowly out to the street where the two dogs are. Sutara growls at him, and starts backing away from him and the pot.

Tajim is big and angry, his smell and anger are warning signs.

Just for once he manages to move silently, allowing Sutara to make a bad judgement for her retreat. Tajim smiles at Sutara. "Finally, you filthy dog, I got you, and you are not smarter than me. You are not more important than me! I am the man of this house, you stupid bitch!"

Tajim lifts up the pot and throws the boiling water on her face.

Sutara is blinded as her eyes are being burnt with the rest of her face.

Her pain is the pain of death, and as she shrieks out to the world, crying for help Tajim then moves towards the puppy, who is heading towards his mother. He throws the rest of the boiling water on his back.

"You filthy dog. I hate you and you are going to die."

The puppy doesn't understand where the pain is coming from; it feels as if his skin will burn up, running down the street, screaming in agony, calling his mother.

In this little life of his, he has been protected from evil until now. His eyes are red, the coat on his back is now red skin that oozes. He tries to run away from the pain, but it is stuck on his back and hurts so much he doesn't know what to do.

Tajim throws the pot away and takes a big stick and walks down the street.

Sutara has managed to stagger away from him with the pain making her whole body spasm, blinded, and eventually has to lie down, ready to die.

If she only had left this place earlier. She should never have gotten comfortable with the human. This is all her fault. The golden eyed puppy runs up to her, screaming. He wants to be protected and he needs his mother.

It's a terrifying sound that make most of the neighbours on the street come out and watch.

The children are crying, watching Sutara and her son in the middle of the street awaiting their death sentence. Sutara has nothing more to give, the pain is overtaking her and death will be a welcomed relief.

She cannot see, cannot hear, but can feel him standing right next to her.

Her wonderful offspring, her beloved son with his soft heart. And the last thought is that is that he will not be weak, that he will get away from here. That he will find safety and make her proud.

She takes her last breaths as she is in that place of smelling him, touching him and sleeping next to him.

His small soft paw playfully touching her nose, her whiskers.

Lying together under the coconut trees in the safety of the country side.

The wonderful smell of his paw. Her son.

She wants to be with her son forever.

As Tajim is coming up to Sutara, ready to beat her with the stick, Mister Badhu, who has been standing watching with the other neighbours, takes a step forward, raises his arm and tries to stop him.

 "Tajim, you have done enough now, leave them alone".

"Shut up you old man, I will kill this ugly parasite, I will kill my wife too".

Mr Badhu tries to take the stick away from him but Tajim punches him and then chases him off with the stick.

He gets close to Sutara and beats her hard on her head.

Sutara doesn't move.

The puppy is walking backwards, howling, screaming, the pain from his burnt back and the pain from inside from seeing his mother lying there, not moving, with blood coming out of her head, not breathing, not protecting him; the screaming has changed to a howling of death. He keeps looking at Sutara, disorientated.

Tajim now prepares to beat the puppy with the stick too.

Mister Badhu manages to grab Tajim from behind, drags him on the floor, and beats him with the stick.

"It's enough now". He beats Tajim over and over.

"Chello! Chello!" The children chase the puppy away, but the puppy can barely move.

Mister Badhu has had enough. He tells Tajim to stand up.

As he gets slowly on his feet he keeps beating him on his head and tells him never to come back to this street again.

Tajim falls a few times as he staggers and limps away without looking back. Mister Badhu chases the puppy away from the crowd and his dead mother. He doesn't trust Tajim, and he has to do the right thing. He makes sure that the puppy disappears, chases him with the stick up into the palm tree plantation behind his street.

• • •

Garati is walking back to her house, carrying the shopping bags and singing.

She turns on to the little road that she lives on.

Then she stops.

Sees Sutara lying on the street, the blood. The body.

She drops her bags and runs up to her, kneels down next to Sutara. Touches her, hoping she will breathe. Looks at her and starts crying, praying and then crying some more.

She is screaming, her crying turns into the same horrific howling sound that Sutara called out in her last living moments. She touches her burns, her eyes, and knows what has happened. She is crying and her tears fall on the burned skin of Sutara. She picks her up and holds her like a baby and cries for her. Rocks her from side to side, sings to her.

The golden eyed puppy is watching her from a distance, hiding behind the trees. Like a shadow, watching his mother and his human helper. He is still trembling, still in terrifying pain, but at least she is back, their protector.

Garati stands up, with Sutara in her lap. Her sari is full of blood and she holds the dead dog's head again her chest.

She turns around, looks for her puppy. She had come up with a name for him today; she didn't want to name him. Just in case. But she had made up her mind. She would have named him today. Raj. The King, because that's what he was like. His kingdom was his heart. With his proud walk and the way he listened and cared for poor people like Garati, like a real King should do. A real king should help the poor people, just like her Raj had done.

As darkness starts to fall, down at the end of the street where the trees are forming into the small palm tree plantation, she sees the shadow of a small dog with a low head. She stands there trembling in silence and looks at him. He is looking at her, wags his tail at her. Just as he is about to come up to her she turns around and walks away.

It's a good bye, where they both know that if he follows her, she will lead him to his death. At some point Tajim will return for Garati and for her Raj. This is the only way she can save him.

The puppy lowers his tail, stands with his tail between his legs. Alone.

He is trembling, doesn't know where to go. Suffering and crying, what before was howling it has slowly turned into a painful low noise.

He looks at Garati and his dead mother from a distance.

He sees her crying and holding Sutara tight to her body. How Garati takes the pillow she bought at the market and puts Sutara on it. Puts a blanket on her, hugs her and keeps crying, kissing her. Stroking her and kissing her, holding her harder and stroking her. Mister Badhu comes to her house, walks up to her on the porch. Tries to take Sutara away from her, but she refuses.

She yells at him, and lies down next to the dead dog. She is inconsolable.

Other neighbours stand outside the house.

The children and the families next door put food on her door step; they pray and stand there outside her house in silence. It's a wake and no one is making fun of Garati now.

Mister Badhu sits down next to Garati, gently strokes her chin and wipes the tears away. His heart is aching. How can he help this young woman who only has known sorrow in her life? How can he make her happy again?

He has an idea, someone owes him a favour and maybe things can be put in place after all this pain. He talks quietly to Garati who eventually nods.

The puppy needs to be removed from the neighbourhood. Even if they all keep their eyes out for Tajim, they have to think about what is best for the puppy and for Garati. It is best this way.

He says that he knows someone all the way in Anjuna that is a kind person that will help them. Garati goes into the house.

She comes back with a bundle of rupees. She has been saving those, hiding them from Tajim. It was the money she needed to take the train back to Mumbai. She gives it to Mister Badhu.

She says it's for food for the dog, and for kindness.

She asks that they be kind to him. Mr Badhu nods. He will do his best.

He takes her money and leaves. He asks the crowd that has gathered to leave Garati alone.

The children are still crying and they ask where the puppy is, the beautiful puppy.

Mr Badhu leads them away telling them all that everything will be fine.

Garati stays on the porch of the house holding Sutara.

She looks up to the sky.

All those hopes and dreams that lit up the sky for one night many months ago are all gone.

The humble servant of the defenceless has been defeated.

• • •

Mr Badhu walks to the back of the neighbourhood looking for the puppy among the palm trees. He hates Tajim, the drunk. He hopes he gets hit by a car and dies.

He stops, in the darkness he can make out a shadow.

He can hear a weak sound of pain and confusion.

He calls out to the shadow.

The puppy walks up to him, slowly and with his tail between his legs.

Mister Badhu can see the burnt skin in the darkness. What a shameful act, what suffering.

He lifts up the puppy and carries him into a rickshaw that is waiting for them.

They drive off.

In the rickshaw the puppy lies quietly on his lap. Shivering, crying.

He tells the driver to head for Anjuna and as the rickshaw drives up the hill leaving Mapusa he wonders if Priya is still living in the same place.

She had lived a few doors down from him on the same street, Priya and her husband Krishna.

Krishna had been once a shop owner, an incense maker in Mapusa. Then he fell ill and couldn't walk anymore.

Mr Badhu had helped Priya get him out of the house and back inside the house every day. When the husband finally died he helped the ambulance men get Krishna out of the house for the last time in his life, Priya was left alone with nothing. Krishna had given the incense shop to his employee and never thought about how Priya would manage. Priya had no money and had to leave her house. She was offered a mud hut by a kind Christian lady who helped poor people. She was also given a small shack by the road to sell sandwiches and drinks from. It was good protection for the Christian lady, to have someone stand outside the property and keep an eye out, and Priya would make a few rupees. Mister Badhu had helped her move to this new place, all the way to Anjuna. Her hut was in the back of a big bright blue house, along with a few other huts for the help and another family that needed somewhere to live. He hadn't seen Priya in years, and maybe she wasn't there anymore. But it was the only place he could think of where he could ask for a favour. This was the least he could ask of Priya after all that carrying of her stingy husband.

• • •

It's night. Garati has fallen asleep next to Sutara.

She is awakened by the sound of a rickshaw stopping by her house and Mister Badhu getting off.

He tells her he has brought the puppy to the new place. He asked for kindness and understanding. God willing, if he survived the burns, he would make a good guard dog.

Garati laughs. "My Raj, a guard dog?!"

Mr Badhu is happy to see her smile.

He hands her back the money. They didn't need the money.

"Why don't you go back to your family in Mumbai for a while? When you return things will be different, I promise you. We will help you."

Garati wants him to have the money. He refuses.

"I will buy a bus ticket for you with this money. It's enough for a return ticket too."

He leaves her with the dead dog.

Garati looks at Sutara.

She smiles. "A guard dog!" Talking to Sutara, she tells her about her life and about the time Sutara has been at her house. About what a wonderful mother Sutara has been.

She picks up the dead dog, and the pillow, and goes to the back of the garden where a grave will be for her dog. Once ready she puts the new pillow on the bottom on the grave so that the dog can rest comfortably. Then the dog, then a blanket and finally earth to cover Sutara.

Garati prays for her, for forgiveness and for a safe journey into a new life, a better life.

For people like her, life is just earth and death, Garati thinks as she covers Sutara's body with the earth.

• • •

It's still quiet on the main road that leads to Anjuna.

Considering that Anjuna has some fame and a lot of tourists, most people would think it's a fancy well paved road with several lanes, but all it is, is one lane with lots of holes in it. In the dry season buses and taxis honk and overtake each other yelling at the other drivers, all in a hurry to get to the market or to the beach.

Along the main road, where Anjuna begins, there is a big blue house and next to it a little shack.

The humidity makes the morning feel cool and everyone is still asleep.

On the sandy patch next to the shack lies one eyed Jimmy.

Jimmy who has never been near the sea or near a bath tub. His whole coat is full of mud, fleas and dirt. It's his sandy patch and he is a fierce guard dog. Jimmy yawns, stretches himself and scratches yet another tick behind his ear. Then he lies down, enjoying the cool earth and the quietness of the morning. He stretches again.

At the last phase of his stretch his rough neck gets a good long last stretch and his one eye is looking at the shack and a box in front of it.

Now he remembers clearly.

How last night a rickshaw drove along the main road in the middle of the night.

The rickshaw had stopped by the shack, a human got out with a box and hid it under the table of the shack and left in a hurry.

Jimmy was all the way behind the chapel then, but could see it all from a distance. When the rickshaw drove off he ran up to the shack, smelling something strange. Not the smell of a dog, more like burnt chicken.

Something in that box under the table was making a noise, a terrible noise. It was painful to hear. Jimmy had sneaked up to the box and looked inside it.

There was a little scared dog in it. A new dog in his territory?

He had stood above the box growling, but the little dog in the box had finally stopped crying and gone to sleep, as if it didn't care.

Jimmy was surprised and didn't really know what to do.

So he went back to his guard place and hoped that the humans would throw the dog away the next day.

MERCY

Priya wakes up; it's nice that her landlady got her the frame for the bed, but without a mattress it does get kind of hard to sleep on it.

Her back is aching and its difficult getting up in the morning. At least she has a home. She gets dressed and gets out of her mud hut, walks down the ten steps, walks past the new house where her landlady rents out rooms in the dry season and then passes the gate to her shack. She has to check every morning that nothing has been stolen and take some water from the landlady's tap so that she can wash herself and cook some food. Now that monsoon is finished she won't be having rain coming in through the holes of her hut, so that's a relief.

She hopes that the tourists will arrive early this year, and she wishes that more foreigners would stop and buy from her, but they all want samosas and chapatis, not her egg sandwiches and Indian sodas.

She sees Jimmy by her shack, and under the table there is a box that is not hers. She kneels down and opens the box – and takes a step back. Gasps.

The stench. Looks again, it's a little dog inside the box. Is he dead? He is not moving – Jimmy growls warning Priya of this intruder. Who put him there? As if she ran a dog cemetery! How shameful! She looks in the box again, holding a piece of her lungi in front of her face.

The little dog is not moving. She touches him, and she can feel he is warm and is breathing. So, not dead. Then he opens his eyes. And Priya sees the gold coloured eyes and his pitiful look. He must be a young dog, and he is hurt. But those eyes, what a beautiful colour.

She sees an envelope in the box, opens it and looks at the content. It's a thousand rupees. Enough money to buy the sodas the foreigners like and make the shack look nice – holy Lord Shiva and Hanuman! – and maybe enough money as well to buy that beautiful sari she had seen at the market – Priya runs back into her hut and hides the envelope. Where is this money coming from? Should she kill the dog? What was she expected to do? That wound smells very bad and medicines cost a lot. He will take care of it himself. If he lives it will be the power of the gods to help him, if he dies then it will be Lord Shiva's way of deciding between life and death.

She finds a bowl and brings some water back down for the dog. She changes her mind, walks back to the hut one more time and puts some of her fish curry in another bowl. Then she walks back to the shack with both bowls and gently lifts the golden eyed puppy out of the box. The dog is crying and howling now. She puts him on the ground, and shows him the food. He eats all of it and drinks all the water. She gets a sponge and tries to clean the wounds on his back but he just cries and cries. She gives up, gets an old piece of fabric and puts it on the floor next to her chair in the shack.

She looks at the little dog and points to the fabric. The dog lies down on it and falls asleep again.

Priya is confused. Who could have done this?

Her mind is already drifting to the market and that beautiful green and gold coloured sari.

The puppy is snoring, Priya smiles at him, how cute, a dog that snores.

• • •

Zâbel is a beautiful and proud woman in the later stage of what people would call middle age, carrying her sorrows disguised under the few extra pounds she has been putting on in the last few years. Her long dark hair is impeccably groomed and she carries a big silver cross that hangs on a thick polished silver necklace.

She is a deeply faithful Catholic Goan woman and the matriarch of the Blue House.

A widow with five adult children, three servants and the honorary care taker of the local chapel, which is something she takes very seriously. Her five children are all idiots and Zâbel strongly believes that Jesus has sent those five children to her as a test of her faith. But why all five of them? If it hadn't been for Saraswati, her best friend and oldest servant, she would have given up or at least killed one of the children.

Now her eldest son Desmond wants to start a taxi business, buy fancy new cars and drive the Russian tourists around. What an idiot – as if he could be bothered to help in the shop or his sister's juice bar. He thinks he can sit there in the house doing nothing hoping the customers will turn up by themselves and that all the Russians will choose his taxi service. Zâbel has been studying the situation, that's what you do when your shop is in the village and you see what kinds of businesses work and which don't. She has this brilliant motorbike taxi idea – call it "Safe Travels" or "Jesus on Wheels". When she is selling cigarettes, beers and the necessities of life in her small shop to the tourists, she listens to what the foreigners say. They always make jokes about how dangerous it is to drive around the area and how fast the taxis and rickshaws drive. Zâbel does think the tourists are idiots too, in their scruffy clothes and un- Christian hair styles, but it has given her this brilliant idea. The drivers will be trained not to drive fast and not kick dogs or cows when they drive the tourists and they will tell the tourists to wear helmets. Show them a church or two, maybe invite them to a sermon and be the true ambassadors of Anjuna. And now Desmond and this stupid car taxi idea. If only her husband hadn't died, may his soul rest in peace, and left her all alone to try and raise their unruly children. This time she will stand up for herself.

And now look at this. Priya standing there in her old sari doing God knows what with that shack. She has to help her to make it look nicer or no one will buy anything and then will have to feed her as well. Praise the Lord that water will turn into wine this dry season.

Then she hears the noise.

The shriek.

And something moving around Priya. Oh no, what has she done now, that silly woman.

She walks up to the shack and stops, cannot believe what she is seeing.

A hairless dog. Screaming like a child.

"Priya, get that thing out there, NOW!"

"It's the new guard dog, for the shack!"

"This? A guard dog? It looks like it's going to die any minute! And who will feed him? I have five useless children, Jimmy and the servants. Get this thing out of here now! Or I will have it killed!"

The tiny hairless dog looks at Zâbel with his terrified look and pitiful state.

"Look! Beautiful!"

Zâbel has had enough. She really wishes she could go away, far away, like the foreigners who come here for the whole of the season. They show up, sit on the beach, do their yoga and talk useless talk at their cafés and bars all day long. Jesus my saviour, please help me. But Priya looks happy, look at her with her old sari and that unkempt hair.

Holy Lourdes, your power over the crippled and the maimed souls is eternal and I always pray for the miracles you perform, but could you come to Goa too sometimes and help me out?

"Priya, I will buy you a proper lock for your drinks and food. Get this animal out NOW!"

Priya looks at Zâbel with her pitiful look, and starts crying. The dog has to stay or she has to find out who gave her the money and return it.

She keeps crying and points at the tiny hairless dog.

Zâbel looks up to the sky and sees one of those air planes flying by. She closes her eyes and sees herself take off, far away. Rome, Italy, eating Italian food and walking along the Italian streets, being happy and not thinking about anyone else but herself. Go to the Vatican and meet the Pope. Pray in the Sistine Chapel.

Her dream is interrupted by a loud cry from Priya.

This woman is a sad servant for my sins, whichever they may be, she sighs.

"You are lucky it is Diwali soon. And no Hindu names now."

"Yes Madam, anything you want, I just want to feel safe. This will be a very good guard dog. But what name?"

Zâbel is tempted to walk up to Priya and hit her on the head with the bible she always holds in her hands. She lifts up the Bible as if aiming at Priya ready to strike her and a bunch of little cards with different Saints fall out and land on the ground.
"You stupid woman, look what you did!"
Zâbel picks up her cards with the saints. On top is Saint Thomas. She looks at the dog.
"Jimmy....and Tommy. That's it. A good Catholic name. Tommy. To remember that our Lord the Saviour Saint Thomas came from Jerusalem all the way to Cochin to save the Indians of Kerala."
And I am one of them, don't you forget that, she whispers to the Lord as she looks up to the sky quickly and kisses her cross.
"Make sure he doesn't stink anymore. And this is not your dog! He is not anyone's dog. If he stays he stays, if he goes he goes. And I will not pay for the food and medicines. You will do that! Remember that, it is not your dog! And you will help me with the celebration of the Madonna!"
Priya nods and smiles.
Zâbel walks away. Sighs. All this for a safe place in heaven.

• • •

Lauren is looking out of the window as the plane is on approach to Goa. She sees the coast line with its miles of beaches and coconut trees. She's restless and anxious to land when the plane suddenly starts circling around above the airport. Apparently a holy cow has occupied the tarmac.
It has been a long journey and she can't wait to get off the plane. With a raging hangover from the previous night at the disco in Cancun she had flown to Miami, touching American soil for the first time in three years. Off to the Indian Embassy to apply for a visa. Wait twenty-four hours and spend a couple of them in an art supply store mostly wondering if her hands were still able to do it. Browsing and then choosing. Buying, just in case, if she still wanted to, felt the need to.
Then out and with a thought of maybe calling Scott. No, not ready yet, he could wait.
Via London and Qatar she then flies halfway across the world to end up waiting to land delayed by a cow.

As the plane eventually touches the ground she spots the delinquent. A few men are holding an old cow by her horns as she tries to get back to the tarmac again. Hello India!

Lauren is excited and is the first one off the plane, waits for her bag at an old screeching conveyor belt and then walks quickly out to the chaos of rickshaws, taxis and food stalls, all fighting for her attention.

She gets into a rickshaw, and tells the driver she wants to go to Anjuna.

She closes her eyes as the rickshaw drives out of the airport and heads up north, along the country roads in the traditional Indian style of driving.

Honking and tooting, spending most of the time on the wrong side of the road, overtaking anything and everything, even if there is a big truck heading straight towards you.

Cows walk along the road, cyclists, dogs, people. The occasional goat. Motorbikes hurrying along; trucks creating invisible lanes giving them right of all ways. Street vendors pulling their carts ringing their bells.

It's the beginning of dry season, as they are driving into Anjuna, she sees how the businesses are starting to build up the restaurants, shacks and shops that had been dismantled during monsoon.

They get yelled at by a local farmer who has just put the harvested rice, the famous and expensive Goa Rice, on the road to dry it and the rickshaw driver happily drives right over it and keeps tooting and yells back some profanities in Konkani at the farmer.

Lauren gets off in the village, her hair is a mess and her arm is killing her after holding on for her life to the side of the rickshaw. She looks at the intersection with the little local shop, the restaurants and the travel agents and the book store. Lauren takes her backpack, and stands next to a cow who has parked herself next to her. Apparently Lauren has taken her place.

She walks down the street, gets a table at a restaurant, orders Chai, and some dahl and rice. Lauren looks at the signs along the road. Guest houses everywhere, but she needs something stable, permanent, maybe she can find a house, or a nice room. Savouring the Indian spices and the garlic from her naan bread she looks at one of her bags. It's a plastic tube with expensive water colour sheets rolled up inside. She touches it and wonders if it will work again, if the magic is still there.

The food is good and she orders some more. She is quietly looking at the street life. A scooter drives up to the little shop by the junction, a middle aged woman with the longest and shiniest hair Lauren has ever seen is sitting behind a young man, apparently arguing with him. As she gets off the scooter the woman slaps her son on the head with her bible, calling him an imbecile and why did God give me such a useless son. The young man laughs and drives off. Once inside the little shop she inspects all the items and takes a seat by the counter reaching for a small battery driven fan and leans back in her chair. She sighs and her eyes meet Lauren's. They smile at each other and then the woman does the sign of the cross on her chest and closes her eyes.

Lauren pays, gets up and walks to the woman's shop. She buys some water and peanuts and asks her about houses to rent.

Zâbel looks at Lauren.

Another unruly Christian who just landed in Goa. They did have a room left for rent in the house next to theirs. It would be good for Priya to have a foreigner there, and maybe Zâbel could bring this foreigner to her church.

Zâbel makes a phone call, yells at the person at the receiving end, and then smiles at Lauren.

"Our Lord Jesus Christ is kind to us today. My son will show you a very nice room next to my house. It's a very good room for a very good price. You will be very happy there. Here, have a cake I just made."

Lauren eats the cake; it is good and very sweet like most things Indian.

The son returns on his scooter, tells Lauren to get on the scooter behind him and takes off at full speed.

Zâbel can tell that Lauren is hesitant to ride with Desmond.

There you go, if I'd had my way, we could have had happy tourists with a trusting faith riding safely with "Jesus on Wheels", but no, your idiot son, now you will drive like a maniac and scare her off.

• • •

It's an empty room, humid, with some stains on the walls.

But it has a high ceiling with a big fan.

A bed casually placed under the fan, in the middle of the room.

The mattress of the usual low quality of being very hard, ensuring backache.

Outside there is a small porch, overlooking a field that overlooks another field, your typical Goan field with plastic bags and garbage everywhere that at the end of the dry season will turn into dust and whatever remaining grass try to grow, it will be eaten by the occasional hungry cow.

A shack stands next to the house on a sandy patch. A scruffy and dirty one eyed dog and another small dog with big ears and a hairless back lie there next to each other resting in the sun. A woman is cleaning the shack and occasionally looking at the servants running in and out of the big blue house across the sandy patch. It's an old colonial Portuguese style house. Bright blue, over a hundred years old with white windows and big white round pillars with steps leading up to the entrance of the house. Well kept with a clean court yard and brand new flower pots. Tropical plants that provide the house with mango and papaya fruits. A servant coming walking into to the back of the house where the kitchen lies, cooking rice and preparing vegetables for dinner.

Back when it was built it had been the only house in the area, where cattle and rice would bring wealth to the owners of the Blue House. The chapel across the road had been constructed by it's first owners, as a gift to the farmers. But now, it had all given way to the future. The main road to Anjuna had been built in front of the house, and the land and its wealth was long gone. Zabel's father had sold most of the land to newcomers who wanted to build around the area and Zabel's husband finally sold the last remaining plot across the street to a developer. Her children inherited the Blue House and all Zabel had to her name was her small shop.

The two dogs and the woman by the shack both look up as Desmond drives up from the chapel to the house at full speed, making the passenger sitting behind scream. He parks violently on the sandy patch so that Lauren almost flies off the scooter. He smiles at her "You like driving fast? I can get you a good scooter to rent for a very good price! Here, follow me; the room is behind the gate."

The dogs look at Lauren as she says "Hi" to Priya and follows Desmond to a newly built house behind the shack.

Lauren walks into the room. It's very simple, almost squalid. She likes the big window, the high ceiling and the porch with the view over the fields.

She goes back out to the shack and the dusty patch.

The location is so unromantic, it's right on the main road to Anjuna, and traffic will get busy in the high season. She looks at the two dogs and at Priya, who smiles at her. So not what I had imagined, Lauren thinks and looks out to the field across the road and the chapel. At the beautiful blue house across the sandy patch where the dogs are lying, and in some way she likes it. No expectations.

Desmond smiles at her, tells her that this is the best quality house built in the last few years in Anjuna, he shows her the lock and claims it's the safest place to stay in Goa. All of Goa.

"Yes, but the room is quite humid, I think maybe you ask a little bit too much, and its right by the road!"

"This is the best location for Anjuna, half way to the beach, half way to the Yoga, and half way to the Hill Top Disco! The best techno music in India!"

"I don't know. I just got here."

"Let me do this, I will give you a very good price, five thousand Rupees for the room, and three thousand for the scooter."

"Four thousand for the room, and two thousand for the scooter. Four months upfront."

Before Desmond can answer, Lauren gets her wallet out and hands him the money.

"This is a very nice place, and my mother will be very happy to have you here. I will bring you the scooter this afternoon."

Lauren takes the keys and goes to the room. Sits down on the bed, under the fan.

Her new temporary home in her new temporary life.

She feels observed, turns around and can see the ears of the little hairless dog sticking out from the corner of the wall on the porch.

Curiosity takes over and the tip of his nose, the whole nose, then the eyes, slowly turning the corner of the wall.

Looking at her with big curious gold coloured eyes.

He moves a paw forward, then tentatively another one.

Lauren looks at him. This is the moment she will always remember.

The first time their eyes met.

He must have had the most striking eyes she had ever seen in a dog. Small but perfectly built, with long slim legs and a curly tail. Not that she was an expert, nowhere near, but she had seen enough varieties of dogs on her travels.

Very young, with a proud posture and a broad chest. Big ears, symmetrically shaped in a triangle standing right up.

She smiles at him and he carefully wags his tail, she looks at him and he looks right back at her. Not in an unfriendly way, but in a very conscious way, like he is figuring her out the way humans do when they meet. It's like that, when you are not aware yet, that what is in front of you will change your life forever. She says "Hi" and he runs off back to the dusty patch.

Jet lag calls in and Lauren feels tired.

It's been a long trip and she lies down on the bed, under the fan, cursing the mattress.

She leaves her door wide open and falls asleep in the humid room.

• • •

He has never seen a white person before; she smells different, has yellow hair and freckles, walks differently from the people he knows.

He has been here a week and she is the first human that has meet his look, like Garati used to do. But it's not that, it's something else too.

As Lauren falls asleep with the door open he sneaks into her room. He stands there looking at her.

Her hand is hanging down from the bed. She snores lightly and mumbles in her sleep something that sounds like "Really, I hate country music".

He tiptoes in to her room, and smells her hand.

In her sleep Lauren puts her hand on his head and strokes him.

He stands next to her for a while, just like he did with Garati.

She smells like home, like safety. He has never been inside a house before and he walks carefully around, smelling at her bag, the strange tube shaped thing lying on the floor, her shoes.

He walks silently back to her and smells her hand again. Lauren opens her hand and he licks it gently taking in the smell of this strange looking human.

When he walks out again, he stops in front of the sandy patch and looks at the shack, at Jimmy, and at the road with all the cars driving by.

His wounds are still hurting and itching and the lack of hair makes the mosquitoes and flies land easily on his back and sting him, eat the wounds and make the infection worse.

He is still waiting for Garati, for Sutara. Why he has to be here he doesn't know, but he doesn't know how to get back to his old house and he feels lonely and deceived.

One eyed Jimmy looks at the skinny young dog. He knows that he is a pure Indian Native dog; he has that sophisticated walk about him that Jimmy never owned, and he has that sixth sense in him that has been carried his blood lines for eight thousand years. Jimmy is a real mutt, born and bred from a multitude of stray events, he was born tough and he lives tough. He is not well mannered and he guards the sandy patch and the house fiercely, knowing it's the way he gets rewarded with food.

But this little prince, this little dog that got dumped on his door step, he doesn't know what to do with him. He should kill him but then again it is nice to have company. And then he made up his mind. He eventually started tolerating this new dog they call Tommy and took him on as his sentinel, started teaching him the things he needed to know to be able to please Jimmy. Look out for dangers when he sleeps and then teach him how to survive. Before you cross any street you always stop and look. When there are no cars or scooters, then you can be safe and cross the road.

Before you approach any humans you need to smell them, you can walk behind them and figure them out. And by the way, your mother was too soft on you, that's what Jimmy tells Tommy. And Tommy listens and learns, does as he is told. But mostly he looks at the field across the road, as if waiting for someone to come and look for him.

Zâbel doesn't mind feeding the little dog, she had told her servants to allow him to come to the Blue House to eat with Jimmy. Otherwise he can stay on the sandy patch and stay out of their way. Hopefully a car would run over him one day, that's what Zâbel is hoping for. But he does look pitiful, so her heart gives in a little bit for him too.

Priya has been nice to Tommy, throws him an occasional egg, and the Indian tourists who stop at the shack to buy the sandwiches think that Tommy is a sad looking dog and throw him a piece of food too. Tommy has learnt to be cute so that the tourists will give him a little bit more food. Sometimes if no one gives him anything he adds a little limp and folds his ears down to look even sadder, and that usually helps make the tourists throw something to eat at him.

He sleeps on the sandy patch by the main road and at night Jimmy takes him on his rounds around the neighbourhood. They chase cars, motorbikes and the buffaloes down by the coconut plantation. They run around the chapel on the field in front of the Blue House. This is their territory and this is his new life.

Jimmy has seen the white woman arrive. He doesn't like strangers, he doesn't really like anyone after a by-passer had thrown a rock at him and Jimmy lost his eye.

When Tommy had followed the white woman to her room Jimmy had gone after him so he could see what he was up to and what the white woman would do to him.

He had stood outside of her door and she hadn't told him off.

How strange. He had never gone to that part of the new house.

The woman had sat on the bed, staring at the ceiling, then lied down and fell asleep.

The little dog had sneaked into the room and as the woman was sleeping he had smelled her. Then had stood next to her, as if on watch. As if she needed someone to be there. She had put her hand on his head and touched him.

Jimmy couldn't understand what this silly hairless dog was up to, but his behaviour was definitely not normal.

* * *

Air, freedom. India.

Lauren is riding her scooter at full speed along one on the country roads.

Her hair flying in the wind, her hands on the brakes, ready for a dog or a cow to run out on the street.

Her restlessness makes her go all the way to Mapusa, where she parks at the market and looks at the colourful stalls.

She needs to feel that she wants to stay, that she is in the right place. It's her first time in India and it's nice to be in a completely new environment, makes her feel awake, curious.

She buys a couple of Indian dresses, a few yards of Indian fabric, with bright patterns, a big blinking Ganesh lamp, the God of the travellers, who removes obstacles, brings wisdom and prosperity. The God of beginnings, says the shop keeper and gives her a good price.

She knew about Ganesh and had always liked the idea of a God with a friendly elephant face, sweet eyes and long eyelashes. India loves Ganesh, tourists love Ganesh. Lauren loves Ganesh.

And then the obligatory Bollywood posters. A carpet for the floor and another soft carpet for the little dog.

Incense, from the friendly young man at the market who flirts with her and asks if she is married. A table. Biscuits for the dogs and samosas for dinner. As in Thailand markets are a big part of life and she loves the stalls, the vendors, the spices and the way it's busy but not really fast paced. You talk, you bargain, you walk away and finally get your price.

She packs the scooter with the table between her legs on the front, the carpet folded on her seat and the rest of the shopping bags on the handles. To start the scooter and drive off is hard, but she gets the hang of it. While getting the balance right, she looks at the bus station which is in front of the market, at people getting ready to leave for some unknown destination. Families with many children getting on; wives bringing presents, husbands going back to see their families.

A woman waiting to board the bus is crying, she has a big bruise on her face.

The older man helping her must be a family friend or maybe an uncle. He hands her the ticket and gives her some money. She doesn't want to take it, but he insists. He consoles her and when she stops crying she gets on the bus.

The man is waving at her, and she waves back at him from inside the bus.

Lauren wonders what has happened to the woman, and who the man is.

She looks so sad and lost. The bus honks and drives off.

The man stands and watches the bus leave.

• • •

Garati's friendly neighbour Mister Badhu is missing Garati already but it will be good for her to go to Mumbai and see her family. He has given her a little money so that she can buy gifts for her family. He has promised to help Garati. Not just with the little dog, but to make sure Garati or anyone in the neighbourhood doesn't get hurt by her evil husband anymore. He hasn't told Garati, but he has a friend who is a policeman in Mapusa, and they will make sure that Tajim will not return to the house anymore. Mister Badhu doesn't want him near his house, the children of the neighbourhood, near Garati and he wants him gone for good.

He will help Garati get a job somewhere and she will have a better life. His own daughter lives so far away from him and he misses her. It would be so nice to help Garati and take care of her.

As the bus leaves he waves at Garati who waves back at him. He smiles at himself and decides to go to the market and buy her a new lungi, as a surprise for when she gets back. And some sweets for his wife. He crosses the street he sees a foreign woman trying to find the right balance with all the things she has packed on the scooter. Mister Badhu runs up to her. She looks at him and starts to laugh. He tells her to get off the scooter and he helps her rearrange all the things. The carpet on the floor and her feet on it, the table on top of the carpet, one bag in the helmet compartment and the two remaining bags on the handles. He tells her to look straight ahead and as soon as she has the balance to give some gas and go without stopping. She thanks him and does as he says.

He sees her drive straight into the jammed traffic lane and laughs as she toots and yells at other cars and bikes to move out of her way.

●   ●   ●

Lauren makes it all the way back to Anjuna without falling and as she drives past the chapel she sees the little dog. She stops her scooter next to the field and looks at him.

He seems to be looking far away, as if day dreaming, beyond the church and the fields.

She calls him. He recognises her and runs to her.

"Come!" She drives up to the house and he runs after her.

Parks the scooter and gets all the stuff off. Priya wants to help Lauren but tells Tommy to go away.

"No! It's OK. No problem!"

Priya smiles. Those tourists are so strange.

"What name?"

"Priya!"

"Priya."

"Lauren."

And then she points at Tommy.

"What name? Dog?"

"Tommy"

Oh, Tommy.

"Your dog? Tommy?"

Priya points to Jimmy and the street, and then makes a funny face.

"OK. Didn't get that! What about his back? Back?"

Lauren points at Tommy's back.

Priya makes another funny face, holding her finger to the nose.

"Bite?"

Lauren curls her hand and makes an effort to show a bite by opening and closing the hand. "Woof Woof".

Priya laughs.

She doesn't know. OK.

Priya helps Lauren carry the table to her room.

Tommy walks behind them, as if supervising the new items arriving to the room.

Lauren wants to thank Priya. She gets a samosa out and hands it to her.

Priya smiles. Samosas. She has to sell the samosas. Look, now the tourist has been buying things elsewhere. Not her egg sandwich.

She takes one then leaves.

As Lauren is unpacking and making the room look nicer, she can feel she is being observed again.

Turning around she figures it has to be the little dog.

"Hi! Tommy?"

He wags his tail. Stands away from her door.

"Biscuit?!"

He backs away as Lauren walks up to him.

She puts the biscuit on the floor and walks away. Tommy doesn't touch it.

Lauren goes out, reaches to touch him. Tommy stands there, cautiously.

She scratches his neck, and then tries to look at his back. Those are some nasty burns. And infected too. How does a dog get burned on his back like this?

Lauren looks in her first aid kit; she finds an antibiotic powder. She sprinkles some on Tommy's back.

"We still need to clean it, but later. OK, take your biscuit."

Tommy takes the biscuit. He looks at her again, with his beautiful eyes.

She looks back at him and he comes closer to her.

Zâbel is looking at that silly tourist, touching that ugly little dog. She has put some white powder on him and feeds him biscuits.

What is it with these people and the dogs? They should be praying and going to church, not get diseases and god knows what else from those filthy street dogs.

She goes up to Lauren, who is at the shack buying some water from Priya.

"What a glorious day our saviour the Lord Jesus Christ has given us today!"

"Hello! Yes, it's wonderful, all wonderful! Tell me, what happened to the dog? Those are nasty burns."

"Oh, you don't worry about the silly dog, they are fine, we feed the dogs."

"I understand that you are a very kind person but the wounds are infected. Look here, and here. I need to know what happened, so I can buy the right medicine. It's a very beautiful dog, you know."

"Oh it's a silly mongrel! We don't know anything; one day he was here. Not everyone is a good Catholic. Sometimes people throw boiling water on the dogs to stop them barking. But we don't do that and Priya is a very good person. Is everything good in your room?"

Lauren nods.

Then Zâbel invites Lauren to the Madonna celebration, it's a very important occasion and she has to come. Lauren agrees. The Madonna celebration?

"It will be wonderful! You must come and celebrate! All the ladies in the neighbourhood will be there so you must come too!"

• • •

"The Temple"

It's a new sign on their gate.

"The Temple"?

Sky is driving up to her house on her roaring motorbike. It's splendid, loud and pink, it's an Enfield.

Her backpack is tied up on the back of the Enfield. She has just returned from Bali, immediately regretting letting Jerome stay at her house this season.

She hits the brakes, gets off her ride and walks into the house with decisive steps.

"Jerome, I said you could live here, but really – The Temple? What is going on with you?"

Jerome runs out of his room, excited, waving a flier.

"They are here! They look great! Look! It's the ultimate labour of love!"

"The Temple?"

"You will see! Come and have a look in the garden!"

She grabs a flier.

"Spring and Sky?"

"My new name. The new me. No more bad karma from Bali. It's all different now. I have it all ready now, in the Temple!"

Oh God. Please.

"Ecstatic Yoga Journey with Sky and Spring at the Temple"

Jerome is wearing a purple lungi, the traditional Indian sarong.

"Sky, I think I will only wear purple this season. It will create a shield, I need protection."

"Jerome, I am tired. Can we talk about this later?"

"Sky, it's a great idea! We do the classes outdoors, at night! No one else is doing it. The students can move freely, let their souls shine under the stars! I can feel a kind of cold front coming from you but I know it's just Mercury Retrograde affecting you. I have written down the whole teaching routine for the night classes and it's perfect. I need to focus my energy into this important transition and this very month Pluto is transmitting new events and big changes. The near future will all be about the connection to your body and releasing inner frustrations!"

"Jerome, OK then, let me release my inner frustration: I will eventually forgive you for Bali, but don't screw things up here in Goa too. OK? And by the way, the "Ecstatic Yoga Journey" was my idea. And how about a "Welcome back?"

"Sky, my lovely friend, come here, let me give you a big hug, I am sorry. Now, what about the workshop?"

· · ·

It's time to do it now, at least try. Don't be a coward.

Lauren is looking at the tube shaped container, takes a deep breath and opens it.

Takes out the papers and rolls them out, puts books on them to flatten the papers.

She is sitting on the floor, staring at them. White, blank sheets.

She takes out the colours from another bag, and the brushes.

A sketch book and a pencil. All white, staring at her.

Tommy is standing by the door, looking at Lauren. What a strange human, to sit there staring on the floor.

She organises her colours, the blues, the reds, oranges, and her favourite colour, Payne's Grey.

"Maybe I should have a coffee." She thinks as her inspiration still runs on nothing.

It's been three years, and she expects her hand and her mind to start up where she left it back then. But things don't work like that.

Lauren lets her hand draw imaginary lines on the big sheets, letting her hand become friends with the paper again.

She tries to keep all thoughts away and it's difficult. This is not how she had intended things to be. Or maybe it was?

What about the beach? She still hasn't gone down to the sea. Tommy is trying to get her attention, but Lauren's mind is travelling fast, trying to escape from the fact that if she still is able to paint, what will that mean? Does she have to go back to... . exactly, it's the "go back". It's all been about "go to". Or was it ever "go to"?

Lauren pushes the papers under the bed, gets up and goes out, slamming the door so hard after her that the little dog jumps across the wall to the other field and hides behind all the garbage.

She gets on her scooter and drives off.

Tommy runs behind her for a while, but gives up when he realizes that she is not really there, she is somewhere else and driving fast to get away from it all.

He stops running at the crossroads with the Holy Cow that always hangs by the fruit shop, and tries to bite the cow on its heels. The Holy Cow lifts her hind leg and aims at Tommy. He backs away from her and starts trotting back home.

Lauren zig zags across small roads that eventually lead to the beach. She is driving too fast, getting away from the thoughts again and almost falls with her scooter on a curve full of gravel. She keeps going and coming closer to the beach she can see the bars, restaurants and night clubs lined up in front of the sea. Bungalows, guest houses and people everywhere. It's like coming to a different world. So this is the real Anjuna. She parks and gets off. Walks down to the beach and walks into the sea. It calms her, it always does. She swims with all her clothes on, turns on her back and lies there floating until she feels the current pushing her out. She makes her way back to the shore and lies there for a while. She gets up, a few people looking at her getting out of the sea fully clothed, drenched.

It's hot and they will dry fast. She goes to a bar and orders a lassi, sweet mango lassi please, and a vodka tonic. Double vodka tonic. She pays with wet bank notes.

On the sun lounge, drying up her clothes, sipping her drinks. Do I really want to do this, and anyway where was "go to"?

I could just as well call that boat captain and go back to the boat. Maybe it's easier. Better for everyone. Or go to Thailand. Go diving again. The drink soothes her mind and as her breathing calms down she says "Hi" to the people next to her.

She leaves the bar and walks on the beach until it ends. Then follows another path along the sea front. Sees a small house on the path with a beautiful garden. Coloured pillows are on the floor, a big couch in the middle of the garden with bright coloured fabric. Fairy lights on the trees, and flags with the Om sign blowing in the wind.

There is a sign on the gate. "The Temple".

And next to it, in a transparent envelope, a bunch of fliers.

"Ecstatic Yoga Journey with Spring and Sky"

She smiles, it has to be the girl she met in Peru all those years ago. She takes a flier and knocks on the gate.

She knocks again but no one at The Temple seems to be home to greet her.

Lauren walks around the house as she can hear two people arguing from inside and as she decides it might be best to leave a woman walks out of the house, down to the outdoors living room.

"And you want to buy purple fabric and turn my room out here into some two pence amateur "find the inner child" shala? Are you out of your mind?"

"But Sky, I have changed, I am onto to something revolutionary here, please, let me try, it will be an instant success! Let keep the momentum going!"

"You made a fool out of yourself in Bali, but I have a chance, and I am not going to lose it because of you. If you want to we can do relaxing yoga at night, but none of that "Ecstatic" bullshit. Things are different now, Jerome and I for one intend to move on. And you are welcome to move on too, as in move out." Lauren looks at Sky, she looks exactly the same, as if fifteen years went by without affecting her. That same dark shiny hair and that perfect posture and olive skin. Actually, she looked even younger now.

Sky feels observed. She turns around and sees that blonde woman with a face full of freckles. She tries to place the face to a name, to an event.

The penny drops and Sky smiles the way she does with that big smile of hers, finally.

"Holy cows and monkeys! How long has it been? Machu Pichu in Peru! The tunnel and the rats! Welcome to seventh heaven, Sister!"

Sky walks up to Lauren and hugs her, welcomes her into her house. Jerome hears Lauren's American accent and is thinking of what was to be of his future in California. The lost dream.

"I am Jerome, but please call me Lord Spring!"

From inside an Indian voice with an American accent can be heard.

"Jewel Sharma? Here? He's on every show in California."

"It's Jerome. Practising again. He plays those CD's over and over again to work on his speech for the yoga classes. He calls it The New Me."

They laugh and start catching up on their travels, or their journeys as Sky calls them.

• • •

As the sun is setting, Jerome is on his best behaviour trying to impress Sky and prepares dinner for the girls, cleans the house, keeps playing Jewel Sharma's talks on life and keeps working on his new accent.

Sky blesses the food and Lauren asks her if she still carries that wonder powder for scars and burns she always used to travel with. "I sell it online on my website now, here have it, it's a gift. It's organic, you know." She gets her a tube.

"Does it work on dogs?"

Jerome frowns.

"The special medicine from Varanasi for a dog?"

At the same time the CD plays one of Jewel Sharma's most famous quotes

"Acceptance is a foundation that leads to harmony in the universe." And the word "acceptance" stays on repeat thanks to a scratch on the CD.

Jerome gets up to turn off the player. Finally, some silence under the stars.

"I think it would be great to do the yoga classes here at night. That's a great idea." Lauren says.

She leans back and looks up at the coconut trees. For Sky it's all about staying in the moment. She doesn't seem to care about anything except the present and her yoga and Goa is her universe. Nothing else is relevant.

And anything bad or inconvenient is written down as another learning experience or Karma. So simple.

Or Jerome, whose strong conviction in re-incarnation makes him label good from evil in the simplest way. But faith has to be more than that? Lauren looks at Sky when they walk down to the beach. A few Holy Cows are walking on the beach, a pack of dogs bark at them and further away the "Umph Umph" of techno music being played at a club down at the beach echoes through the night.

"You know, Lauren, we are a very blessed generation. We were the first generation of women who could go out in the world all by ourselves and travel, discover the world, on our own terms. I am going to focus my spiritual work next year on that theme. It's all about gratitude and abundance. What are you going to work on?"

"This." She points at the sea and what goes on around them.

· · ·

It's late when Lauren drives home and when she gets back to the Blue House the little dog is there waiting for her.

Priya is still up standing by her shack waiting patiently for customers. Lauren buys some soda from her and compliments Priya on her beautiful sari. It's obviously new and Priya is very proud when she touches the sari as if it was pure silk. "Thank you" she says and smiles.

Tommy follows the human with the yellow hair back to her room and stands outside looking at her.

Lauren gets a biscuit.

She gets close to him and gives him a biscuit which he takes in the gentlest way. As he chews on it she slowly gets the miracle cream out. The little dog starts shivering and backs away. She starts talking gently to him, and he stands there quietly while she applies the medicine on it. It soothes his pain and she can see how his back is more relaxed. "Enough for one day, but I think we need some betadine and antibiotics. I just wish I knew what happened to you." He looks at her and she smiles at him.

"Sooner than you know you will look like a fabulous Indian dog." She kisses him on his forehead and Tommy looks into her eyes. "Be careful or I'll take you with me."

● ● ●

The first market day of the season is in full swing. Lauren is out for a ride on her scooter and the traffic is manic. Adding to the amount of heavy traffic on the small Indian roads a temple elephant is walking in the middle of the road, he is painted with bright colours and has golden tassels and blankets on him.

Tourists stop and take photos, Indian drivers toot and try to over-take the large animal. His ears are flapping; he is getting agitated. The Mahout yells at the drivers, at the elephant, at the tourists. The elephant starts to walk faster and when a rickshaw driver keeps tooting and drives his rickshaw into the elephant's rear end, the elephant panics and runs wildly out into a field. The rickshaw speeds away, the Mahout cursing and swearing. The elephant stops and pants.

Then the rickshaw drives straight into a scooter with a couple of tourists on it. They fall, and all the Indians who are in the vicinity run up to them. Some to help, some to take photos, some to talk and the rickshaw keeps driving, honking on its horn without even looking back. The paradox of India. Drive like a maniac with a smile on your face and then help those who get hurt. It's all very surreal. Lauren wonders about the connection between religion and behaviour. Is it really a reaction of your Karma if you get hit by a car? Or if you are born into a poor family, is it really a consequence of your previous lives and therefore you have to accept your faith? She is standing by the side of the road watching the elephant. The Mahout is looking at the back side of the elephant, to see if he is injured. Lauren can see Jerome driving up towards her and turns away from him. Too late. Jerome has seen the freckles and their owner.

"Are you coming to the German Bakery?"

Jerome shouts at her, from his purple Enfield. The motorbike is so noisy she can barely hear what he says. She points to her ears and the motorbike. He switches off the engine.

"Are you coming to the German Bakery?"

She barely recognizes his voice, it's got a faint German accent now, the other night he sounded like Jewel Sharma, the famous Indian philosopher and talk show host.

"I have to go back to the house soon, I am invited to the Madonna celebration."

"The Madonna? Such ridiculousness. Come with me!"

"OK, but just for half an hour."

Tommy has been following Lauren all the way from the Blue House. With light paws and keeping a safe distance he runs after her scooter. He was thrilled to see the elephant and was very close to run after him and try to bite him when he remembered he had to keep quiet and not be seen by the human with the yellow hair. He is afraid that she will leave him and wants to make sure he knows where she goes, so he can find her.

And now she is following that big man, and he has to keep running after her.

He slows down when they park their bikes and walk into the German Bakery, the Anjuna café to see and be seen in. The yogis and the local foreigner's home away from home.

Walking in Jerome says hi to everyone and leads Lauren to a low table where they sit down in the traditional Asian way. Pillows on the floor, sitting in lotus position and eat under large images of Indian Gods on the walls. Tibetan prayer flags hanging above them and under the trees that cover the coffee shop. A huge orange flag with an OM, the sacred Hindu sound, is hanging above the counter and the waiters all wear colourful Indian shirts. Jerome says hi to Shakti, the tantric coach, then Anita the Soul Dancer, Venus, the Universal Theory Meditation teacher and Tim, wow, a normal name, the poet who publishes his books at the post office Xerox machine and gives everyone his books for free.

"Why does he give them away for free?" Lauren asks.

"Tim is a fantastic poet. Here, take a book. Read and learn. Oh look, here is the fabulous Nirvana! My colour therapist!"

They great each other with a Namaste, the Asian greeting, placing their hands together in prayer pose in front of their chest.

Tommy is standing at the entrance of the German Bakery. He can smell all the food sitting on the low sitting tables, and watches the people with the funny looking hair and clothes eating their food. He spots Lauren sitting next to that man again, and a woman smelling like Frangipani standing with them.

Lauren opens the poetry book and reads randomly from a page in the middle.

The poem is called "My Lingam is my space ship".

Talk about a change of scenery from the Caribbean.

She reads the poem.

"My Lingam. A spaceship en route to the orbit of ejaculation.

I am in the land of the rainbow and a sound of intrusion. Is. Now. Bang.

Orbit is approaching. I need. Now. The Lingam. Let the honey of peace and intricacy rule."

Lauren starts to laugh.

Jerome looks deep into her eyes.

"Like I said, Tim is amazing, don't you think? You know, Lauren, I am a painter too. I wanted to get to know you better, so we can share this experience together. And then you can take me with you to America!"

Lauren looks at Jerome, tries to get eye contact with him, as he stares at her breasts.

"Well, I would love to, but I have no plans to go back any time soon.

I just move wherever the wind takes me. Like a space ship, you know, like the poem." He smiles at her and laughs.

"So tell me, really, you paint?"

"I paint the soul." Jerome answers proudly.

"That sounds ambitious. What does the soul look like?"

"It's the soul! What do you think it would look like?!"

"Well, I think it's interesting. I would love to know what the soul looks like. I don't think any painter has ever made such a powerful comment."

"I haven't really started painting yet, but maybe we can, you know, discover the soul together?"

"So, you are not a painter?"

"It's all about the learning experience, Lauren, art is such great therapy! It will be another way to work with my yoga students. And you, mostly you!"

"Well why don't you start and then tell me when you have finished a masterpiece? So what does a colour therapist do?"

"She matches the mood to a colour. To either calm you or energize you. The soul.... I will work on that and make you proud...and you have all those Karmic layers that need to be let free and -"

Lauren pretends to look at her watch.

"Namaste, have to run!"

"But Lauren, time is just an illusion!"

Tommy runs and hides behind the motorbikes when Lauren walks out to her scooter, and as she drives off towards towards the Blue House he trots along behind her, happy that she is on her way back.

● ● ●

Lauren barely has time to drive up to the sandy patch and park her scooter before it's time for another ritual, another religion.

She really should be trying to paint again, but she has promised Zâbel, and honestly, the idea of going back for the third time to that big white sheet of paper staring at her in the face makes it easy for Lauren to go have a look at the celebration.

All the women from the neighbourhood are there as the Madonna is being carried inside Zâbels house. Once a year the Madonna gets taken out of the local chapel and is carried in a procession from house to house in the neighbourhood that lies between Baga and Anjuna. She spends a couple of nights in each house and celebrations are held blessing the house and long prayer meetings are held in front of the Madonna.

Zâbel has prepared a table with blinking Christmas lights and metallic gift wrapping paper for the Madonna.

The Madonna will stay there for the three nights. The whole living room is filled with local women and they are singing loudly. Priya and Saraswati are running around with incense, serving drinks and food and making sure that everyone has a prayer book. Priya hands Lauren a prayer book and smiles at her. The singing quietens down and turns into praying as Zâbel makes a special prayer for her house and her family. The singing resumes, louder and clearer. The women hold their hands up high and Priya is singing too, wearing her new sari.

Zâbel smiles at Lauren and waves at her with enthusiasm. Lauren smiles back and tries to sing along in the Konkani songs. The lack of sense of time in India makes the ceremony go on for what seems a lifetime. The women have been standing all this time singing and praying and none of them seem tired.

Maybe Jerome is right, maybe time is just an illusion.

When it's finally over Lauren tries to leave but Saraswati hands her a big plate of Indian sweets and makes Lauren take a seat with the other women and eat the sweets. Zâbel hands her a baby to hold, it's her granddaughter, and then gets introduced to the whole family. The sons, the cousins, the second cousins and the uncles and aunts.

• • •

It's sunset when Lauren finally manages to leave, so full from eating all the sweets and cakes that she has to get some air, walk a little.

Heading down towards the main road it doesn't take long before the little dog shows up from nowhere and follows her. He is wagging his tail and stays right behind Lauren as she walks on down the road along the buffalo fields. She hears the roaring sound of a big motorbike approaching and sees Sky driving towards her. It seems as if the size and noise of your motorbike is a way to tell if you are a local or just a simple tourist. The longer you have stayed in Goa, the bigger the bike. They wave at each other. Sky stops and Tommy runs up to her.

"Oh, so this is the injured dog? He's really cute! I will ask my homoeopath about a better remedy. Are you coming to the Shamanic meeting next full moon? It will be very powerful!" Lauren laughs. "I just spent three hours with the whole local community praying to the Madonna! I could use a nice bar and a Strawberry Daiquiri right now!"

"Embrace Goa, embrace it! The universe has great things in mind for you! Come to Yoga tomorrow!"

Sky starts up her metallic pink Enfield and roars away. After a narrow bridge there are a few local shops. Lauren sees a video rental place with mostly Bollywood movies. She walks in with Tommy by her side and looks at foreign titles.

The shop keeper recommends "Om Shanti Om" with the now world famous Shahrukh Khan. "Madam, this is the best of the best, it is a very happy and tantalizing films" He says as his head moves from right to left in the typical way most Indians do when they mean Yes.

"Tommy, did you ever watch a movie? No, I didn't think so. What about Beverly Hills Chihuaua? Or Marley and Me?"

"Oh Madam, your dog will love the films with the American dog! If you rent one more films, you will get this sticker for free! And your Indian Dog, he is for free too!" Lauren rents another movie, a real love story in true Bollywood fashion and the man in the shop gives her a Ganesh sticker. "You will bring back the films in three days, Madam. Or four days if you like. It is not a problem. And you will enjoy very much! This is my special promise to you! Yes. You will be so happy! So very happy! And the dog will be happy too!"

Lauren has to shake the man's hand and walks out with a smile on her face.

And so with four movies and a little dog in tow Lauren walks back to the Blue House, enjoying the cool dry air and the slow pace of walking. Back in her room, she turns her laptop on, and plays Beverly Hills Chihuahua. She tells Tommy to sit next to her on a pillow.

Together they watch the movie, as Lauren starts sketching on the large white paper. She thinks about important moments that we will never forget that shape us into who we are, about religion and the ongoing rituals that go on here.

She draws the outline of hands in prayer pose. She thinks of this strange place in the world where faith is so important, and how funny it is that the prayer pose that Christians use is also the way Asians greet each other. We are not as different as we think we are. From that she will turn into an abstract shape, but that's for later. Not too much pressure, it's just the beginning.

She looks at Tommy watching the film. He is totally focused on the sounds coming from the screen and when one of the Chihuahuas in the movie barks, he barks too.

They sit together, like two best friends and Lauren isn't feeling lonely, for the first time in a long time.

• • •

The Golden Lotus Yoga School is the biggest Yoga school in Goa and Jerome is its uncrowned prince. It's the first class of the season and as he walks into the grounds all the students salute him and he hugs each one of them trying to remember which one of the students he slept with the previous season. The Yoga Shala is made out like a big tent, with large Buddha's standing in the entrance of the tent and a big Ganesh wooden statue in the front of the shala. The yoga students follow Jerome inside the tent, they take their mats while Jerome hands them yoga blocks, wooden coloured blocks to help the students with their postures. Sky walks in, she is late and apologizes. She waves Lauren into the tent and gives her a mat.

Then everyone lies down, and Jerome starts the class.

"Close your eyes and start focusing your mind on how you breathe. Let the shallow upper breathing get deeper; let it move gently down, to a conscious place of peace and serenity. For each breath you will feel how you regain strength, how you feel an independent adjustment happening to your life, your Karma and your Asanas.

We will take ten breaths, slow deep breath, for each breath feel how each of your Chakras gets fed oxygen and rejuvenates into energy. On the tenth breath you will slowly sit up and then stand up. Yes, very beautiful. We are all breathing."

They all slowly sit and then stand up. Sky leads them through the first few postures and walks around the group making sure everyone is doing the postures correctly. Jerome helps adjusting the students when they do mistakes and it doesn't take long before he has his hands around Laurens waist. Lauren takes his hands away and gently puts them on his own hips. Jerome puts his hands on her back and starts talking to the class about finding your soul, and winks at Lauren as he moves on to help another student.

"He really does sound like Jewel Sharma!" Lauren says to a student next to her.

"You are right; I was trying the place the voice – he really sounds like him!"

Jerome is on a roll today, it's the first class of the season and he does have a lot to say.

"It's all about finding your inner creative child, your pure individual persona, your true you. Let Goa embrace you and cherish you, let the you inside the you blossom in this safe place of harmony and growth. This is our time to take responsibility for our current reincarnation. This is the life we have when we have the capacity to change, to help, to do. To You.

I will be offering a special workshop this season called "Ecstatic Yoga Journey" and I cannot tell you how important it is for your personal growth to attend this event.

We can talk about this after the class. And now it's time for my favourite pose, the pigeon!"

Tommy has been following Lauren to the Yoga school, as usual from a safe distance.

There are so many places to see and discover that he never imagined in his little life, and running after the human with the yellow hair makes him feel safe. So many different smells, dogs, houses and roads to find. Not to mention goats and cows and the buffalo lying in the mud on the fields far away from the Blue House.

He stands outside the tent, watching. He then sneaks in to the Shala and goes up to Lauren, who is lying face down with one leg folded in front of her and the other leg stretched out behind her. Lauren feels that someone is licking her forehead and for a moment she thinks its Jerome. She looks up and sees Tommy's face in front of her. Lauren continues her exercise as if nothing has happened and hopes that no one has seen Tommy.

"Now everyone come and join me and Jerome in the circle."
Sky announces, and tells everyone to hold their hands high, to breathe in and to ask the Universe for anything they want. "Now close your eyes and let's hold each other's hands here in the circle and share that abundance of wishes. Oh yes, I can feel so much hope and power from our Goddesses here! All right, release the hands and just stand, slowly open your eyes and look at the person in front of you. Yes, wonderful, now stand and feel your feet, your toes, look at your feet" In the middle of the circle Tommy is standing staring straight at Lauren.

"Well, apparently we have a four legged Yogi here today; look, he can feel how every little paw is carrying the whole weight of his body. Open up those toes, wiggle and move them. And look here, he is doing a perfect downward dog! Ok, let's shake those beautiful bodies and thank you very much! See you here again on Wednesday for our early morning session!"

Jerome smiles at Lauren, but gets a cloth out and starts scrubbing the place where Tommy was standing. "The dog is filthy! It is not a healthy reincarnation, Sky! It shouldn't be allowed in our space of worship!"

Sky is already walking out of the shala with Lauren and all the women in the group who are fussing over Tommy. All the attention that the women usually give to Jerome is now directed at the dog.

THE GOD OF BEGINNINGS

Garati is a different person now as she gets on the bus to go back to Goa.

She is feeling better after spending some time with her family in Mumbai. They have fed her and taken care of her.

She has regained some of her beauty and happy spirit, and sitting by the window on the bus she enjoys looking at the views and wondering what if she was born here, in this little village they just passed, would her life have been any different? Or this town here, what would her name be and where would she have lived? Would she be the same person?

The family got her the cheapest ticket on the slowest bus. They wanted her to stay with them, and in the end the whole family was arguing with her when she said she wanted to stay in Goa. How would it look for a young woman to live on her own? People would think she would be loose, a prostitute! Garati was holding on to her belief, that she had a better life in Goa, that she would be happy there. And she promised her family that she had Mister Badhu protecting her and helping her.

What she really wanted to be able to take care of Sutara's grave, to be able to wake up every day and look at the place where she rested, and pray with her every day. In the end the family gave in and reluctantly let her leave.

The bus drives slowly along the coast and stops at every village, suffering through every turn, ready to die any minute. And eventually the bus does break down. The driver gets out, looks at the engine, kicks the wheel and walks off. Garati walks out of the bus and realizes that they are near Ganpatipule, where the Ganapati temple is.

The bus will be stuck here for hours, they have to wait for a spare part and someone points at a shack and they see the bus driver having another beer. No one is going anywhere for a while. She wants to go to the temple, but alone?

That wouldn't be good. And how would that look? People would think…but girls do go places alone nowadays, so why can't she? But how would she get there? She barely has any money.

There are two tourists on the bus, and they are talking to each other with a big map asking people things about Ganatipule, which apparently is a famous tourist attraction for the adventurous traveller. It's two girls with red and blonde hair – she slowly walks up to them, she has never been so close to foreigners before. Staring at the girls' red hair, wondering how could any God create such a strange looking hair colour, she gets a crazy idea – maybe she could go with them? Who would know? She looks at the girls, and the girls look at this young Indian woman with the beautiful long black hair and her simple polyester sari, and they smile at each other. The girls start talking to her. Garati keeps smiling. She points at the redheads t-shirt; it has a print of Ganesh on it. The girls go "Yes! Yes! Ganesh! Temple? You know where it is? Is it far? Can we go there?" Garati looks at the girls. She replies speaking Maharati: "I don't know where the temple is, but please take me with you!"

The blonde girl speaks to her friend "I think she knows where it is, she's on our bus, isn't she? Why don't we ask her to go with us, so we know where we are going?"

The girls look at Garati, and point at the T-shirt. "You, us, Ganesh Temple?"

Garati smiles, and does the typical Indian "Yes" moving her head from one side to the other and laughs.

"Ah, she means yes. Good! Bus? Taxi? Rickshaw? How much?"

The girls point at a rickshaw and the driver speaks to Garati. She doesn't have the money for a rickshaw. What if they think she will pay for the ride? Isn't it customary that the Indian pays for the tourist to see the great places in her country?

She talks to the driver and when he looks at the tourist girls he gives a very high price. Garati thinks that this part of India only has rich people living in it considering the exorbitant price for the ride, but it's strange, no one in the streets or villages look like they have any money. She tells the driver that she is only a poor house-wife from Mapusa and she can't pay that kind of money.

"How much" The girls ask. Garati starts explaining to them in Maharati that this is a very expensive place and maybe its best just to wait here, this is not a place for poor women like them, who travel on a simple bus. They should wait by the bus and accept their fate, like she will do now.

The driver is talking back to Garati and tells her she can have a good price, he will wait for them and make sure they return in time to catch the bus.

Its money Garati doesn't have. The girls ask Garati again "How much?"

Garati shows the girls seven fingers – seven hundred rupees, and sighs.

"God that's cheap! You, you, no pay, come with us?"

They point at the rickshaw and tell her to hop in with them. She doesn't understand what they mean, and starts looking in her pocket for the money, to show she can't afford to pay. The girls go "No no no!!! OK, come!"

Garati does a very happy Indian nod and gets into the rickshaw next to them.

The driver honks away and the three young women laugh as the driver tries to impress them by driving the old rickshaw at full speed all the way down to the temple.

● ● ●

Oh, Holy Lord Shiva and Parvati all the Holy Cows in the world! Look at this!

The three young women get off the rickshaw and stare in awe at the never ending beach spreading out in front of them, the sea, and the Swayambhu Temple with its ochre colour and humble splendour.

It's a square shaped temple right by the beach, with pillars supporting the roof and the white tower in the back. Ochre coloured Ganeshes are sculpted into the walls and Garati is crying as she walks into the temple. The girls follow her curiously.

There he is! Garati's uncle told her that the only Ganesh inside the temple is four hundred years old and faces West instead of East.

Garati kneels and prays in front of the legendary Ganesh, this one according to legend, sprung from the soil.

She interrupts her prayers and stares at the deity. Facing West instead of East.

Doing things differently. What if she can do that too? What if she can have the courage to face West instead of East? What if this idea she has is a good idea and not just a silly whim like her mother told her?

She is here now, and she is not afraid. She takes some scented flowers and throws them at the deity's feet, praying for strength and courage. She also prays for Sutara and for her puppy with the gold coloured eyes.

Ganesh, the God of beginnings. Garati prays for protection for the beginning of her new journey and for guidance in this change of life she wants to embark on. She prays that the Holy Lord Ganesh will help her and teach her along the way how to overcome the obstacles put before her and prays for her good fortune and for some happiness.

The two girls kneel beside her and give her more flowers, Garati smiles and she shows the girls where to put the flowers and how she prays.

Garati closes her eyes, and prays for her beloved Sutara.

And there she is again, smelling Garati's hair and telling her that she has forgiven her, and she thanks Garati for all that she tried to do for her. Garati listens, nods.

Sutara also tells her that the golden eyed puppy is alive and that she should always be proud of him. That their beautiful Raj will make them all proud one day.

Sutara tells her as well that Garati is a good person with a big heart, and that she should never forget that.

They sit next to each other, Garati and Sutara's ghost.

Garati strokes her head, her back and kisses her on the nose.

Sutara walks slowly away, out of the temple and disappears on the beach. Garati looks at her walk away, and the two Western girls ask her if she is OK.

Garati nods and follows the girls out of the temple, wiping a tear away.

• • •

It's late in the evening when the bus finally drives into the small state of Goa and for a moment Garati is taken over by fear. What if he comes back to kill her? What if Mister Badhu couldn't keep him away?

She starts stirring in her seat, worried she looks at the road ahead of them and the two tourist girls look at her, wondering what is going on with their new Indian friend. The girl with the red hair puts her hand gently on Garati's shoulder and she can feel that the young Indian woman is shaking. Garati looks at her, smiles and tells her, as she tries to tell herself that it's OK, I will deal with problems as they come. The Lord Ganesh puts obstacles in front of us to test us, to make us learn and be stronger. Eventually the fear will go, she hopes. The girl with the red hair says she doesn't understand, but in some way she does, as Garati calms down and offers the girls some more of her laddhu sweets.

As if operating by some divine intervention the bus manages to arrive to Mapusa bus station without breaking down again. The tourist girls take Garati's luggage and help her to get off the bus. Garati thanks them for being so generous and taking her with them to the temple. They shake hands and say farewell and Garati looks at them walk away with their backpacks on their backs and their carefree walk. They turn around and wave one last time at Garati as Mister Badhu arrives to pick her up.

It is nice to see Garati smile again, he thinks as he sees her. And she looks so young now. He helps her get on behind him on his scooter and as they drive back to their street he tells her that she doesn't need to need to be afraid anymore.

That Tajim would no longer return.

Mr Badhu's wife is waiting for them at Garati's house. She has cleaned it and brought some food home for her.

She greets Garati who reluctantly walks to the house, up the stairs to the porch.

She sits down on the porch, it is so clean and Mr Badhu has replaced the rotten planks on the floor with new ones. Garati looks towards the street.

She asks Mr Badhu about the golden eyed puppy. He looks at her. "I am sure he's fine, Garati. Now, don't think any more about the sad things. Why don't you come and have dinner with us?"

Mr Badhu's wife greets Garati like a long lost child. She tells her she looks so beautiful and that she will be very happy to invite her for dinner whenever Garati wants, she is happy with some company and wants to hear all her stories about the big city up north. Mrs Badhu feels sad that her son is so far away and disappointed that he doesn't take care of his old parents like a good Indian son should do. Still, she loves looking at the photo he sent her where he stands next to his new fancy car.

He must be very busy with job as he rarely replies to their letters, especially the ones where they ask for money. She sighs, at least now she has Garati to dote on.

Mrs Badhu has made her favourite dish for her. Goan rice with mackerel and a very spicy sauce. Garati tells them that she is has an idea.

She has seen the tourists at the market ask for Ganesh pillows, and she wants to make those and sell them.

She shows them the fabric she bought in Mumbai. She could only afford a couple of yards, but she looked in so many shops until she found the perfect fabric.

And here, she shows another piece of fabric, a layer of gold, and then in the back, a last layer of dark blue fabric. One pillow long and round, and another like a normal pillow, square. Just two models, to start with. Two different pillows, two different deities, Ganesh and Saraswati.

But she can't speak English and doesn't have any money to buy all the fabric and a sewing machine.

Mr Badhu says he thinks it's a good idea. He could ask his son if they could borrow some money to buy the sewing machine. Both he and Mrs Badhu speak a little English and they really need to make more money. Maybe they could work together? Be partners? Garati nods. She would be very happy if they could. Mrs Badhu clears the table and thinks about her son again. No she will not write to him this time, she will call him, and tell him a nice big lie. She smiles and knows that this time he will send her the money they need for this new business. And for another set of teeth she badly needs. Yes, it will be a good thing. In the kitchen she hears Garati cry of joy as she opens the present Mr Badu has given her. Things will be good, she smiles and brings out some sweets for their young neighbour.

● ● ●

The sheet of watercolour paper is rolled out, staring at her.
The sketch she had started last week is now intricate, the hands in prayer pose have turned into flowers and Lauren is preparing the colours that will be in the background.
Tommy is sitting on a pillow in her room studying his yellow haired human.
The wound on his back is almost gone and hair is growing back.
Lauren knows better than to feed him, once you do that the dog stays with you and he does get fed at the Blue House. She always laughs when she sees him and Jimmy show up at sunset for food, how he trots up to the back of the house and wait for Saraswati to bring out their food. She has seen how he eats gently and how Jimmy waits for him to finish his food.
Lauren gets up to put hot water in a bowl and when she walks into room she spills some of it on the floor. Tommy shrieks and runs out of the room, terrified. He runs out to the field and hides under a tree, trembling with his tail between his legs.
Lauren goes out running after him, wondering what happened.
She walks on the field looking for him, and when she finds him, he backs away from her with fear.
"It's nothing, little dog, nothing. Come!"
But he can smell the hot water on her hands and the memories are clear. Death, pain and separation. He runs away from her.
Lauren stays there, looking at him, and then she understands. The hot water in the bowl.
She gets closer to him, kneels down and starts talking softly to him. "Nothing will happen, the water wasn't for you, it's for my paintings, nothing will harm you little guy. Come!"
Tommy stands at a distance looking at Lauren. He takes a few steps towards her. His whole body is trembling and he can barely

walk. Lauren slowly moves towards him. She keeps talking to him in a soft voice and Tommy takes a few more steps towards her.

Lauren can touch him now, and sees how his eyes are full of fear and how his body is shaking.

She keeps talking to him and lies down on the field next to him.

Eventually the tail comes up a little bit and he goes to stands next to Lauren.

She strokes him and tells him beautiful things. Most of all she tells him that bathing him is out of the question now, and that we need to find another way to clean you up.

Priya is preparing to open her shack and is careful so that her beautiful sari doesn't get dirty. She has seen Tommy run away in fear and Lauren trying to get him to come back to her. All this talk and fussing about this dog, she never even pampered her husband like that.

It's funny, she thinks, they do belong together, like a married couple, that little dog and the blonde woman with the spotty looking face.

Lauren needs to get the colours on the paper. It's taken her days to prepare for this and she needs to concentrate – once it's done, it can't be changed.

But she wants to make sure Tommy is OK. What kind of a name is Tommy anyway?

She strokes him on his forehead and he is calmer now.

She leaves him in the field and walks back to her room and takes the big paper out on her porch.

Gets the water out again, and prepares the paint, gets the brush out.

Dips the brush in the hot water, then in the colour, lifts the brush and splashes colour all over the big sheet of paper. Her mind is concentrated on a train of thought. All this faith in God, that she once had and once discarded and now faced with it again like a storm. Wherever she looks there it is. Faith. Another splash with her colours and another correction with her brush. It's all about detail and momentum. It all takes a few moments and it all has to be perfect. God on command, she laughs out loud to herself.

Payne's grey in the background. Let it dry just a little bit. Marine blue and finally Indigo.

Celebrations, wherever she looks its celebrations everywhere.

Colours and prayers.

Miracles.

Royal blue and Phthalo blue, another splash of colour over the previous layer.

Now to the fastidious but most important part. With a soft tissue she absorbs thick layers of water, creating new abstract shapes in the background, allowing the five colours to create new shapes. Magic. Now it has to dry, and then later on today she can start with the next layer.

She goes back into her room, into the bathroom to wash off the paint from her hands. She is sweating and hot, but relieved. Maybe it will work again.

Leaning over the sink in the small bathroom she breathes slower, in a satisfied way, thinking about her previous life, before all the bad happened. Back then, she had never imagined that her life could have been different. But that was then.

By the time she comes out of the bathroom she is curious to see what the colour will end up looking like when it starts to dry.

She walks out to the porch and in front of her is Tommy wagging his tail, walking all over the wet paint, leaving nice paw marks everywhere on the painting.

* * *

Jerome is not going to accept his defeat. Bali and California might be out of the picture at the moment, but he needs to turn the volume up, get back on track and persevere to get what he wants. It's always Sky here and Sky there, but not now. His new name is going to bring him back in the game to get the big groups that he wants and the tours that he longs for in California.

He walks out to the garden, taking slow steps down from the house, as if he is a Lord, yes, Lord Spring. He walks ten steps and for each one he memorizes his lines, his new credo, and the opening speech at the first "The Temple" workshop. As he takes another ten steps, straight towards the beach, he memorizes the next part of his new speech. This sequence is to be called "The memory of the foot, the rebirth of balance".

No, it cannot be called "Ecstatic Yoga Weekend" – it has to be about the outer boundaries of our bodies. "Ecstatic Soul Weekend" or what about "Ecstatic Body Movement Weekend"? Oh well, the fliers are printed and handed out.

Jerome opens his arms, takes a deep breath and slowly exhales, letting the air empty from the lower part of the lungs, the middle part, the top part and when there is no air left he holds the breath, closing his eyes below the stars.

Complete harmony and stillness in the non-breathing.

"Jerome, move your stuff out of the way, the ceremony starts soon! I need to clear the space of all male energy! Out!"

Jerome falls backwards, startled by Sky's presence.

"I will participate tonight!"

"No Jerome, its full moon and it's a women's ritual. Get out."

Jerome sighs and walks out of the garden. Memorizing his ideas, he stands in the garden as Sky prepares tonight's event. She places pillows in a circle, lights sage and walks around the garden waving the sage around, making Jerome cough.

The noise of motorbikes and scooters is the sign that the participants are arriving. Soon enough all the female residents of the alternative scene in Anjuna are in Sky's garden. All beautifully dressed in tribal inspired dresses with Indian fabrics: the latest Goa style designer outfits. From a former royalty in a refitted golden sari with bright red nails and silver hair to Shakti, the Tantric coach who grew up in a grey town with grey weather not far from London with a grey job she hated. She went with a friend to a weekend festival of spiritual dance and left her grey world the following Monday.

Soon enough she was in Goa and it was full of colours and tastes, exploring the body and the mind in every single possible way, it was all here! Yoga and shamanism. Tantric workshops, creative dance and meditation. Therapy and fun if that's the way you wanted it. From a country with no Gods and no rituals she found her way to a haven for her to create her own.

Lauren is wearing her favourite dress that she bought in Thailand ten years ago. "It's so ethnic", says Shakti and looks deep into Laurens eyes. Sky introduces Lauren to Adnah, the Soul Dancer with a Namaste.

"A soul dancer?" says Lauren.

"Yeah, like Osho, Krishna and the spiritual connection that unleashes our inner cosmic journey."

"Oh."

"It's all about letting go in the flow of the movements, you know."

"I know, tell me about it! Caribbean style! You like Reggaeton?"

Adnah gives her a condescending stare.

And as Sky calls all the women to join her in the circle the last participant arrives. It's Venus, the Universal Theory Meditation teacher. She is dressed like a big pink butterfly and as she spreads out her arms, a set of huge pink butterfly wings open wide as she trots towards the women. Lauren can't stop laughing at the middle aged woman in the bright coloured spandex dress, and as Sky goes from woman to woman to put a few drops of a golden coloured potion on their wrists, she shushes at Lauren and starts giggling too. "This is all about being divine."

Sky takes her position in the middle and talks to the group.

"Good evening Goddesses. Welcome to this full moon meeting. Let's call in the directions!"

The whole group faces to the East, the direction of the air.

Sky calls the forces of the East and then whole group says "AHUM" in unison.

As the women turn to face the next direction Anita opens her arms and her big butterfly wing hits Lauren right on her face.

Jerome is watching the scene from the porch. He watches Sky's friend, the one with the freckles and laughs out loud as Lauren takes the wings and ties them up in one big sailor knot much to Venus' dismay.

When Sky calls the direction of Grandmother Moon, Lauren gets interested.

How beautiful, Grandmother Moon.

Grandfather Sun, Mother Earth, Father Sky.

And then Sky calls the direction of The Above, The below and finally, The Within.

Lauren stands there with all these women and looks up to the sky remembering the days when magic was never called upon, it just presented itself with a smile when you least expected it.

• • •

As Lauren focuses on her painting, Jerome spends more time working on his new "Me" and Sky spends a lot of time riding around on her Enfield thinking about her future and where it may lead her. She loved Bali, and is secretly dreaming of moving there. As different as two people could be, Sky likes having Lauren around and spends time getting to know her better. They go on drives together and sometimes the little dog rides on the bike too. They bring Tommy to the beach, and he curiously studies this giant blue water world in front of him. He is amazed by the space and the horizon, and the sensation of freedom that running on a beach can bring you. He rolls in the sand and in fits of pure joy he starts digging a massive hole. He barks when Lauren gets in the water for a swim and runs along the beach with other young dogs. Lauren can see him actually smiling and wagging his tail with joy. This is the life, Lauren thinks, making someone else feel this happy, not just fighting for them to stay alive. She is absorbed by this little life that has four legs and a curly tail, seeing how he grows every day, finding new ways to communicate with her, and learn new things about life without any fear. She wonders if he will make it, if he will live longer than the average three years that street dogs live.

The season carries on with tourists and yogis coming and going and things on the outside seem to go on like always.

Jerome has started his "Ecstatic yoga journey", and as it turns out that it's more a class where he talks about his future in America and his divine reincarnation and less about yoga under stars, leaving people bored and not showing up for the next class. Sky reclaims her garden from him and invites her friends over every night for some fun. Enough of the ranting now, she would like to tell him.

Tommy has become Jimmy's perfect assistant. He has learnt to go up to strangers in a safe way, to chase by-passing dogs away from their territory, to arrive at just the right time for his meal at the Blue House to be sure that they get that extra piece of chicken instead of just rice and broth. And to master the most important skill of a street dog: Tommy always stops before crossing the street, looks to the right, looks to the left to make sure no cars or scooters are driving past. There have already been a few dogs killed by cars in front of their eyes.

One time Lauren was there with Tommy and a little puppy with a red ribbon tied around his neck just walked out in the middle of the street and a jeep drove over it.

Lauren cried and picked up Tommy, put her hand in front of his eyes and held him so hard he almost choked. Saraswati came out with a shovel, picked up the puppy and threw it in the ditch.

At night, Jimmy takes Tommy with him on his rounds, always warning Jimmy first of any danger. They meet other dogs, look for food or simply tease cats and cows.

Come morning Tommy waits for Lauren to open her door so that he can sleep under her bed where it's cool and safe.

In the afternoons he sits next to her when she is painting.

When he gets bored he lies down and makes a funny face, stretching his paw like a person does to get someone's attention. When Lauren looks at him, he opens his mouth, shows his teeth and stretches his paw again touching her hand, then curls up like a bad wolf and cringes with his whole face. Lauren takes one of her painting brushes and teases him while he grabs it with his teeth and makes another funny face. She ends up tickling him on his stomach until Tommy kicks his legs and runs off with her brush.

There are now three finished paintings and Lauren knows that it's soon time to send them to Scott.

Scott, my saviour and best friend, she thinks. How I let you down. She rolls the paintings up and wraps them in brown paper to make a parcel. All those times you looked out for me, helped me and all I did was to leave you without a word. Will you ever forgive me for my silence?

She doesn't attach a note or a letter. Just the paintings. Writes his address on the brown wrapping paper and heads to the post office on her scooter.

• • •

New Year's Eve is approaching and Goa is preparing itself for the big night.

Everyone is making plans for the evening and the locals are busy making decorations and special menus for the big night to come.

Sky and Jerome are organizing a party at the beach house and Lauren is helping them decorate the trees and the gate, and hang more fairy lights – a star clad sky in the garden. Sky is going through the play list with the DJ and it's starting to look like a party everyone will remember.

Lauren had learnt to hate New Year's Eve. It had been the night she realized that it was the beginning of the end and every New Year's Eve after that she had made sure she couldn't remember any of it. The last one had been the worst. A "has-been" band with a couple of hits in the nineties was playing on an island party and she had gone there with a few people. She couldn't handle it, standing there with in the crowd with their clapping, cheering and singing. She quickly got drunk and by the time the fireworks started and everyone was wishing each other a happy new year she had passed out under the stage where the band played. The third time the band had played the only hit everyone knew she woke up as the drummer had decided to do a long solo and the cymbals were right above her. With a splitting headache she crawled out from under the stage and went to the beach. Sat there alone and had no wishes for the New Year or any year to come.

The DJ starts playing a few songs and it's loud, knocking Lauren back to present time as she gets dragged to the dance floor by Jerome. "Look!" he turns on all the lights and a rainbow of colours in the trees makes her laugh. Then he turns the disco lights on and a blinking array of infuriated little stars isn't enough. Turning spotlights in neon colours make the temporary dance floor look like Studio 54 on steroids.

Jerome stands there looking at her very proud. She applauds him and Jerome looks at the lights as he re arranges his purple outfit. The guests arrive and Jerome announces that from now on he will be Lord Spring. No one seems to care that much and the dance floor fills with people, and as more guests arrive the music gets louder. Sky and Lauren dance under the blinking lights, Jerome is comfortable on a couch with a couple of young women around him and a young Indian priest with the most magnificent hair style. They argue and laugh in a lively discussion about the afterlife. And as any other place all other the world, when the music is too loud and people are having too much fun, the police show up and ask the DJ to turn off the music. No one can hear what the police officers are saying and the DJ waves to them with a big smile. Shakti, the Tantric sex priestess invites the police officers for a drink and asks them if they would like to share their tantric moves with her on the dance floor. The DJ starts the countdown. Lauren stands in front of Sky, who is raising her arms to the sky. "Ask the New Year for whatever you want!!! Happy New Year!"

The fireworks go off and everyone greets each other and makes their wishes. Lauren can't get away, getting caught in the middle of the party. She gets hugged and kissed by the guests and greets them back. Jerome gets there just in time and gives Lauren a big kiss on the mouth. The police officers get too close to all the girls and the young Indian priest manages to get them out and leave. Eventually Lauren finds a way to leave the dance floor and walks down to the beach and looks out, far away. The fireworks are above her and the noise is deafening. Like a happy war zone, she thinks.

In the midst of the celebration Lauren gets on her scooter and drives off. Everywhere there are people, tourists, locals, all shooting fire-crackers and shouting, fireworks are covering all the sky of Anjuna. As she drives up to the sandy patch Tommy runs up to her. He has been waiting for her all night. The bypassing cars throw fire crackers at him and keep tooting their car horns to let the world know this year will be so much better than the last one.

He seeks shelter walking right behind her as they go to her room. She opens the door and Tommy jumps up on the bed next to her. She looks at Tommy and he looks back at her.

"We made it, little man. Now, what's your New Year's resolution?"

She strokes him and when her hand is next to him, he curls up and locks her hand with his body, so that she can't leave him.

He closes his eyes and rests with her hand beneath him.

Lauren looks at Tommy and wishes him happy New Year with some pieces of chicken she has taken from the party. She strokes him gently and he puts his head in her cupped hand and rests there.

It had been New Year's Eve, and Lauren had gone to a party at someone's fancy house in Los Angeles with Scott. At sunrise she had left and driving back home in her car she made a detour, passing the area where Heather lived. She knew she was with her friends, that's what she had said but still she drove up to her place, parked and went up to her apartment.

Stood outside for a while surprised at the silence. Or maybe no one was in. She rang the doorbell and it took a while then the door opened. She was there on her own.

"I thought you were with your friends."

"I am."

Lauren followed Heather into the living room and sat next to her in front of the TV.

There was no trace of a party, of other people. Heather focused on the TV.

Lauren reached out to her older sister holding out her hand to her. Her sister looked at her, and took her hand and held it hard.

"You were always my favourite sister." Heather finally said.

"I am the only sister you have."

"Exactly."

"You wanna come with me? Take a break? Go somewhere?"

Same old questions, same old answers. This is as far as Heather would ever go. And as much as Lauren kept the volume up to make some sense of her life and find energy for the both of them, Heather had turned the volume down.

She smiled at Lauren and they laughed quietly. Lauren put her arm around her big sister.

"And you will always be my favourite sister too."

"Always."

No more nagging and no more pressure, Lauren had promised herself as she got back in the car and waved good bye to Heather. Whenever she was ready to come back, to change, she would say so herself.

It is when you understand how lonely someone is that it gets hard to live with yourself. When you realize that whatever you do, it is not enough to help someone who has shut down.

Lauren had turned back, gone back to Heather's home. Had looked in through the window and as she was about to knock on the door again, she stood there looking at her. How she wanted to tell her that she knew how she felt, that it was the same for her, just in a different way. She saw Heather dozing off on the couch and let her be, feeling the loneliest Lauren had ever felt in her whole life.

"You finally made it" Heather tells her younger sister. "That's who I was, and this is who you are."

Heather's ghost hovers above Lauren. She looks at the dog and wishes she could have had a beautiful dog like that.

She whispers to her little sister that her life should be full of colours and she should not be afraid to be happy or to love again. That's all they wanted from her, Heather and her dad, that she could be free and happy.

And keep that cute little dog, he is really special.

Before Lauren was born Heather had asked for a dog but she never got one, all she got was a little sister, not a dog.

Heather reaches down to Lauren and touches her head, strokes her freckles, like she used to do to her when she was a little girl. She strokes the little dog on his head, and he looks up, he can see her and wags his tail at her.

It was as if it was Heather that was the younger of the two. It was all a lie, the story with the magazines, she never read National Geographic or watched documentaries like she told her. She never travelled through shows or books, she had lived through Lauren's letters, reading them over and over again. The adventures, detailed with all the flavours and how different people's lives were out there in another continent.

Heather so wants her to know that she could never have been what Lauren wanted her to be. Lauren was the warrior, and Heather the silent one who got lost early and found solace in silence.

Heather tells Lauren that it's OK, that she is allowed to live and try to be happy. No regrets, little sister. No regrets.

Tommy looks at his blonde human and tears are running down her cheeks. He licks them dry and she kisses him on his forehead. She sighs and by the time the sun comes up on this first day of the New Year, he leaves Lauren and goes back to sandy patch. He lies down next to Jimmy and together they watch this new day and year begin.

• • •

This New Year is starting well, all those hopes and promises didn't vanish with the remains of the party, and everyone is concentrating on making this year better than the previous one.

The party decorations at Sky's beach house are long gone and Sky is in contact with Ganges, they send each other messages with ideas about what their future should be and how they can work together again. Sky is starting to feel detached from Goa, to

Jerome and since her trip in Bali her travelling spirit has been awakened.

She spends hours on the beach meditating and mostly dreaming about being that young girl again with a small back pack going wherever she felt. Maybe she needs new ideas, to let go of what she knows and learn to look at things from another point of view. Lauren parks her scooter at the beach bar and Tommy recognises Sky from a distance, runs up to her, kisses her and then runs back and forth on the beach with his tail high and barking of joy. He chases the holy cows down the beach and then proudly trots back to Sky and Lauren who applaud him.

He lies under their chairs in the shade as the girls drink wine looking at the sunset talking about their destiny and how their lives brought them to where they are. Sky who believes everything is meant to be, everything is Karma, and Lauren who believes that innocent people die for nothing and doesn't accept Karma the way Sky does. They argue and they laugh and they both know that at some point it will be time for Lauren to move on. Her visa is running out soon, and she will have to leave Goa.

Jerome is getting restless. His new idea, the night classes have been a failure. He blames it on the tourists, on the yogis, not on his monologues where the students became bored and fall asleep under the stars instead of listening attentively like they do with Sky. He decides to let things be and save his energy for the cleansing ritual he will do once the season is finished.

He will go to America…he will, one day.

He looks at the tourists sunbathing, at the Holy Cows lying on the beach, the dogs lying under the sun beds sleeping.

Another month and it will be over. The crowds, the cool nights and the dry season will turn into a humid and hot pre monsoon. And then all the restaurants and shacks will close, the roads will be empty again and the tourists will disappear. He loves the circle of nothing and everything. Where will he be next dry season?

Lauren looks at Sky walking back home along the beach. Thinking about her life, her new life and where she should head next. She has sent Scott another couple of new paintings, and is curious to know what he will think.

And Tommy, what about Tommy? Lauren has spoken to Zâbel who promises he will be fine and that he will have food and shelter.

She has given Priya money to make sure she keeps an eye on Tommy. She cannot take him with her, she doesn't know where she is going and its better he stays here where he knows his neighbourhood and has Jimmy to protect him. This is his world, and here is free to come and go as he pleases.

Lauren looks out at the scenery, the Holy Cows on the beach. One of them gets up and walks slowly towards the sun chairs where a couple of Russian tourists are lying. The Holy Cow sticks her head in a hand bag and gets a fruit out, chews it and then looks at the tourists who are taking photos of the Holy Cow. The Holy Cow then decides that the hand bag tastes quite good too and starts eating it. The tourists try to grab the hand bag, the horns, and the tail of the Holy Cow. All that is left of their hand bag is the strap and as the Holy Cow burps, she spits out the chewed up credit card of the Russian tourist.

TAKE ME WITH YOU

Lauren is packing, Tommy lies on her bed, and he keeps looking at her, asking questions she cannot answer. How do you tell a little dog that when your visa expires you have to leave? That sometimes places have a time limit and then you move on? That you might have finished what you came here to do. And then she stops herself – what did I really here come here to do?

"I promise I will make sure that you are OK, this is the place where you have food, you have Jimmy to protect you and you are safe here. This is your home. I am just a visitor in your country, Tommy. I am so sorry. I will try to come again one day. "

Tommy doesn't move. Lauren holds him for a long time. Tommy chose Lauren a long time ago. She is his new Garati, his new Sutara.

It happened the first day she arrived, when she first touched him. He became hers that day, feeling as much an alien at the Blue House as she did with her foreign looks and different smell. He has given her his heart and his trust.

And now he can sense change again, he can feel how life will change again, just not how.

Zâbel and Priya help Lauren carry her bag out to the sandy patch. As they wait for her taxi, Lauren gives them a piece paper with phone numbers to Sky, to a veterinary someone knows, she gives them money for Tommy. Zâbel says "No, you silly girl, you don't worry, he eats here and the Lord will make sure that the mongrel will be fine." She gives them de-worming pills, a flea collar and a little bag with medicines for Jimmy and Tommy.

Zâbel takes them and hugs Lauren. She will miss the silly tourist who is crazy about a dog and who stained the walls of the rooms with her un-Christian paintings.

Lauren turns around and looks at Jimmy staring at them. As always that little prince of a dog is the centre of everyone's attention. Lauren walks up to Jimmy and kneels down next to him. She has never touched him, been close to him. He always stayed away from her, from everyone, even though she always noticed how he kept an eye on her, to make sure she wouldn't hurt his companion. She leans forward towards him and touches him, then kisses him on the nose and asks him to take care of their precious friend. She says thank you and walks away.

Jimmy feels her lips on his nose. It's a soft touch, a nice kiss. He doesn't clean his nose at once, surprised, he keeps the first and last moment in his life a human touched him as a memory to reflect on. He looks at her walking away as the taxi arrives. It has a big mattress on the roof. As the driver gets out and takes the mattress down, Lauren points to Priya and tells her that she should have a nice mattress. Priya walks up to the mattress and touches it. It's brand new and firm. She has never seen such a nice mattress. She starts to cry and hugs Lauren.

"Take care of Tommy now, Priya."

The driver puts her bags in the car.

Lauren picks up Tommy, a long last smell of the most comforting smell she has known in a long time, another long last hug.

Tears on Tommy's forehead.

Tommy whining, worried, here it is again, the smell of change.

Lauren puts Tommy back on the ground.

"You will be fine here, I will have people come and check on you, I promise. You will be fine and you know that you are in my heart forever. I will come back one day, I promise that."

She gets into the taxi and drives off.

In the small world that he lives in, by a dusty patch alongside a busy road, he has found someone that he loves and wants to be with, who can understand him and the love he has to offer.

He is only a young dog, but he has already understood that life is full of hardships and that nothing lasts forever. But this one, he can't let go of.

He runs after the taxi, chases it and barks. Lauren hears the barking and sees Tommy running after the taxi in the back mirror. She tells the driver to stop and gets out of the car.

Tommy greets her happily and Lauren picks him up, carries him back. He has to stay here and she has to leave. "I know, it's just as hard for me as it is for you, you know." She hands him to Priya and Zâbel who have to hold him as she says farewell to him once more and then runs to the taxi. Lauren gets quickly into the car and tells the driver to drive fast. She looks back to see Tommy who desperately tries to free himself from the women's grip barking and crying, scratching Priya's hands and sari. As the taxi drives off and leaves the Blue House and Anjuna for the last time she closes her eyes and the tears keeps coming. Why did she come to India? Like most people who come to India, it rarely is what they think they came for. Like most people, India will give them something completely unexpected. Lauren realizes that India gave her back her life and dreams and that they came in the shape of a little Indian dog.

• • •

As the taxi drives off, Tommy eventually manages to free himself from the women holding him.

He runs the same direction as the taxi, but it's too late.

He can't see it, can't smell it. He keeps running, way beyond his territory. Gets chased by other dogs, by a man who herds his goats, get stopped by fifteen buffaloes crossing the road. He hates water, but decides anyway to wade through the irrigation canal, and keeps going until a pack of wild dogs stop his way. He can't go forward anymore. It doesn't matter if he surrenders to them, they won't let him through. They chase him back through the water, the buffalo herd and the goats. But he refuses to go back. Who brought him to the Blue House anyway? She is supposed to be with him and he is supposed to be with her. That's the way things were meant to be. She has to be somewhere.

• • •

Through the noise on the roof, Priya can hear the first Monsoon rain arriving.

She is sitting on her new mattress, with the plastic cover still on, and hasn't noticed that Tommy has been gone all night.

She hasn't slept this well in her whole life and her back isn't hurting like it usually does.

She doesn't notice Jimmy standing outside her hut, worried, pacing back and forth. She doesn't notice much right now, and decides to lie down again on her new beautiful mattress and sleep some more.

Jimmy is getting worried, that spoiled little dog has been gone all night, leaving him to protect the sandy patch all alone. But it's not like him to stay away this long. He wonders where he could be.

• • •

Even if it's the beginning of monsoon and the yoga school officially has closed, Jerome still teaches a few classes until the shala get taken down. It's starting to get very hot and humid and the students get quickly tired. Jerome is telling them to breathe slowly and concentrate more, not wipe the sweat away from their foreheads all the time.

Tommy is standing outside the shala, looking for Lauren, he silently sneaks inside the tent to get a better look and stands behind Jerome, looking at the class taking their lotus poses and quietly putting their hands in prayer position with their eyes closed.

Jerome is seated in front of them. His new yoga tights are a bit too tight, especially around the crotch, so he stretches his legs in front of him as he addresses his class.

"Tomorrow I will start my silent meditation, it will last for three months, and after that I will no longer be Jerome. I will be Spring, like the season. New and inspiring, bringing promises of change. Next season I will bring a workshop on the purity of our souls, on the divinity of being Human Beings. Spring Time, I will call it." He takes a long slow breath and adjusts his tights around his crotch.

"We are in this sacred place called our body. We can feel how our previous lives are joined together with us in the now. With each exhale feel how the ego is leaving you, allowing the inhale welcome the divine. It's a rhythm, a dance called Peace of the Self.

Feel how your Ego is no-longer. We are the powerful selfless servants of our bodies; we are of service to the Divine.
And Breathe in.....breathe out..... Breathe in...breathe out....."
Jerome walks around the tent, pulling his tights as he adjusts postures. As he is facing the front of the tent he sees the small dog. He grabs a wooden yoga block and tosses it at Tommy. He misses and Tommy runs out.
"OUT! That stupid dog! RAUS!!!"
A ripping sound is heard, and Jerome's tights burst from all the commotion happening to his ego.
"That stupid ugly animal again!"
Tommy looks in to the shala again, wagging his tail; Jerome throws another yoga block at him.
The students are silent, not sure what to say. The all look at the little dog feeling sorry for him.
Jerome walks slowly around the room, catching his breath, holding his hands in front of his crotch to hide the broken tights.
"Ok, everyone breathe in....breathe out....the ego is the home of all the evil...."
The students see the broken tights, and they all start to laugh.
"We are not like the animals. Our time is now, this is the perfect re-incarnation. Animals are a living proof of past sinful lives!"
A student stands up, looks at Jerome.
"That dog seems lost."
"The dog shouldn't be in this place! It is not lost; it is just his reincarnation that reminds him of the suffering it needs to endure!"
Another rip is heard. The tights have surrendered to the pressure and now the back side is torn too.
The class laughs again and Jerome needs to take control.
"OK, OK. Let's just stand in a circle and sing Om. It is the last class of the season and then we can all do what we want to do."
As the group stands united and sings Om, the purest sound in the world, Tommy stands outside looking at the people in the tent with his tail between his legs. Everything has changed.

• • •

Trotting along the road in this first monsoon rain, he remembers the short cut to the German Bakery, all the way down behind the school and the soccer field. The entrance is closed, the restaurant shut down and the guest workers have all started heading back to their families in other states in India, or all the way back to Nepal. Tommy continues to the Anjuna flea market.

The whole area is standing empty, only the bamboo frames are left, as skeletons that were once covered with colourful clothes, bags and carpets with sellers ready to make a good price. As soon as the heavy rains will arrive, the market will turn into rice paddies and when monsoon ends, and the grounds are dry, the market will return.

Big waves are washing up on the beach and they frighten him. Lauren brought him here a few times and he had never seen such endlessness before and the sea smelled salty and the sand felt so good on his stomach when he lied on it. And now she is gone and the beach is disappearing under the dark waves.

He is cold, wet, far away from home and as the sun is setting Tommy decides to hide from the rain under a tree. Eventually tiredness takes over and the little dog falls asleep all alone.

Later on he is dreaming of Jimmy, he can smell him and feel one of the many fleas that cover his body jump from his dirty coat unto his wet body. He wakes up from the dream and looks up. It isn't a dream. He is standing there, growling at him, right in front of him. Jimmy has been looking for him for hours. He does know where the human with the yellow hair used to go, and wherever she went, Jimmy could always see that stupid little dog running after her. So, yes, I know where you go, Jimmy lets Tommy know in an annoyed way. Tommy puts his head down again. His eyes are gloomy, is body wet and he is shivering. Jimmy waits for Tommy to follow him home, but Tommy doesn't move. Jimmy gets angry and tells the stupid little dog to get up, and to go with him back to the Blue House.

Tommy drags himself out of his hiding place. He walks slowly behind Jimmy, following him back, over the bridge, past the liquor shop, the chapel and back to the place they all tell him is his home. But Tommy doesn't lie down next to him on the sandy patch. Jimmy is surprised as the little dog walks past the Blue House and stops further down, in the direction that the taxi drove off to, and keeps staring that direction throughout the night, over the bend of the road for car lights to appear.

• • •

Two friends are out driving on their scooters. Anjuna is so nice now that almost all the tourists are gone. They arrived recently as the season is ending and decided to stay on, enjoying Goa in a quieter way. The deserted roads are safer with little traffic and the locals having more time, giving them good prices on rooms and souvenirs and the rain feels refreshing after a long hot and dusty dry season.

They yell at each other and laugh while driving, without the street vendors chasing them, and the boys at the corner shops running after them yelling "Petrol! Buy Petrol! Petroooooooool!"

They are driving past the Blue House and see a cute little dog sitting alone by the road, staring straight ahead. They stop and look at him and take some photos of the chapel on the other side of the road, of Priya who is standing by her shack, of the little dog.

"Oh so cute, look at his eyes! He must be waiting for his owner."

They offer him a couple of treats, but he doesn't touch the food. Doesn't look at them, doesn't greet them like he usually greets humans and he doesn't chase the scooters as the two girls drive off.

Jimmy goes up to Tommy, takes his treats and walks off. He worries about Tommy, if he doesn't eat he will get sick and monsoon is not kind to the weak and wounded.

Another night approaches, and for another night he will lie next to the road, looking at the direction of where the taxi left. Waiting.

He falls asleep. On the tenth day of waiting he finally walks back the one hundred yards to the Blue House.

Priya sees the dog walking with his head down towards the house, and as he lies down in front of her shack she brings some food for him.

She knows Tommy likes fish and has saved a piece for him.

He eats all the food Priya gives him. She takes some food from her own plate and gives it to him. Jimmy is standing next to Tommy, to protect him while he eats.

When done, Tommy lies down on his usual place on the sandy patch, but his eyes are still fixed towards the road that leads away from Anjuna.

Priya is missing Lauren too. She goes to her old room and opens the door to it, looking at it all empty and silent. She turns on the fan and sits down on the bed, looking around in the empty room. Giggles when she sees the red and blue stains on the wall, a souvenir from one of her painting sessions.

That silly tourist that was so kind to her. Next season she will sell samosas, just like she told her to do.

SO FAR AWAY FROM YOU

It's sunset time and the crowds are gathering on the beach to enjoy the view and start the evening with a drink before the partying. Lotus Island is in full swing, as popular as it's ever been and still as beautiful as Lauren knew it when she first stepped off the ferry for the first time many years ago. She found her love for the sea here, with all the tropical fish coated with bright colours and intricate patterns. The corals, spreading out with reds, ochre and burgundy colours and outrageous shapes. The Whale Shark with its white spots and dark grey body. And the sunsets, the beautiful purple and red colours blending and just before it says it's time to say goodbye for this day it turns bright orange and it's like watching fireworks in slow motion. Beautiful Thailand.

• • •

It's been like this since she left India. The sinking feeling was back, but this time it hit her harder, and in places she couldn't protect herself from.

When she landed in Bangkok she did her usual temple rounds, not so much out of need or interest, just out of habit. It was happening again. But it was more than that. It was as if she forgot to take something with her, that feeling of having forgotten something and not knowing what it was.

Almost like when she was fourteen and went to camp. All the other kids had brought changes of underwear and socks with them, but not Lauren. She had been teased because she smelled bad, dirty and her clothes didn't match. There was no mother to wash her clothes, to teach her to change every day. The boys would lure her to come close, and she had been charmed by the attention, but they all ganged up around her and started mocking her. Lauren looked at the toughest of the guys and said "All I need is a shower, but the filth that comes out of your mouth will never change. Loser." She turned around and walked away. Heather would have been proud, she taught her well. As Lauren was ready to pull down the curtain yet again and disappear into her solitary world she noticed how the other girls gave her the thumbs up and admired her. The next day a camp volunteer brought her to a store and got her a change of clothes, shampoo and a hair brush. Lauren always had a mother and father, just not her own. Help had always come from strangers, and her life had depended on the ones you didn't know. The girls at the camp liked her and Lauren realized that this was the first time in her life that she had made friends her own age. She learnt to sail in the lake and sang with the other children around the fire in the evening. No parties in Los Angeles or San Diego with adults who were high.

Where had her mother been? Lauren thought, looking up at the giant Buddha with the most seductive and understanding eyes. Where were the memories? It couldn't have been just medicines and hospitals, and then nothing. As she sat in the temple with her eyes closed, trying to remember she realized that they had never talked about her. Heather and her. There had never been any "Do you remember when Mom did this...." stories, just this great void inside of her that was starting to eat her up from inside. Why was that? And when had everyone's grief really started? No one had cried, no one had talked about it, they had all just vanished into a daze, Heather and her dad.

· · ·

Sky is riding her Enfield, not entirely happy to be sent out on yet another mission from a friend in need. She has received an email from Lauren. "Please can you drive by the Blue House and see if

Tommy is OK. And take a photo of him."

Holy Goddesses and Karmic forces. This dog.

She loves monsoon in Goa, it is easy to meditate, to be with nature and to enjoy life. The weeks go by and the weather decides what can be done or not.

Jerome is doing his silent vow and it is nice not to hear him ranting on about his new found faith and how he will save the world by sharing "The Intention". What intention? To kick him in the butt? And Sky has other things to think about. She has been invited to go back to Bali. By herself this time, and lead the classes all on her own. Her name in big letters on the posters and invitations. It's all a message from the Universe, her thoughts and prayers were answered. She can't wait to go, to see where this trip will take her this time.

She turns up to the street where the Blue House lies and looks around if she can see the little dog that Lauren likes so much.

The ugly dog is there, but not Tommy. She drives around the neighbourhood and doesn't see him. There is another dog, a big black dog with a sad face tied on a short chain to a pole.

Rain is approaching, she'll come back another day and look again. She gets her Enfield on full speed and drives off back to her house.

• • •

She is out on a big wooden Thai fishing boat converted into a free diving boat. The latest trend among young holiday makers, to hold your breath and go as deep as you can. Everyone signs up to learn how to be free underwater, without heavy scuba tanks, noise or restrictions. All the students are on deck with their teacher doing breathing exercises.

Lotus Island is promising a bright future but Lauren is stuck.

That shadow following her is making itself heard and she cannot shake it off.

She is on the surface, breathing slowly, with her mask on, looking down.

Beautiful blue, beautiful sun rays reflecting back to her. Life, art at its best.

It's her turn and she takes a last deep breath, and off she goes. The long fins taking her deep down, as she follows the sun rays to show her the way.

It's supposed to make her happy, all of this, but as she turns around at 90 feet and start making her way up, she just wants to stop. Let it all end now. Please, it's enough. Mother, Father, Sister, Indian Dog, please let it all stop. This constant restlessness of never finding peace. What is the point?

She is ascending, up to 65 feet, without wanting to. Her head hurts and the body is screaming for oxygen. Let time just stop for a minute.

And she knows it at this moment that it's time to start the process, it's been three years and now is the time. Grief is not about suffering or about you, it's about letting go of our loved ones. The path needs to be clear, to be selfless, without personal agendas in the way.

And Heather looks at her from above and again she has to tell her that she is OK, that it's fine and now finally Lauren knows what love is. She just needs to make up her mind and move on. You are not alone anymore, just choose to do the right thing.

I am so tired, Lauren thinks as she is ready to pass out, let herself go with the sea. And Heather tells her that no, you are not, you are ready now, and this is when the journey really starts.

"It was never my intention to hurt you" she says and smiles at her. And Lauren decides to ascend, to follow her body's instinct to survive, to follow through and surface. Heather holds her hand and makes sure that Lauren makes it all the way up and as the other divers help her little sister as she gasps for her Heather takes her hand away and says farewell.

• • •

Tommy has been wandering in the fields behind the Blue House. The other day Zabel's son Desmond came to the house with a big black dog and tied him to a pole by the tin roof where the cars park, on a tight short chain. He took the dog as payment from someone who owed him money. And he is getting married, so the bride's family will be impressed with this German shepherd. A European breed dog. Impressive, costs a lot of money. Not just some Indian dog that shows up at your door step one day.

More changes will come, he has to show the family that they are not simple country people but they are business owners and have a high standing in the village. The mongrels will have to go, Desmond thinks and looks at the sandy patch and Gita's shack with disgust.

The German shepherd looks confused, out of place, when Desmond calls "Zorro", he doesn't listen. He has never been out of the yard where he grew up, he has never met any other dogs and has never known the world. Now he stands alone chained by a pole. He cannot reach the food, or the water. He keeps pulling and pulling at the chain, trying to free himself, to get away from this place. It's a hot day and he is thirsty. He sees Tommy and Jimmy walking past him. Jimmy growls at the new intruder, Tommy stays behind Jimmy.

As Tommy is walking up to Zorro, Saraswati comes and shoos Tommy away.

She takes the chain off the pole, and takes him for a walk so the dog can relieve himself. As if she doesn't have enough to do. Zorro pulls and pulls, trying to get away from the chain. He makes the housekeeper fall and drag her along the road, in front of a passing rickshaw. The rickshaw driver honks, brakes, almost hitting Zorro. Saraswati gets up, gets a stick and hits Zorro several times. The giant black German shepherd dog keeps pulling, trying to get away from this human, from the pain she inflicts him. The chain is choking him; he can barely breathe. Tommy wants to help Zorro, but Jimmy stops him. Never get too close, or you'll end up like him.

Saraswati manages to drag Zorro back to the pole, ties him up again and beats him with the stick again. Desmond comes out and looks at him. Makes sure the chain is tight, makes sure he can't get away. He looks at Jimmy and tries to kick him. Zâbel stands from afar and watches. That German shepherd will be a good guard dog and now they can show the neighbourhood that they are respectable people.

• • •

The last few nights Tommy and Jimmy have been barking a lot.
A stranger has been passing by the Blue House several times.
Jimmy tried to bite him, and chased him off the grounds when he
tried to climb the gate.
This night the thief is back, and Jimmy attacks him again.
Zorro is lying on the ground, not caring about the thief or
anything else, all he wants is to get away from this horrible place.
The next day Desmond comes out and tells Zorro he is a good
dog, to bark and scare strangers off. He gives him a piece of meat
and pats him on the head.
He tells Saraswati to stop feeding the mongrels and to clean up
the sandy patch.

· · ·

Priya is lying comfortably in her new mattress, dreaming, long
beautiful dreams. Every morning when she wakes up she carefully
covers the mattress with plastic and a blanket, so that it will stay as
new.
She makes some Chai and looks forward to the day.
She will go to the temple beyond Mapusa and celebrate the annual
Hanuman celebration. There will be a lot of people and a lot of
good food.
She puts on her beautiful green and gold sari, brushes her hair and
places a colourful bindi on her forehead. Takes her handbag and
leaves.
She crosses the sandy patch and sees the new black dog tied to the
chain. He is pulling and pulling and she sees that he cannot reach
his food or his water.
She goes up to him, pushes the bowls closer to him. He doesn't
care about food and water, he just cares about pulling the chain
and try to get away.
Tommy sees Priya and runs up to her. Follows her to the bus stop,
and waits with her for the bus to turn up.
Priya is happy that Tommy is feeling better and strokes him on the
head as he looks at her.
She gets on the bus and Tommy runs after her, happily chasing the
bus for a while until he gets tired.
Priya waves at Tommy from inside the bus, promising him she will
pray for the silly tourist to come back soon.

The thief is lurking behind the chapel. He throws a piece of meat and Jimmy runs up to eat it.

Normally he wouldn't take food from strangers, but since the new black dog arrived they have barely been given any food from Saraswati. He is hungry and on his nightly rounds there is less food around. The restaurants are closed, the seasonal travellers and workers have left and so the garbage areas are almost empty in monsoon.

He is so hungry that he doesn't even smell the piece of meat. He chews it quickly and it tastes good.

• • •

After chasing the bus, Tommy has been barking at the Holy cows on the other side of the bridge and then trots off for a visit to the local shop waiting for a treat or two.

Heading back to the Blue House he feels proud, he made those cows run! And the bus! He knows to run along the road on the left side, like the cars do. He always runs on the edge of the road, keeping a careful eye so that a driver won't run over him.

He takes the shortcut across the chapel, runs across the field and crosses the road to the Blue House.

He sees Jimmy on the dusty patch. He is lying down, panting, and froth is coming out of his mouth. He can barely breathe and his pain is apparent.

Tommy freezes, not again, not more pain. He runs up to the Blue House, barking. Saraswati comes out, takes a broom and shushes Tommy away.

He keeps barking, but no one opens the door for him.

He barks at passing cars, who all yell at him, barks at Zorro, who is not looking, not caring, just pulling the chain and staring straight ahead.

Jimmy vomits, struggles for each breath, the pain in his stomach is excruciating.

The poisoned food from a simple thief has destroyed the toughest dog in Anjuna.

Tommy stands hovering over him not knowing what to do, except bark to get anyone's attention. As each of Jimmy's breaths becomes more difficult, Tommy turns more and more quiet.

All he can do now is to stand by the only one in the world who hasn't deserted him. It's a long and painful afternoon and whatever Tommy tries to do; it isn't helping Jimmy.

By evening, Priya gets off the bus with a stomach full of delicious blessed food and a lighter mind as Jimmy is taking his last suffering breath.

One eyed Jimmy looks back at his life. It has been a tough life. He lived all his life at the Blue House and most days were good. No human ever touched him, except when someone threw a rock on him and Saraswati had to take him to the animal clinic and they had to take his eye out. Jimmy never needed anyone and never wanted anything from anyone. Until the little dog arrived. He looks above him and there he is. Standing right next to him, eternally faithful and kind.

As his soul is ready to leave this earth, he wishes him a life safe from more dangers. His last thought will be that the human with the yellow hair will return and take care of his young companion before he will be harmed too. He will not be able to survive on his own, Jimmy thinks and looks for the last time into Tommy's eyes. And during his last breath he smells that sweet smell of the little dog with a soft heart that was the only friend he ever knew.

Priya returns to the Blue House, she is singing "Om naja Shiva". She stops abruptly. The silence. No happiness, just silence and Tommy standing over Jimmy, watching over him.

Priya runs up to Jimmy, kneels down. He is dead and she prays for him. But who will watch her shack now? Not Tommy, not the black dog, that's for sure.

The blood coming out of Jimmy's mouth is a sign of pain, the poor dog. She is crying for him and tries to comfort Tommy, who is so silent and shivering.

Saraswati looks out of the Blue House and sees Priya and the dogs, yells at her to be quiet. Priya keeps crying. Saraswati goes up to Priya, telling her to be quiet, and then sees the dead dog,

Oh holy Krishna, the work never ends and now with the wedding it will just get worse. She returns with a shovel.

Picks up Jimmy and carries him to the field next door.

Dumps the body, throws some earth on Jimmy and walks back into the house swearing.

Priya looks at Tommy, how he runs up to Jimmy's dead boy and stands above the dead body. All night Tommy stands there as a silent statue, waiting for Jimmy to wake up.

Priya feels as lonely as Tommy does. She calls him, tries to get him to follow her to her hut, but he is not listening. He is with Jimmy, keeping him company in that middle land between life and death. Priya walks slowly back to her hut. As she prepares her bed for the night she looks out to the field to see Tommy lie down next to the dead dog. What sadness. All those prayers were for nothing.

The next morning, she finds him standing alone by the road looking at the direction Lauren left, where the taxi drove off.

He barely remembers why he stands there or why he is looking at that direction, but that's where his eyes are and that's where his hope lies, that someday he will not feel this lonely again.

And while Tommy is standing by the road, waiting for the pain to leave him and Priya is lonely in her hut eating the blessed sweets, the thief returns to the Blue House undisturbed.

He gets in through the kitchen, steals all of Zâbel's money that she had secretly put away to start her motorbike taxi business, the wedding rings and the new laptop for the youngest son. Spoiled by Jimmy's fierce guardianship they all sleep without worries and get on with their dreams.

Zâbel is the first one to wake up, she prays as she always does and then puts on her morning robe. Half asleep she goes to the kitchen and then she sees it. The kitchen door is open.

Before she wakes everyone up she quickly checks her hiding place, the money is gone. She can't tell anyone about the money, because no one knew she had put money away. So how could the thief have known? She suspects her son has something to do with this and she curses him in her prayers. Her dream is gone, the safest motorbike taxi business in Goa. And now back to her shop for the rest of her life. She will talk to people and find the thief, eventually. She looks up to the sky and prays to Jesus that he will one day give her comfort in this only life she knows.

· · ·

When Ganges calls Sky again and says the magic words "Your future in Bali" she packs her bags quickly and gets the first flight out of Goa, forgetting all about checking on Tommy and forgetting all about Jerome staring at a wall chanting some self-composed mantra.

As Sky is getting on the plane at the airport and the rain keeps pouring down and the humidity hits a maximum where it's almost painful to breathe or even think about walking, Tommy is hiding under the roof of Priya's shack.

The busy road in front of the sandy patch is deserted and with the never ending rain, not a soul is in sight, not a scooter to chase and no one walks past. Priya is in her hut, Jimmy is dead and Zorro keeps pulling the chain, like he always does.

Darkness falls and it's feeding time. Tommy goes to the Blue House for food, at least it's worth trying even if they haven't given him anything in days now.

The son of the house, Desmond, is shouting at Zâbel when he sees Tommy.

"Now we have the big dog, we don't need those ugly mongrels around. Where was he when the thieves came?"

"It's not a problem, no one says anything. And what did the big dog do to stop the thief?"

Desmond is furious. Why does his mother always have to talk against him? This is not the way it's supposed to be.

"But the wedding, all the guests from Mumbai will come, and what will they think? We are not poor; this is what they will think when they see the dirty dog on the sandy patch!"

He points at Tommy, points at his mother.

"He has to go! I have the taxi business now! The father of Anita will invest money in the business! Soon we will be driving every tourist between Calangute and Morjiim! This place has to look decent! That shack makes our house look like a slum! And the mud huts in the back with all the poor people you have to help and feed! That has to change! This will become a respectable home and when I marry I will become the master of this house and you will have to submit to my decisions. That is the way it is and this house will no longer be a haven for charitable needs."

Zâbel sighs and walks away, she is tired of always being so understanding and helping everyone and what does she get in the end? Having her money stolen? Being yelled at by her stupid son? Tommy is standing there, looking at Zâbel. The son takes a rock and throws it at Tommy. Misses and takes several rocks and throws them at him.

"I will kill this mongrel!"

Priya hears the commotion from her hut, she runs to the Blue House and for the first time in her life she takes a tone that no one knew she possessed. Little quiet invisible Priya yells at the top of her voice at Desmond. She tells him to stop hurting her watchdog, to stop yelling at Zâbel and as she builds up the courage she needs to tell him what she thinks about a lot of other things she gets hit on the head by Desmond throwing another rock at her. And as Priya runs back to her hut Desmond picks up a last rock from the ground and finally gets a good hit, hitting Tommy in the head too. Quietness returns to the Blue House. Only the subdued sobs are heard from Prya who is sitting on her comfortable mattress, but it doesn't feel very welcoming tonight. Everything is falling apart. The holy lord Shiva and Krishna, and please Ganesh, give me some guidance, she prays in desperation. She had heard what the son had said, what would happen next, they would chase her off too? And where would she go?

In the rainiest night this monsoon, Tommy stands far away from the Blue House, bleeding from his head.

He is still hungry and understands now that the way Jimmy was looking at him in his last living moments was a warning to watch out, to be careful. To grow up. To be better, to stop hoping. Welcome to reality, little dog.

• • •

He stands by the chapel, he has been standing there for two days, waiting.

For food, for shelter, for forgiveness. Whatever he had done that is bad he doesn't know but he keeps hoping to be forgiven, because he is so hungry he doesn't know what to do anymore.

He sees from a distance how Desmond brings out nice pieces of chicken to Zorro. But Zorro has stopped eating. He has stopped pulling on the chain.

He just stays there, swaying back and forth. There is no more longing back for him, to that happy garden and a happy youth.

When Desmond is gone, Tommy can't help himself anymore. He knows it's wrong but hunger takes over logic or justice. He sneaks up to the sandy patch and eats Zorro's food, drinks his water.

Tommy looks at Zorro, but the big dog's soul is spent, he is like a ghost. The chain is cutting into the skin of his neck. Where once his thick black coat was, the chain has now cut through the skin and the flesh, and it keeps cutting deeper, but Zorro no longer feels pain. Tommy licks his ears, trying to get some life back into him, licks his whiskers, to tease him, but Zorro just sways to the left and to the right, and doesn't care. It's useless. Tommy returns to the chapel, and looks at the sandy patch and the Blue House from a distance under the rain. He sees how Priya walks to the shack, how she goes to Zorro, to check on him.

How she stands looking out towards the chapel looking for Tommy.

How she strokes her beautiful green and gold sari, worried and sad. Priya leaves Zorro, goes back to her hut. There is a hole on the tin roof of her hut and she has to try and cover it somehow before the whole hut gets full of rain.

● ● ●

Monsoon isn't kind tonight. As the hours pass the rain is making its way into Priya's hut and soaking her new mattress, Zorro has turned around, and the chain has double turned around his neck. He leans towards the chain, pulls all his weight, almost enjoying the pain it inflicts him.

Tommy is sneaking up to the sandy patch again, he is cold and he wants to see if Priya is up. When Zorro sees Tommy, he lunges at him.

It is almost premeditated, an excuse for a last desperate action to get away from a life he never knew could be so cruel.

Slowly the chain blocks the last little bit of air and Zorro keeps pulling until he is freed from this horrible thing called life.

It's over and Zorro looks happy in his death. This time Tommy doesn't stand over Zorro's dead body to grieve him. His body isn't shivering with sadness but what kicks in is uncertainty and the realization that he has to get far away from this place.

Desmond needs to get out and get some air, even if it's raining and it will ruin his hair. Zâbel is driving him mad, all those questions about the thief this and the thief that. He is thinking about sending away his mother as well, why not, he has her money, he will have her house, so he doesn't need her anymore. Find a tiny house somewhere with a cheap rent and dump her there. He lights a cigarette and closes his eyes, satisfied with this new idea.

He sees Zorro lying on the ground, in the mud. He goes up to him and sees that he is dead. He kicks the German shepherd, what a useless dog! What a useless place. How will he get things to look presentable when the bride arrives? He swears at how messy his hair is in the rain and when he looks up, in the distance he can see the silhouette of a small dog with his tail between his legs running away, who will never return to the Blue House again.

● ● ●

Jerome is feeling lonely in the Shanti house. The waves are washing up on the path and it's humid, cold, wet everywhere.

He is tired of his silent vow but he has to purify himself. Go back to the origins, the pure and selfless journey baring the soul, cleansing his Karma. He spends hours every day writing down the outline for "The Intention". It's dragging on and he has no one to talk to. He finishes a chapter on divine evolution.

"Only the human soul can understand what pain and suffering is. That is how we are different from animals, how we keep being reincarnated into animals until our Karma has reached a state of development where we are allowed back to Mother Earth as Homo Sapiens. All animals have no feelings or know no pain. They should be treated with indifference as the choices of their previous lives is the result of their current form."

He needs to develop this, but his mind keeps drifting back to Sky leaving in a hurry for Bali. He feels betrayed. His mind is bored and he needs sex, not silence. Women's names come up in his head, for each name a body, a beautiful body.

Jerome decides to go for a ride. The rain will do him some good, calm down his libido and help him regain control. Maybe this whole silent vow was just a stupid idea, maybe this new dogma is just stupid. Maybe he should just lick his wounds and move on. His mistakes in Bali is his Karma punishing him. Oh well, he could always go to Nepal for a few months, enjoy the mountains and not think about taking life too seriously.

He drives out of Anjuna, away from the village, along the road up to Vagator, looks out to the big field where the techno parties used to be. What memories he has from this place, as he looks over the empty green fields, he thinks about the good old days in Goa. The parties going on all night, all day and then all night again. His ears deafened by the loud music. Pumping with energy, dancing on and on until he would pass out next to a beautiful woman or two, and then wake up and start all over again. Oh, the brilliant younger days!

He continues past the restaurants; a group of Holy Cows are lying down under the roof of the tourist restaurants that are now shut for the season.

He drives back onto the main road, keeps driving, the rain is helping, his mind is concentrating, he feels calm, his sexual tension is slowly calming down.

And there, there is a dog crossing the street. Jerome slows down, he recognises the dog.

It's the dog that lived at Lauren's house. The stupid dog at the Yoga school that ruined his class. He sees Lauren in front of him. When she was painting and leaned forward to reach the paper with her brush, he used to be able to see her bra, the shape of her breasts, oh man, breasts. And instead of talking to him, she would talk to that dog. Oh, pure Divinity. I need to have some fun again!

Then he stops the Enfield.

He remembers now. Sky had been looking for him. Lauren wanted to know he was OK. Jerome gets off the bike, gets his phone out, calls him. "Dog, Dog!"

The little dog runs up to him, crying, wagging his tail.

He looks skinny and miserable and dried blood is on his head around a big open wound.

Jerome takes a few photos.

He is not sure it's him, but keeps taking photos. He is dirty, making a ridiculous begging noise and smells really bad. Yuck.

The little dog follows him as he walks back to the Enfield. He gets on the Enfield, emails the photos of the dog to Sky straight away from his phone. The wonders of modern life. If Sky can see that he can be a good friend to her maybe she will ask him to come back to Bali, or anywhere. He has to make sure that she doesn't forget all about him, whatever it takes. He starts the engine and drives off. The little dog runs after him for a while, Jerome tries to kick him and the little dog stops running.

Tommy stands in the middle of the road, soaking wet, crying and begging for food, for shelter.

Jerome drives fast. That stupid dog.

It's starting to rain harder now and water is filling up the puddles. He gets his Enfield on full throttle and shouts out of joy. Ah, the reason Goa is the best place in the world! Wide open roads in monsoon! He accelerates the motorbike to top speed and a few moments later the shouting turns into surprise and then fear. Fear of death and suffering.

A holy cow walks out to the road from a country path right in front of him.

It's a small black and white cow with gentle eyes. She has red and green marks on her forehead from being blessed by Hindus in the neighbourhood. This small and beautiful holy cow is staring him straight into his eyes as he hits the brakes and the motorbike drives straight into the cow.

The crash is loud and as the holy cow is crushed underneath the motorbike Jerome flies with the Enfield across the road and skids down into the ditch. The Enfield coughs a last time and dies. Jerome lies in the field; the holy cow is on the ground in the middle of the road. Screaming in agony, trying to move, trying to live.

By some miracle Jerome regains consciousness. The only reason he used his helmet today was because he didn't want to get his long beautiful hair wet in the rain.

He is hurting everywhere and bleeding. He can't feel his left leg, but still he gets up and limps to the cow. The animal.

And then he sees it. Her eyes are wide open, so full of suffering and pain. Looking at him asking for help. Her legs are broken and blood is everywhere. A few peasants who live nearby come running. They see the tall white man with the purple helmet standing by the cow. He is crying and kneeling down next to her. Suffering is everywhere and Jerome can see kindness in the animal's eyes, despite her unbearable pain.

They see him go to his Enfield and get something out, and return to the holy cow. They see him lifting his arm and it's a knife he is holding. Jerome needs to help end the suffering. He lifts his knife and kills the holy cow.

Everything he has believed in ends here. Suffering is everywhere and he has caused it. He is as culpable as the next man. Nothing he has learned in the past twenty years has helped him be superior or protect himself. And suffering, emotions or pain is not just for human beings as he has been preaching. What a liar he is.

As the holy cow takes her last breath, and her eyes stare straight into the void, he falls down to the ground with the cow's blood on his hands.

He doesn't hear the villagers approach. They come up to him from behind and start beating him with sticks and shovels and anything they can get their hands on.

Jerome's damaged leg can't carry him and he takes the pain and the humiliation as it comes. But when he lies down next to the cow and tries to hold her the villagers stop beating him. A big white man asking for forgiveness. By the time the ambulance and the police arrive Jerome has lost consciousness and the villagers are all blaming the big white man for the death of their holy cow. The paramedics have a hard time getting the long haired man to loosen his grip around the holy cow. It takes five men to put him on the stretcher and carry him to the small ambulance.

· · ·

Sky has landed in Bali and instantly feels at home.

She is helping Ganges with the last preparations for the festival, and it's as if she's been there forever. Her and Ganges, side by side, as if they were meant to be together.

Ganges takes Sky to dinner, a real romantic date at a five-star restaurant. Asks for the best table and the best Italian wine.

Balinese dancers and musicians are performing on a stage and Sky is loving it all. Ganges looks at her and asks her to come and live with him in Bali.

With him, in his Balinese house in the rice fields and his collection of Italian records. She smiles and says. "Let me think about this."

Actually she doesn't, it's a yes straight away. And as Ganges pours another glass of Italian wine and she is about to say "Yes" her phone rings.

She neglects it, and it rings again.

Annoyed she picks up the call and with surprise she hears an Indian man on the phone, from Saint Joseph's hospital in Mapusa. Does

Sky know a Jurgen Hesseldorf? Jurgen? Oh, Jerome. Yes, she does. Will she pay for the hospital charges? What?

The man describes how this Mister Jerome is lying in the hospital with a broken leg and some broken ribs. He has a serious concussion as well and talks a lot to himself. Will he be OK? Sky asks. "Yes Madam, he will be very fine, he will need to stay here for one week and that will be two thousand rupees per night, plus the twenty thousand rupees for the operation and the plaster for the leg. And the crutches and the drugs. And four thousand rupees for the cow."

The cow?

Sky says "Yes, that's fine, I'll cover the expenses."

The cow?

She tells Ganges that something has happened. Does she need to go back to Goa? What about the Festival?

She will stay. He looks at her, waiting for that answer.

"And Yes. I will live with you here in Bali."

And Ganges leans over the table and kisses her. "Thank you, my Goddess, my beautiful Sky Goddess!"

He holds her hand, but she is restless, she asks him to wait, she needs to check her messages, takes her phone out again and yes, there it is, an email from Jerome. It's from last week. She has forgotten all about the rest of the world, and didn't that feel great. She sighs.

It's from the day of the accident. There are photos attached.

"Here is the dog your friend was looking for. Please send her the photos and also my email address. It is very empty here without you and I will make sure to take care of your house."

She opens the photos and looks at Tommy. She emails Lauren the photos. Done. Enough now. Goa is so complicated. Time to move on.

What is all this about a Cow? She apologizes to Ganges, everything is confusing.

Ganges tells her to look around her, look at how beautiful Bali is. So green and lush. Tropical. He lifts his glass of wine and so does Sky. "To Bali. To our bright future."

• • •

Saint Joseph's hospital in Mapusa is the ultimate Goa experience. It can be called anything but clean or high class and most Indians would barely call it a hospital, let alone choose to be hospitalized here, with or without money. It was a clever doctor in the heydays of the party times in Anjuna that came up with a recovery hospital, as he called it. "Cheap and cheerful" and "Detox with a smile!" was written on the entrance to the hospital. Obviously along with the "All credit cards accepted".

The patients in the ward are lying in a row on squeaky beds with stained sheets. At the end of the long narrow room there is one toilet. It's extremely dirty and the smell from it wanders down the ward, reminding every single patient that they are indeed staying in the cheapest hospital in the area. The ambulance driver that arrived to the accident scene looked at Jerome's long hair, his motorbike, his purple lungi and bare feet and figured that this was another wannabe hippy tourist who experimented with drugs and probably would need his parents to pay for the hospital bills so he drove him off to the nearest and cheapest place. He looked a bit old for having parents pay for him, but one never knows with these tourists.

The doctor smiled as the big man was carried off the ambulance and into the surgery room. Big man with big wounds and a broken leg. Great for business in the low season.

Jerome feels nauseous and sick most of the time. A patient next to him is vomiting for the fifth time in a rusty bucket and on the other side a woman is screaming in agony. Jerome is begging the doctor to let him go home, but the doctor is insisting he stays put here for another week and gives him more sedatives. He needs to stay calm and get better. Jerome fights the sleep, his mind is on fire, and he wants out of this torrid place.

Flies are everywhere and the one fan in the whole ward has broken down causing all the patients to sweat profusely and create even more bad smells.

His concussion and God knows what drugs they have given him is making him drift in and out of hazy clouds of consciousness. His leg is broken and in a cast that hurts and is itchy. He can barely breathe, his ribcage isn't doing too well, and he can't really understand what is wrong with it, but it does need some expensive medication. He doesn't want to lie here because all he thinks about is the Holy Cow.

He needs to know, because if he is wrong then all he believes in needs to be dissected and rearranged into something that is unknown and he will be bared and dissected too. Another cross road.

It takes another two days of begging before the doctor lets him leave and as he is wheeled out to a rickshaw he is handed a small bag full of medicines for him to take several times a day and a pair of crutches.

As they drive off under the cloudy sky Jerome is happy to see the world again. He feels the wind hit his face and the fresh air feels cooling after lying in a bed surrounded by disease ridden people. They drive past a sign on the road: "Goa Animal Rescue, NGO". He tells the driver to turn off and drive up to that place. The rickshaw driver swears and tells Jerome he has to pay extra for washing all the mud off. Jerome's ribs are killing him as they ride up the bumpy and muddy hill. As he takes another painkiller he says "Yes, whatever you want, just drive." They stop in front of the entrance and Jerome takes his crutches and hops to the reception, asking for a veterinary.

He explains what happened with the Holy Cow and asks "I need to know that I did the right thing."

The veterinary asks him to go with her. She takes him to the cow rescue shed.

Points at Laxmi, a small cow with three legs. "Laxmi here had been lying in a ditch for a week with two broken legs, we picked her up and here she is, a month later. Yes, she has suffered a lot, but she is alive and now she is OK. If the cow you hit could have survived? I don't know, I wasn't there, no one called us. But we would have tried. So, maybe you did kill her for nothing. Who knows? Let me show you Tanner, come with me."

The vet takes him to the dog shelter.

A little dog is trying to hide in a corner, he has a big bandage around his neck and his tail is wagging shyly.

"One of our volunteers found him tied to a rope that was cutting through his throat. Someone must have tied him up on a chain when he was a small puppy and then forgotten all about him as he grew older. We were sure he was going to die, but he made it. The rope was stuck to his throat digging into the flesh. Should we have killed him? Now he is fine. All he needs now is a good home. All stray dogs are being released back to freedom once they are healed from their injuries, but Tanner here, he is not a stray. Should we bring him back to the place that almost killed him? And look, here is Lola. Two months ago her whole body was covered in mange, she had no hair, and the illness was literally eating up her body from inside. That was just one of the problems. We handled that with medicines. Someone also kicked her on the back repeatedly, and she ended up lying in a bush ready to die. Luckily, another volunteer saw her. Look at how beautiful she is now! But she has been here too long now, so she might have lost her territory and it will be hard for her to release her again as she will be chased out of her old patch. We will put her up for adoption. Suffering is everywhere, but we try to beat it, one soul at the time."

Jerome's eyes are filled with tears. "But it's their Karma! It's a part of their reincarnation!"

The vet looks at him. "You think these poor animals understand Karma? They only know that they have one life and this one life is what happens right now. Not a nice way to live your only life, is it? What if it happened to you?"

"But the Universe – The Universe says..... "

He stops himself. Lowers his head and sobs. Takes out another pain killer and swallows it quickly.

"I'll take them, both of them. And the cow."

And for the third time in his life, Jerome walked away from everything he had ready to start a new chapter in his life.

• • •

Lauren is standing on the beach looking out over the emerald coloured sea. She is holding a photo in her hand. Looks at it and then looks out to the sea again.

She turns around and goes quickly back to her bungalow.

On the floor her big sheets of paper are spread out, several attempts at doing intricate decorations are lying unfinished.

A couple of photos are posted on the wall. It's of her and Tommy, of Scott and Heather.

The new photo is the one Jerome took of Tommy before the accident, and Lauren cannot believe the state of him. Again she has let someone down and driven them to suffering and despair. It's as if she is programmed to cause death.

A cockroach is walking happily across the floor. A big gecko runs across the ceiling and poops right on her painting. Lauren swears at the gecko, and notices that ants have been eating some of the colours. Lauren had believed it had been her words that drove him to his death, but as she is standing here in a shabby bungalow in Thailand, looking at these photos she wonders for the first time in three years if it really was the argument they had that led to her father's suicide. It had happened short after she stormed out of the house, after she blamed him for everything.

But he had heard worse things in his life, the way Heather used to yell at him. She had been sure it was her fault, and she had carried that cross for a long time. How can you do any good when you cause such pain? Maybe he was just tired of it all, of trying to find a reason to live when all he ever wanted was to be with the one he really loved. A neighbour had called her, wondering why the door had been open for two days. She said she didn't know. He had gone in and found her dad on the couch. Yes, it was pills, yes it had happened the day Heather died. Yes, she had said, I'll be there soon. They had taken her dad's body to the morgue, she signed the obligatory documents and then left it all to Scott. Took a taxi and went to the airport and left for good. Always leaving everyone, that's what she did. And then what?

Lauren keeps staring at the photo Jerome took of Tommy. Of that look in his eyes of being let down. Of begging for help.

What happened? They promised her everything was going to be fine. Now look at him. Bleeding? Hungry and lost? And what was Jerome doing?

How could he have left him there? That selfish self-absorbed pompous prick.

She needs to breathe, to get away. Again she has tried to help and all she did was to ruin someone's life.

Lauren drives her scooter back and forth on the small island. She finally stops at a beach bar.

Dance music is blaring out. It's sunset and the party is just getting started.

She orders one drink after the other, dances and stumbles around, falls into a few people and walks down to the sea.

She walks out wading in the sea, looking up to the stars.

Where did it all start, this moment of change and hope? And why was she failing again?

She picks up her phone. Stares at it. Punches the numbers. It's time to make the call. God knows what time it is in California.

He answers the phone.

"Scott. Hi, it's me."

"Are you OK?"

"Hm. No."

"Do you need money?"

"No. I don't know what I need."

"You sound drunk."

No answer.

"Everything is different now. Not like it used to be."

"I know. Where are you, by the way?"

"On a beach. I met someone."

"Listen, if you are calling me about some guy and pretend like it was yesterday and I am supposed to comfort you then forget it, OK? I don't know where you are, if you are alive or dead. I don't know how to help you and I have been waiting a long time for your call."

Lauren is silent.

"I haven't heard your voice in three years, you can do whatever you want, but maybe sometimes I need to hear your voice too. It's just that I can't because I don't know where you are and you never answer my emails. I have been going through a really tough time here and I could really use talking to my friend sometimes."

"It's not like that. I think that I should come back, at least for a while. And this Tommy is not just some guy."

"Tommy? Who the hell is Tommy?"

"He is injured and sleeping on the street somewhere. I have let him down. I let everyone down."

"Well if this Tommy has lived on the streets for a long time, I am sure that he will know how get back on his feet again. And what kind of name is Tommy anyway? How much have you been drinking?"

"A lot."

"I'll pick you up at the airport."

"I think I am going to be sick. OK, I'll see in a week or so."

• • •

The Awakening Festival is on its last day and it has been a huge success. More yogis are here than last year, and they have come from all over the world. Sky is looking at the poster again. She does it all the time. Her name right up there with all the famous yoga teachers in Asia and America. It really is happening! She is going to lead the closing ceremony with Ganges. It will be a Love ceremony from the Buddhist meta mediation. She did it once at a silent retreat in Thailand and now she will engage the whole world in it.

She has asked everyone she knows to participate from wherever they are. All participants have been asked to do the same creating a global meditation.

Ganges proposed to her last night, they will get married and she will move to Bali. She needs to go back to Goa to pack up her house and get her belongings, and say good bye to Jerome. And then they will get married.

Ganges is standing behind her and he whispers to her. "Are you ready to go and do some magic for the world?" Sky backs away from him, overwhelmed by her feelings for him. She nods yes as he takes her hand and leads her to the tent.

Close to a thousand people are present and Ganges and Sky look at each other smiling. Ganges makes a gesture to let Sky lead the meditation. She asks everyone to sit in the Lotus position and to close their eyes and reminds everyone participating to concentrate on only sending love, not words of regret or wishes. This is a meditation, not a place to make up for lost opportunities, she says and thanks everyone for sharing this important moment with her.

• • •

It's early in the afternoon at the Shanti house in Goa. Jerome is lying on the couch with Lola and Tanner next to him. The three legged cow is eating the bushes and all the flowers Sky planted last year. Jerome turns his computer on and logs onto the Bali website.

He clicks on a link and he can hear Sky's voice. He smiles proudly and closes his eyes. It's time to start.

Sky asks all the participants to send love to someone they love. Jerome thinks about the Holy Cow he killed, that one girl he fell madly in love with in Berlin, he thinks about his mother who refused to talk to him when he left for the West leaving the old ideas of East Germany for a frivolous life out there without constraints or judgement from your neighbours.

He decides to send love to her. He sits in silence sending this love, as Sky far, far away sends love to her family she hasn't seen in a long time. She will invite them to Bali, she thinks and share her life with them. Maybe when they meet Ganges they will finally accept her path. Settled and all, like her father wants her to be.

After a while she asks that everyone send love to someone who needs love.

The whole tent is silent and Ganges is the only one who opens his eyes. He looks around his tent at all the participants and at Sky, and his heart is happy.

• • •

Lauren is in her bungalow in Thailand. She has closed all the doors and windows. She is sitting in front of her computer, with her legs crossed in front of her and with her eyes closed.

She is listening to Sky and sends love to Scott. Her knight in shining armour that was always there to help her. He needs love right now.

When asked by Sky to send love to someone they like, Jerome sends it to the veterinary at the animal rescue centre and smiles. She really is quite cute when she gets angry.

Sky sends it to Lauren, wherever she is knowing she needs love right now.

Then it's time to send love to someone they are indifferent to.

Jerome sends his love to his accountant in Anjuna, for letting him have such a great life in India. Lauren sends it to all those people she has met in these last few years, that she couldn't see or care about, that were just there, dancing with her on a beach for a whole night keeping a stranger company.

And the last person to send love to is to someone you don't like.

In the big tent in Bali the silence and surprise causes the meditation to get interrupted. Sky reminds everyone to take their time, to keep breathing and not to lose their focus.

Ganges sends his love to Jerome. He doesn't not like him, he hates him, for ridiculing him, for taking his wife. But then again, here is Sky next to him and if hadn't been for him, Sky would never be here.

Lauren is having a hard time concentrating on this last step of the meditation. It's such a contradiction, sending love to someone you don't like? How stupid, what does it mean anyway? She takes a deep breath and chooses a name. The most difficult one. She decides to send love to her father.

Because if she does, she has to accept his mistakes and let go of him and all his faults and somehow stop blaming him and mostly herself for everything. What kind of father was he anyway? Show up at the house every couple of weeks expecting her and Heather to take care of themselves?

Where had he been, anyway? There had been no letters to trace his travels or whereabouts, no friends to call and ask, no phone book nor diaries. An empty life, after his wife died.

We don't choose our parents, but we can choose how to move on without anger. Yeah, right, we've heard that one before. Or was it his pain that kept him away and made him ill? How can we send love to someone who can't work past his pain? How easy it is to judge.

She opens her eyes wide in anger, when it comes to acceptance it's a big thing to ask when it comes to him. Skip all the adjectives and point of views, it's just about sending love. She leans forward and tries really hard, one little tiny drop of love, that's all it takes. She forces her mind to do this one thing and it is so difficult. The shutting out everything else that is associated with this one simple action. Almost there.... she can see it now, and she is doing it. One second. Enough now, this is painful, two seconds and it's even harder. Three seconds and the whole world feels empty. Four seconds and she can see him for what he was, as he was. And it wasn't her fault. It wasn't my fault, it was not my fault.

She slams down the screen of the computer and stands up screaming "This is a waste of time! Stupid hippie bullshit! I hate you!" She runs out of the bungalow, stops herself and runs back inside, gets her bag out and starts packing her things in a frenzy. It's time to go.

• • •

As Jerome is trying to clean up the garden after Laxmi has turned it into a mud field and the dogs happily play tug of war with one of Sky's yoga mats, yet another plane is making its way to Goa International airport. This time the plane gets held up again circling above the smallest state in India, but not because of a cow, it's the approaching storm that creates strong winds and the control tower and the pilots are trying to decide whether it's safe to land or not. Lauren is waiting impatiently to do the right thing, to get off the plane and make things right this time. She is looking around at the other passengers and finally the plane starts preparing for landing.

The pilot makes a decision, he will try to land the plane. A bumpy landing in the strong wind and the passengers clap their hands at the pilot for being so brave.

As the cabin crew open the doors of the aircraft Lauren pushes herself past all the other passengers and is the first one through immigration and the first one to run out to the taxi stand.

A different rickshaw but the same destination is called out by the impatient blonde woman with the freckles. The driver looks at her and decides he has time to take her all the way to Anjuna before the cricket match starts. It's his favourite team and he really doesn't want to miss the match.

The hour long drive seems to take forever and as they are driving into Anjuna, Lauren sees how it all looks very different in the rainy season. All restaurants and bars are closed, the roads are full of holes and fields stand empty, houses shut down, no one is around. It's pouring down with rain now and the whole place is deserted. Not one person as far as the eye can see.

She tells the driver she will pay him for another hour, she needs to look for someone. They agree on a new price and the driver follows her directions. First to the Blue House.

Jimmy is not there. Tommy is not there.

Lauren tells the driver to wait. She walks around the property in the rain, knocks on Priya's bungalow, looks if someone is in the Blue House, looks in her old room. She goes to Priya's bungalow again and knocks harder on the door that eventually opens up by itself. All of Priya's belongings are gone, the mattress is gone too. Priya is gone and so is her beautiful sari.

No one and nothing. She walks out to the field in front of the blue house, looks in the chapel. Nothing.

While Lauren is getting back in the rickshaw and drives off Zâbel has been looking at the silly tourist walking around her property. She has been hiding behind the curtains.

Her shame is apparent, she let the tourist down. She let everyone down. Desmond kicked Priya out and took all her belongings shouting and throwing rocks at her, telling her to get lost. He even took her new mattress. All of this for a wedding and she did nothing to protect the weak and poor when they needed her the most. Zâbel knows that the thief is a friend of Desmond. She put two and two together. She will not forget, and her mind is occupied with how to confront Desmond.

She will do it on his wedding day. When the parents of the bride hand over the dowry, she will take care of it. Move out of the Blue House, and live her own life with the money from the dowry. An eye for an eye. She will find Priya and ask her to be her house-keeper. And will not care if people will speak ill of her, a widow from a good family living on her own in a small house? She cannot bear staying in this place anymore.

Oh Holy Saint Thomas, please take care of me and give me the strength I need to be able to do right this time.

She sits down in front of the television and starts to pray for forgiveness.

• • •

Lauren tells the rickshaw to head for the yoga school.

It now lies empty, the bamboo roof been taken down and the rain has flooded the grounds. The guest house next door lies deserted. They continue to the German bakery, it's shut.

Lauren shows the driver the photo of Tommy, asks him to keep an eye out for him. She tells him to drive until they find him.

"Madam. This is not a good thing to do for a young lady to look for a mongrel. You know they carry a lot of diseases and they are very bad dogs. My uncle's cousin has very nice dogs, he is in Chaphora, not far from here, I am sure it is the Pits Bulls. Very nice the Pits Bulls. Not dirty, Madam, not disease, Madam. Very cheap, Madam."

"This is the dog we need to find. He has to be here somewhere."

"Yes Madam, this is what I am telling you, the Pits Bull of my uncle's cousin could even be a mixture of Labrador and Pits Bulls. Only ten thousand rupees each, Madam."

"Just keep driving along the rice paddies, and then turn left on the beach"

"Madam, it is not suitable to drive around in the rain. And Panjim will play Arpora in an hour's time! I simply cannot miss this big event! It's the quarter finals!" Lauren tells the driver to keep going. They ride through the rice paddies, Lauren scans for something with big ears and a curly tail everywhere. She gets off, and walks down to the beach, where a pack of dogs bark at her and follow her back to the rickshaw. All her clothes are wet and fog is forming, not helping her in her search.

"OK, let's go to my friend's house. I'll continue the search tomorrow; you can't see anything in this rain. Take the short cut to the left and turn right after the Hindu temple, please."

Lauren sees in the distance a camp of nomads that have stayed for monsoon.

"Slow down".

She jumps off the rickshaw. Runs towards the camp, looks at the dogs standing around the camp.

She zigzags through the tents, her feet are caught in the mud and her flip flops disappear underneath the mud. She doesn't care, keeps walking barefoot in the mud and the dirt.

Then, in the furthest part of the camp she sees a small dog, chained to a small tent.

Roughly the same size but different colour. The rickshaw driver is running after her.

"Madam all these dogs are gipsy dog, they have the evil eye on them! Now, I think seven thousand rupees is a good price for my cousins' uncles' Pits Bulls."

She starts walking in the direction of the dog. It's in the dirtiest part of the camp, plastic and garbage form layers and the mud path runs between the garbage and the small tents.

The dog is standing with his eyes closed, his ears back and his neck low. Mosquitoes are biting him everywhere and he doesn't even try to chase them off. He is shaking and the wound on his head is not healing, the flies are covering his head feasting on the infected flesh. He does not move when she gets closer. He is very thin, frail and full of bites and scars. He is standing there, with mud up to his stomach.

His eyes slowly open. They are in another place, in a happier place, not at this end place.

Lauren stops.

"Tommy?"

Tommy keeps looking down, as if his name belonged to another life.

"Tommy! Tommy Boy!"

Tommy turns away.

The distant world that he once knew, the happiness and the person he once loved.

The person that disappeared in a taxi and took all the joy and hope with her.

Tommy slowly turns his head.

"Little man, it's me."

It has taken a long time to erase hope and the memories. But slowly something stirs in the little dog's mind. It's her voice.

And the person that he loved so much has a face and a past and the memories are happy. The memory of freedom and running along a road chasing buffaloes slowly work themselves back without hurting.

Tommy lifts his ears, turns to her.

He looks at her as she walks up to him and kneels next to him in the mud.

Holds him as he silently wags his tail and hides his head in her arms. They stand there in the rain as the realization that her words were true, that she would come back for him, start making sense in his head. It has been a long journey and he is exhausted. He leans on Lauren, his whole weight is on her and she holds him so he can rest. He smells her without moving and wants to stay like this the rest of his life, hidden in her arms. She speaks words of kindness and asks him to go with her, to stay with her. He is listening to her and for the first time in a very long time the words from a human are kind again.

The taxi driver watches them from a distance. He is smiling and the cricket game starting in ten minutes is forgotten.

Lauren removes Tommy from his chain. She lifts him up and holds him.

A few children run to a group of people that are picking garbage on a field next to the camp. They point to the woman with the yellow hair and one of the men in the field picks up his big machete and walks towards her. As the man approaches Lauren, Tommy's tail goes between his legs. He starts shaking and pushes himself towards Lauren.

It must be the head of the family who lives in the tent. More men follow and then behind them, a woman and the children.

They are all heading towards Lauren, all the men holding either a stick or a knife in their hands.

Lauren greets them with a Namaste and hands the photo of her and Tommy to the head man of the group.

"My dog"

The rain makes the photo all wet and the man can barely see what is on it.

The man looks at Tommy and then looks at Lauren.

He starts talking to the other men showing the photo while looking at her. His look is intimidating, and he holds his machete with a stern grip

"Two thousand rupees"

"I give you five hundred"

"Many rice, many water."

Lauren points at Tommy "Many doctor, many expensive – here look – this, five hundred rupees, this – three hundred rupees – stomach problem two hundred –here, this wound, at least four hundred!"

"Ok, one thousand five hundred"

"Seven hundred"

"One thousand"

"OK. "

Lauren carries Tommy to the rickshaw. The whole group walks behind them.

As she opens her bag to look for her wallet, the man sees the clothes in the bag.

"T-shirt?"

She looks at the man and his dirty old clothes. She shows him a few nice t- shirts she had bought in Thailand for Scott.

"This."

She gives him the t-shirt. He nods.

He takes it out, puts his machete down and looks at it. Smiles.

"Rolling Stones! Mick Jagger! Very good!"

Lauren looks at the men, at the woman and the children. Such poverty. She gives him another thousand rupees and all the t-shirts she has. And she finds a nice sarong to give to the woman.

The man nods, they shake hands. The woman smiles at Lauren.

She gets into the rickshaw with Tommy and looks at the man one last time. He waves at her, and Lauren tells the driver to leave.

Next to a garbage field in Goa a transaction was made that would change two lives forever.

One of them would have her life back and her lost years of guilt traded in for an agreement at the price of a thousand rupees and for the other one, his destiny would fall back into place.

In a rickshaw in Goa, in the middle of monsoon, a little dog that fought so hard to win someone's love finally won.

• • •

Sky had triumphed at The Awakening Festival.

She wants more from life now, wants to go her own way and she wants to be in Bali and she has no idea how to tell Jerome it is time for them to go separate ways.

On her way back to the Shanti house she has been thinking so hard about how to break the news gently and she hadn't recognized her own house when the rickshaw driver had stopped in front of it.

Two dogs, one with a big bandage around his neck and the other one limping with another big bandage around her stomach had run out of the house and barked at her.

A three legged cow was standing in her garden, happily eating all the plants. What was going on?

Jerome had walked out on the porch with his crutches, greeting her and laughing with joy.

He hugged her for a long time in the rain, the dogs jumping on her, the cow standing next to them, happily eating Sky's organic hemp bag that had cost her a small fortune.

She had walked into the house and the dogs had jumped on the couches and on the beds. The place looked like a mess.

Gone were the Jewel Sharma CD's, his purple clothes. He was wearing a volunteer t-shirt from the animal shelter and jeans.

He looked so happy. And not knowing whether she should be yelling at him for ruining her house, her labour of love, or using

the cow as an excuse to tell him she would leave, she went quiet
and looked at Jerome.

She realized that she had never really seen Jerome entirely happy.
Until now.

He had helped her unpack and had taken care of her bag that the
cow had been chewing on.

He had made her dinner and told her he would quit the whole
yoga circus.

The Cow had shown him that everything he believed in was
wrong.

"This cow?"

Sky asked pointing at the cow in the garden.

"No, the dead cow. The holy cow."

"So this isn't a holy cow?"

"No, it's a normal three legged cow."

"The holy cow I had to pay four thousand rupees for?"

"Yes, that one."

He continued.

The protection he thought he had, because of his belief system,
was just an illusion.

He had caused so much pain, because of his faith. Or lack of faith.
If he hadn't been so arrogant, he wouldn't have killed the poor
cow.

Karma was here and now and suffering is everywhere. It was time
to change and he could help people better with teaching them how
to recover after injuries or with overcoming their handicaps.
Hands on removal of suffering. He was going to become a
physiotherapist.

And then Sky said: "I am moving to Bali. And I am getting married
to Ganges."

And Jerome replied "That is great for you, it's time for change, for
all of us! Can I keep the house?"

• • •

The heavy rain welcomes the new day and Sky is going through all her stuff. Jerome and her laugh at old memories as she decides what to keep and what to give away.

They spend the day going through ten years of Sky's life and it's with sadness she decides to give away her whole collection of Indian shirts. One for each year. Jerome remembers exactly who was there that year, what students they liked and made them laugh, and what dress she had worn to each party.

Laxmi the cow stands outside the gate, waiting for food. She gets spooked and runs back in the garden when a rickshaw drives up to the house, tooting at the cow.

Sky looks out to see who it could be. Oh no. Another dog. Has Jerome gone insane? Then she sees Lauren get off the rickshaw. The dog is standing right next to her. Sky walks out to the gate. What is going on? Lauren is supposed to be in Thailand. They look at each other. Lauren is covered in mud and all wet from the rain. She is looking different. Determined.

"Hi! How was Bali?"

Tommy stands between Lauren's legs.

"He stinks!"

Jerome comes out to the porch on his crutches, sees Tommy. He doesn't say hi to Lauren, he takes Tommy in his arms and hops back into the house on one leg.

"This place is turning into a nightmare! What are you going to do?" Lauren shrugs her shoulders. "I don't know. I think I might have to take him with me."

Sky tells Lauren to get into her house. "Here, you can sleep with the other dogs on the couch. Oh by the way, I am moving to Bali and Jerome doesn't sound like Jewel Sharma anymore."

Lauren looks for Tommy. Jerome has taken him into the bath room and is cleaning him, washing his wounds and talking softly to him. She looks at him. "You hate dogs." and goes up to Tommy. Jerome shows her how to clean the wounds, and what creams and powders to use. Tommy is crying but looks constantly at Lauren. Jerome dries him and makes some food for the dogs. "Free range chicken with broth and Goan rice."

They all eat and then Tommy lies down next to Lauren. She picks him up and he falls asleep next to her on the couch. Sky opens a bottle of wine and fills three glasses.

"We will celebrate tonight the great changes in our lives. Me to
Bali, you to your happiness, wherever that might be and Jerome,
to wearing jeans! To us! And I just want to say, that I think both
of you have lost your minds!"
"And you, Mrs Ganges? To life!" Lauren laughs at Sky.

• • •

The heat and the humidity is on top form today. Francisco d'Souza
is not so worried about his hair anymore. After his sermon at the
Saint Thomas celebration complaints had been made. Francisco
had talked about the joy of living, of travelling to foreign lands,
just like Saint Thomas had, and adjusting to modern times. He
had cracked a joke about Anjuna and the full moon parties and
the joy of dancing and embracing Jesus Christ on a dance floor.
He had quickly been offered a job in a church by the river, close
to the sea, near the beaches. He took the offer and moved away.
Mapusa wasn't ready for him. Not yet. But one day they would.
Almost a year later he had managed to double his congregation
and led amusing masses that the young people loved. He had
started a meditation room in the former offices and was so proud
that he had bought new chairs and built a cross all by himself to
celebrate this new group of adventurous Catholics. He had talked
about the Pet Shop Boys, Bryan Adams and Blue. All good
Christians, he proclaimed and after the meditation hour he would
turn up the volume on his CD player and make the congregation
dance. God and dancing, one unity. Wonderful days for Francisco.

He is dusting his meditation room, getting everything ready for
the next meeting when he sees a blonde woman with a face full of
freckles walk in. He is thinking about the new tunes he hears on
the radio and what he will play for the youngsters this week.
She is breathing heavily; it's the monsoon heat affecting her. Even
under the fans of the church it makes you want to lie down, do
nothing, and disappear far away to some Arctic place. You can
feel the heaviness in your lungs as you inhale.
She walks through the courtyard straight to his meditation room
where a big sign that must be a century old says "SILENCE". It
stands above a big black door that leads to a small, dark room.

His place, his creation, his future and his idea about what the future in this church should be. He keeps dusting and cleaning away while observing her.

Lauren casually takes a seat on one of the cheap plastic chairs. She is not meditating, not praying. Just thinking, staring at a black crucifix.

Overnight things had changed. It wasn't supposed to be like this. Bring Tommy to America? She didn't even live there, she didn't live anywhere.

Like a stubborn child she keeps repeating to herself that she wants her freedom and she wants to move on, not go back. Why go back? To do what? It hadn't been a drunken realization, it had been there lurking in the background for a while, waiting to come out, something that needed to be done to clear the way. What way? As she is sitting there she realises that she misses being on a boat. How on land nothing really moves sideways, how she misses sleeping with the gentle rocking of a boat.

She can feel the wind, the spray from the waves washing up, the salt of the sea sticking to her face and the stars at night. And then she sees Tommy's eyes, and she smiles. Maybe she can have both? With a little patience? An Indian dog that can't swim, can he go sailing? She is sure if he can run on Indian beaches then he can run on Caribbean beaches. They do make life jackets for dogs don't they?

She walks out of the meditation room and walks into the church. Francisco follows her, curious about this foreigner with the freckles and why not, let's admit it, she is cute. We're all human after all.

The psalm books in Konkani are dusting in a corner and the ceiling fans are turning at full speed. Lauren stands in the middle of the church. This is the moment she has to choose.

If only life could be like this, still and permanent like in a temple, all the time.

She lights a candle for Heather, puts the candle in front of the Madonna, and sits for a long time praying to her sister, praying for guidance while looking at the candle burning together with all the other lit candles. Well, the Caribbean isn't that far from California, she sighs and then looks at a statue of Saint Thomas. She puts a coin in the charity box below the statue, thinking about Zâbel and her bible.

From behind she can hear someone, turns around and sees this young priest with gentle eyes smiling at her. She smiles back at him as he walks up to her and takes a candle, lights it and puts it next to hers.

"My sister". The young priest nods and asks to sit down next to her. She nods back at him. He says something about forgiving the sins of the past and then asks her about a playlist. Would she care to look at it?

• • •

Lauren had called the airline company, tried to book a ticket for the dog.

No she couldn't just take him with her. No, she couldn't buy a seat for the dog.

He needed paperwork, vaccinations, documentation. It had to be stamped by official veterinaries and customs officers. It would take at least a month and Lauren only had a short stay visa.

Jerome tells Lauren to get a rickshaw, they need to go and see his veterinary friend at the animal shelter.

They have clinic hours and even though it's low season many local people are there waiting to see the vet with their pets.

Cats, dogs and a pig patiently waiting tied up to a pole.

They sit with the other people under a covered porch. A loud, painful meowing can be heard from inside the clinic. Everyone holds their pets a little tighter. The meowing abruptly ends and three women walk out from the clinic and sit down next to Lauren and Jerome. One of the women is holding a black cat. She rocks it back and forth, and the cat has a drip attached to its paw. The cat opens its eyes and they are bright yellow, staring straight ahead. The woman holding the black cat starts wailing and crying out loud, screaming and holding the dead cat hard. The other two young women, who must be the woman's daughters, cry too and hold their mother. Everyone in the clinic is silent. Death is everywhere in India, and Lauren thinks how again, India is like a roller coaster of emotions. Animals treated so badly and left to die. Animals so loved that an ageing mother mourns her cat the same way she mourns a child. The crying doesn't end. The daughters and the mother make a circle together around the cat and cry together. They eventually wrap the cat in a blanket, and close its eyes, help the mother up and hold her as they walk out of the clinic.

They're up next and the vet greets Jerome, they talk about his dogs and she compliments him on having treated Tommy's wounds so well. She gets a vaccination certificate and two syringes out. "It won't hurt." she tells Lauren and gives Tommy the rabies shot and the annual vaccines, then a worm tablet and flea drops. She fills in the vaccination certificate and a health certificate. Now they have to wait 28 days before flying. It's the rule for exporting an animal to the USA.

After that he will need to have another health certificate from the state veterinary that has the official stamp, and then another health certificate from the government vet and from the customs department. And he needs to put on more weight, so that he is healthy when he leaves. But not too much!

What is the name of the owner? She needs to write that on the certificate.

Lauren says her name proudly, it's official now.

"The end of my freedom." She says, and the vet laughs at her.

The vet hands Lauren the certificates and shakes her hand. Jerome has Lauren buy a volunteer T-shirt as well and a collar and leash from their small shop.

Over dinner Lauren barely eats, she leaves the table with her food untouched and goes out. Beautiful stars illuminate the sky.

How is she going to do this?

Jerome calls her back into the house. He has been on the internet and has found a solution. Why doesn't she go back to America, and leave Tommy with him, and in a month or so he can fly to New York with a direct flight from Mumbai. She can pick him up and then fly together to Los Angeles. He has found an agent that can handle the paperwork and take care of Tommy at the airport in Mumbai.

Jerome will drive him to the airport in Goa and from there he will be taken care of. Lauren can go back and organize for Tommy's arrival.

"It will be good. You can be calm; I will take good care of him."

"Why are you doing this? You hated my dog. And you know I thought you were a pompous ass."

Jerome looks at her.

"I saw your dog before the accident. And I didn't care. Now I do. And I never hated you. You were just different; you didn't need all the soul searching to find your truth. You are tough and brave and you know your truth."

"You look good in jeans. Next thing we know you'll be wearing a Yankees baseball hat. Thank you for helping me."

"Lauren, I know what the soul looks like now."

"So tell me!"

"It's a secret! But it helps if you take a lot of pain killers at the local hospital!"

Lauren looks at Jerome and then looks up at the stars. Maybe it is like they say that when you make the right decision help will come from the most unexpected places.

In the background they can hear Sky yelling "I will not have another dog in this house and sweep up the porch after him! Do you hear me? Jerome! They peed on my favourite blanket!"

HAPPINESS HAS A NAME

"Two hundred dollars. You just cost me two hundred dollars."
Lauren is lost in thoughts, looking out of the car window as they
drive along the Pacific Coast Highway down towards Newport
Beach. California is hot at this time of the year and traffic is slow.
Surfboards on car roofs, girls roller blading along the board walk.
Beautiful big waves crushing on the sandy beaches of Southern
California. It's as if she has never been here before and as if she
has never left.
"Did you hear anything I said?"
She nods.
"Holistic dog food? A blinking stuffed cow? Harmonising
blanket? Buffalo scented bones? Ergonomically correct dog bed?
Bling bling collar for an Indian street dog?"
"I just want him to feel welcome."
Lauren smiles at him.
"We still haven't been to the pet store in Beverly Hills, you know
the one next to the Chanel boutique?"
He slaps her on the knee and turns off the highway onto a street
that leads to the hills above Newport Beach.
It's a wealthy area with big mansions and the higher the street
takes them, the bigger the mansions get.
Security cameras and big fences protect the owners from intruders,

through the gates Lauren gets a glimpse of big swimming pools and picture perfect lawns.

As they reach the top of the hill Scott parks his car.

"Lauren, wake up. You have to be on your best behaviour now, this is my best client and he is being very nice to me. He loves your work and loves investing in lost souls like you – hey are you listening?"

"Yes, I am. Don't worry, I'm back in the game."

"Just smile and say yes to him, OK? I need to be able to trust you on this. It hasn't been easy moving back here to Orange County for me, you know?"

"I know. I promise. But I still think you made a mistake moving back."

Lauren nods and gets out of the car, the view is quite stunning, up here on top of the world. The Pacific Ocean below her, with its big waves and bright dark blue colour, reaching all the way to the other side of the world.

They enter the house and an elderly impeccably groomed man dressed in a perfectly ironed white linen suit greets them. He sees Lauren and smiles at her, reaching out his hand to her and then forces her to give him a kiss on his cheek.

"Scott, welcome! And you must be the wonderful Lauren! Finally, I was giving up on you, but Scott said wait, wait, she is on her way! All the way from Thailand! Then, no, wait, now she is in India! We were losing track of you! How exotic! Look at that dress you are wearing! Very Asian! Is it batik?"

"We finally got her back! I picked her up at the airport to make sure she didn't run away again! How are you, Stuart?!"

"Very busy, darling, just back from Provence, my social agenda is killing me!

Here, come inside, let me show what I have in mind."

The sumptuous living room, all in white and with big windows that open up to an even bigger patio with an infinity pool. A white grand piano is standing next to the pool.

"Come through here, so Scott, those lamps, have they arrived yet? I am just loving my white chandelier!"

"The lamps are here next week and the carpets are on their way. I will make sure you have them before your party."

"Great, I can't wait. And I changed my mind about the new sofas.

I want to go Asian for the pool area. Ibiza feels a bit yesterday, you know. Could you find something from Sumatra?"

Scott nods and takes notes.

"Now, let's go upstairs to my bedroom."

The spiral staircase takes them to a big room all in white. The windows open up to the sea.

"I was thinking I wanted two paintings hanging above the bed, like this, and then in the guest bedroom another one, but in a different colour. How soon can you have them done? I want those beautiful swirly curves that you do and just a touch of that turquoise you always use. "And what about gold? Just a touch of it. And the orange and red, and maybe purple. "

Lauren is standing in the middle of the bedroom looking at the white wall, then turns to the windows looking out to the sea.

"Stuart, when you wake up, the first thing you see is the ocean. So, I think we should stick to a blue palette. Subtle, not to disturb all the white in the house. But strong enough to let it have a presence. Stand here, and look first to the wall above the bed, and then turn around, and look out to the sea."

Stuart does as she says.

"All the reds you want, let's use them for the painting in the guest room. So we create two different experiences."

"What do you mean? I just love this red, I want that red."

Stuart points at Lauren's bright red Indian shirt.

"I will give you the red, but in the other room. Red is quite a strong colour to wake up to, don't you think?"

Stuart looks at her, then looks at Scott who smiles angrily at Lauren.

"Come, stand here by the window, and look at the wall. "

"All right, you win. Wonderful. I love it. Do it. How about two weeks from now, Scott?"

"Two weeks, sounds great, I am sure that you can have it ready by then, Lauren?"

"Two weeks?"

"Two weeks it is; I want everything to be perfect for my party. Thank you Scott, I just love everything you do. Isn't it a beautiful day today? Oh, and Lauren, you must come to the party. So, good. All settled."

• • •

"Art supply store?"

Lauren nods as they get in the car and drive off.

"Present for you."

Scott reaches into the glove compartment and hands her a wrapped case.

"Wait."

He presses a button and the top of the car starts folding down.

"You passed. Well done! Welcome to Newport Beach!"

She opens the present. It's a pair of expensive sunglasses. She laughs and puts them on.

The wind makes her blonde hair fly and she lifts her arms up towards the sky.

"You ready to spend another two hundred dollars?"

Scott turns the music up loud, pretending not to hear her.

Lauren looks out to the sea, Tommy will be running on beaches of the Pacific Coast soon. She sends him a kiss all the way to India and then her mind drifts back to the paintings she has to do. The transition back to a place of sad memories. The transition back to putting some lightness and happiness in them. That's the theme. Keep looking at the ocean, Lauren thinks, and don't look towards land until you can deal with it.

• • •

Scott helps Lauren carry the big sheets of paper into the house.

They put them on her table and she looks around her new home trying to figure out how to turn it into a work place.

Scott shows her how to make the table bigger and pushes the couch away, back against the wall.

It's a smart solution he came up with when he turned the garage into a small apartment. The ground floor is a kitchen and living room, and then a staircase leads up to a loft to use as a bedroom or storage.

The garage doors had been replaced by big windows and he had closed the drive way turning it into a patio.

As Lauren rolls out the sheets of paper he carries the dog supplies into the apartment and carries them upstairs, puts the dog bed next to Lauren's bed.

He stands up, and looks down, smiles at Lauren as she gets her materials out and moving the table and chairs around. She looks up at him and smiles back.

"It's good to have you back, you know."

She walks up to the loft and as he organizes her things upstairs she laughs at him.

"I'm not twelve anymore! This is strange you know, your Mustang used to be parked in here. And you parents yelling at you at night for being too loud. And now it's all different. You did a good job with this place. I like it. Next thing I know is you don't want to have any homeless artist living in your house and kick me out."

"Actually, you paid for this renovation."

Lauren looks at him, surprised.

"There was a bit of money left from when I sold your father's house so when you refused to answer any of my letters or calls, I kept it. I decided not to sell my parents' house but renovate it and rent it out. And I built this little grandma flat in case you ever needed somewhere to live, if you ever came back. I have been renting it out, but it is yours. You don't have to stay here the rest of your life, and I know you won't, but at least you have a place to stay. I know I won't stay here the rest of my life either but after the divorce I just needed to land so I came down here. And as I was renovating it I kept thinking about how nice it would be to have you here, living with me. Not too close and not too far away!"

Scott hugs her.

"I couldn't do it; I couldn't talk to you."

"I know, it's been tough, but I have missed you so much. It was hard to leave Santa Barbara."

"Why did you?"

"She slept with my boss. I needed some distance to places and memories."

"Do you think he's going to like it here?"

"Of course he will. Stop worrying now, he'll be fine. Who doesn't like California?"

And finally Lauren starts telling him about her journeys, about nights out at sea full of stars and countless miles travelled to find peace.

• • •

On two different continents, two different types of preparations are under way. One is Lauren's, the other is Tommy's. Jerome is cooking special meals for him, to make sure he puts on weight and gets exercise to get back into shape. He takes him on beach walks in the mornings and afternoons with Lola and Tanner every day. Tommy is happy to be back on the beach, even in the rain he runs and races on the beach, chasing the other dogs. Jerome smiles as he watches the little dog recover and spends hours brushing him and pampering him.

The handling agent in Mumbai will take care of all paperwork and organize the flights. It will be a long trip, it's literally to the other side of the world, twenty-two hours on a plane. Will a little dog from India be able to survive such a long flight?

Jerome will have to bring him to the airport in Goa, and Adnah, the handling agent, will meet Tommy in Mumbai, and get him ready for the next flight.

Tommy seems aware of the changes to come. He is not crying, not waiting for Lauren, it's as if he knows that he will not be abandoned again and Lauren is working hard on the paintings, with that money she will be able to pay for Tommy's flights and then have some time off with him.

But the pressure to work so fast is overwhelming her. After several failed attempts she yells out, throws the stuffed cow against the wall and starts crying. All this for money. No, it can't be. It's not what it's about. It's about more than this. I am not like that. OK, calm down. She slams the door behind her and walks to the park. All is white, green and beige. Where are the shacks, the food stalls and where is the street life she so loves in Asia? There is nothing here that reminds her of what she has become. Someone is walking a dog and she thinks that she is wrong, she has done everything wrong. How will Tommy like walking on a leash, in a park with nothing going on around him?

Or is she not seeing what lies behind all of this? What does he like? He likes to run, to be free and to follow her everywhere. He loves the beach and he loves adventures. And he likes to observe, to think. To make his own decisions. Oh please, help me! She almost yells out, but then she looks around again, tries to see things in a different way. Removing the obstacles and letting the possibilities move forward. Just like Ganesh would have wanted. She won't be able to see if this is right or wrong until he gets here. Maybe there is a reason for him coming here. But is it fair on him?

She sighs and looks at the dogs playing in the park with a worried look.

Then she knows, it clicks. The paintings will be about making way for something good to come. Giving it a name and a purpose, to ensure happiness for someone you love.

GODSPEED

Jerome holds a steady grip around Tommy's collar. The vet at the state clinic in Mapusa is checking his ears, his teeth, his rear, his coat and his eyes. Jerome strokes Tommy gently on his back.

"This is the first step of getting you to America, young man. You know it should have been me going to California, and look at us now. You go and I stay here. That's really kind of strange. "

As the veterinary opens his mouth and checks Tommy's teeth, he cries and Jerome comforts him.

"I have been dreaming my whole life of going to America, making something big of myself, but now I decided to go a different way. Don't tell anyone, but I was getting tired of teaching Yoga. All those expectations, all those women who just wanted me for my body, it's a lot of pressure you know."

The vet smiles as she gently lets go of Tommy and as she signs all the certificates she looks at Jerome.

"Here, I have signed that he is in good health and that all the vaccines are up to date. You have to bring him here for the official documentation two days before departure. I will order the proper crate for him to travel in as well. You will need to train him, to teach him to be in the crate before he flies out. This way he will stay calm during the flight. But he seems like a smart dog, so don't worry too much, he will be fine."

She hands him the signed document.
"You must have been a very passionate yoga teacher."
The vet winks at him.
"I was."
He winks back at her.

● ● ●

Tommy's paws are on the steering wheel. He is standing up leaning against Jerome's stomach as he drives his Enfield, barking at dogs on the street and his big ears are flapping in the wind. He turns to Jerome as if smiling, his tail wagging with excitement.
They drive past the cinema, the market and the church.
As they continue past the poorer area of Mapusa, the Enfield starts to cough and eventually dies on Jerome.
A few young men run up to him and start talking away in Konkani and English. They are pointing at a house and yell "Uncle, uncle!"
Jerome gets off the bike, ties Tommy to a tree and starts getting his tools out. A man comes running, with the two young men right behind shouting "Uncle! Uncle! Very good with motorbike!"
Together they go through the engine trying to figure out what is wrong with it.
Tommy is pulling to the right and left, he seems restless. The uncle and Jerome help each other and the young men play with the shining Enfield taking photographs of themselves in front of it.
The uncle starts up the engine. No luck. He digs his hands into the engine again and does his magic as Jerome is sweating. It's a hot day and all he wants is to ride his bike to get some fresh air. His leg is hurting and he swears at himself for forgetting to bring his crutches.
The uncle starts the Enfield one more time. It works. Jerome is relieved. He turns around to pick up Tommy, but all that is there is a chewed off leash and no dog.
"Holy Cow and Buddha!" He yells out. "I lost her dog!"
He pays the uncle and rides off on the Enfield into the small dirty streets of the poor neighbourhood. Children are playing on the street, a few dogs are roaming around, and women are standing outside their houses chatting.
She asks the women, no, no little dog. No, Mister.
Then a few children run up to him.

"RAJ! RAJ!!! Mister come! Raj this way!!!"
They start running and he drives after them.

* * *

Garati is on the porch of the house.
A sewing machine is on the table on the porch and a lot of fabric
is next to it.
She is smiling proudly as she is sowing pieces of fabric together
creating colourful pillows.
Some with Ganesh printed on it, some not. Some with her hand
embroidered decorations, some just fancy fabrics in different
shapes. She stops, leans back with a happy face and takes a sip of
tea. As she puts the tea cup back on the table she looks out to the
street. Instead of seeing her imaginary shop that she is dreaming
of every day she sees a little dog trotting towards her. It cannot be!
Tommy knows this street, he runs on it on instinct, knowing where
he is going and as he reaches Garati's house he stops and stares at
the new gate, at the house. At Garati.
"Raj?"
She stands up and walks down to the gate. Opens it and Tommy
runs in, up to her and cries and barks of joy.
She cries too, kneels down, her Raj jumping on her, kissing her
and licking her face, wagging his tail.
She holds him and kisses him.
He is so clean, so strong and beautiful!
She sits down next to him on the porch and holds him, smells him,
praises him.
Her Raj still alive, coming back to her!
Jerome is following the children. They stop outside of a rickety
house and they all point to a woman and Tommy.
He stops, turns off the engine and looks at Tommy and this
woman.
It's as if it's two friends who haven't met in a long time are sharing
old stories.
Jerome wonders if this is where it all started and how on earth did
he end up in Anjuna?
The woman is talking to Tommy and he is listening to her.
How do you know who belongs to whom in India?

Jerome is starting to worry that he might have to leave Tommy here. What will he tell Lauren?

When the little dog sees Jerome he runs up to him and brings him to Garati, welcomes Jerome into the privacy of his and Garati's friendship.

Jerome greets Garati with a Namaste.

"Raj!" and some words in Maharati, actually a never ending stream of words.

Tommy was once Raj.

Garati points at Tommy's eyes, and then at her heart, then gestures small, and holds the imaginary puppy in her arms.

She points at the place under the steps.

"Tommy mama?" Jerome asks.

Garati's joy turns into sadness, she starts gesturing with her hands, and points at Jerome to follow her into the yard. They walk to the back, where there are flowers planted on the ground in a specific spot.

She points at Tommy. "Raj Mama".

Garati starts talking to Tommy again, stroking him and pointing to what must be the grave of his Mother.

Then she points at Jerome. "You?"

"My friend. It's her dog – I mean, how do I explain this, well, she is taking Tommy – Raj, to America soon."

He gets his phone out, and then starts showing Garati photos of Lauren and Tommy.

Garati smiles, and laughs when she sees a photo of Tommy standing between Lauren's legs as she does a Yoga pose. And smiles when he shows her a photo of Lauren and Tommy lying together in bed.

Garati invites Jerome to the porch. She makes space for him, and as she takes the fabric and half-finished pillows away, Jerome sees the designs. "Very nice! You make this? How much?"

Garati shouts at a man standing on the other side of the street. It's Mister Badhu. The older gentleman walks up to Jerome, wondering what this hippie looking Westerner could be doing with the young and beautiful Garati. Then he sees Tommy, and then he sees Garati's tears and her joy.

And Jerome asks again about the pillows and if he can buy a few of the large ones.

They agree on a price and a delivery date.

Then Jerome needs to be sure. He needs to ask.

He shows her the paperwork from the veterinary.

"Here, Tommy – Raj, go to America next week."

Garati is silent, looks at Tommy who is lying by her feet, looking at her, waiting for her to stroke him one more time.

"Raj? America?" She doesn't understand.

Mister Badhu explains to her that the dog and may the Holy Lord Krishna forgive all those foreigners for all the stupid things they do, will go in an airplane to this other foreign woman next week. Mister Badhu points to the sky and looks at Tommy.

Garati points under the porch. With big gestures she describes a storm, this is where he was born, and his mother apparently was very beautiful and Tommy looks just like her. Then something very bad happened.

She tells Jerome to walk out with her up the street.

Tommy is walking right next to Garati.

She points up the road and stands on the place where Sutara was killed. She shows how someone beat her and killed her.

Mr Badhu translates as best as he can, as he tells Garati to calm down. All this fuss again for the dogs.

Then Tommy walks up to the exact place where all the bad things happened, he smells the ground and his tails goes between his legs and he starts crying. He sneaks away from Garati, from Jerome and Mister Badhu. All the horror and pain and death are again clear and present in his mind and there is only so much pain a little dog can deal with.

Garati tells Tommy to come to her, but he stands far away from them, shaking, lifting his paw showing he is afraid.

"No problem, Raj America. America good." Garati says with tears in her eyes.

Jerome goes to Tommy, calms him down and lifts him up, afraid he will lose him again.

He tells Mister Badhu he will pick up the pillows when they are ready and that he will make sure that Lauren will send photos of Tommy, sorry, Raj, from America.

As he starts walking with Tommy to the motorbike Garati asks him to wait.

She takes off her Ganesh necklace. Garati puts the necklace around Tommy's neck and says a prayer. Tommy listens to her. Then she starts kissing him and hugs him. Her tears fall on Tommy's forehead.

Tommy who once was Raj. Who now stands quietly with this young Indian woman and has an important conversation with her. But this time it is not Tommy who gives comfort to Garati, it is Garati who tells him tales of love and foreign lands and that everything will be good.

She picks him up and gives him one last kiss on his forehead. One last hug and she hands him over to Jerome.

"Go, go now. America good."

Because it is in this moment of a definitive farewell that we know what someone means to us.

The act of wishing someone a good life even if it means us not being a part of it is the purest act of love. To know what is best for someone.

It is Garati's way of thanking her Raj for all he has done for her.

Here, Tommy was born here. Lauren was right; he did know kindness when he was very young.

As Jerome starts up the engine and puts Tommy on the front of the bike, Garati smells him one last time and says one last prayer for him. Their eyes fixed on each other, loyal to their bond.

As Jerome drives away he notices Tommy looking back at Garati. In some strange way the past is now linked to the present and all the pieces come together.

The neighbourhood children run along after Jerome and Tommy until he turns off on onto the main road. Their joyful cries of "Raj! America!" echo in the background and as the motorbike disappears from sight around the corner Garati stands watching from her house.

Jerome is thoughtful on his drive back. It is almost as if from now on Tommy is carrying a legacy that is bigger than him. He will take a piece of India with him and share it with America.

. . .

It's 4 am in Goa and Jerome is up waiting for the taxi that will take him and Tommy to the airport. He has washed Tommy, brushed him and prepared him for the long journey ahead.

As they ride towards the airport, Tommy looks out of the window in the night. They ride past the Blue House, the yoga school, the tents where the nomads are sleeping and the field where the buffaloes lie in the mud. It's a goodbye, and Jerome wonders if Tommy knows this will be the last time he ever sees this place. "Tommy, say goodbye to your Motherland, and remember to do your downward dog in America!"

Tommy wags his tail, and as the taxi drives past the outskirts of Anjuna he starts crying at something. It's a woman sweeping the porch of a small house, still dreaming of selling samosas. Priya looks at the taxi driving on the road past her house, wondering who could be going somewhere so early in the morning in monsoon. She walks silently, not to wake up Zâbel, who snores loudly inside the house. So lucky she is, she thinks, that Zâbel found her and took her to her house. She had been sleeping behind the local church for a week after Desmond kicked her out, and the local priest had given her food. She had no water, no clean clothes and no money. And one day Zâbel had found her and told her that she would come with her, that they would live in a small house and that Zâbel would take care of her. Priya had started to cry, and Zâbel had led her to the waiting rickshaw and drove her to her new house. Zâbel had said that she would teach Priya simple book keeping, and that they would open a little shop, eventually, and Priya would help out in the house and in the shop. Priya had kept crying all the way to the new house and all that evening she prayed to Hanuman and Ganesh thanking them for helping her.

As the back lights of the taxi disappear in the darkness Priya wonders what it would be like to go to foreign places. And then she wonders what happened to the little dog with the golden eyes, if he ever found a new home, like she did.

As the sun rises the taxi drives into the taxi stand at the airport. Two betel chewing men run to the car and take out the crate. Jerome pays the driver and goes to the check in counter.

He double checks the crate one last time and before it's time to put Tommy in it, he takes out an envelope to go with the rest of all the other paperwork. It's for Lauren.

He tells Tommy to get in the crate and before he locks him in, he kisses him on his forehead. "Make us proud over there in the big country, young man. You have a lot on your shoulders now. And take care of that crazy girl for me."

The betel chewing men wheel Tommy away, and he looks at Jerome with a worried look.

"You'll be fine, King Tommy, we are making sure of that! Godspeed!"

Jerome stands there until he sees the men putting the crate on a truck that drives Tommy to the plane.

Jerome says a silent prayer for him and gets his phone out.

King Tommy is on his way.

• • •

Adnah is standing in the cargo area at the airport in Mumbai with her van. She is on the phone and as she speaks she dusts off the Indian deities placed on the front of her van.

She is on the phone as she sees the truck arriving with a crate on it.

"I don't know, yaar, it is a tourist who wants to take a mongrel to America. I hope it doesn't bite me! And he has to be here all day long! Can you imagine? A mongrel in my office of all places? Oh well, no darling, have the maid make my favourite sweets for tonight, I will need it. Yes, I love you too. Oh, here it is."

The truck stops in front of Adnah, and she looks in the crate.

"Oh goodness gracious me, is this the mongrel?"

She opens the cage, and Tommy, terrified, comes crawling out. He wags his tail at her and she carefully touches him. Tommy licks her hand and she sits down next to him. "You are not a dirty mongrel! You smell like expensive shampoo and perfume! What a horrible person I am to say bad things about you! What a beautiful dog you are! Come!" Tommy follows her and she tells him to jump up in the van next to her. As she drives he stares at her, wondering where he is and what is going on. She puts her arm around him and he sits closer to her.

As they arrive at her office, he runs in and greets her employees.

"Now, you have to wait here with us today."

"Here Tommy! Biscuit! Sit!" Tommy sits, and does "Paw" making a funny face.

"OK young man, your Mummy is waiting for you in New York! You lucky boy!"

She puts a blanket next to her desk and Tommy lies down next to her. "You are a very well behaved young dog; I will have to tell my husband to bring you some chicken when he comes over for lunch. Yaar, yes, you stay right here next to me! We will show you what true Mumbai hospitality is! Girls, call the airline, I want to have everything to work smoothly for his departure. Double check everything one more time!"

• • •

Lauren is at the hotel, looking around the room. She has landed in Newark, the airport in New Jersey across the Hudson River from New York. Her eyes are closed and she holds a new collar and leash in her hand. The weight of responsibility is making her hesitant.

It's so close now, everything is perfect, then why is she scared?

In what way would her life have been different now? What if she had decided to go a different way? Would it all lead to the same place anyway? What is the price of freedom and the price of belonging to someone?

Now it was time to change, because someone needed her. Not because he was sick, but because he wanted to live. And as she is sitting there on the cheap polyester bed cover and opens her eyes to look out at the Manhattan skyline, she remembers a beautiful kiss on an island and how that man had told her that she was going to see it right in front of her, the day she accepted love to come running back into her life again.

• • •

Adnah, her husband and all her employees get in the van and bring the little golden eyed dog to the cargo area to drop him off and say good bye to him. When she prepared the crate for the flight, she also put a few Om and Ganesh stickers on the crate for spiritual safety. Her husband says a prayer, blessing the dog and the crate and tells his wife that this is a magnificent looking Indian dog. "He has the true spirit of India in him! And look at his eyes, they are like gold, it's an auspicious sign! He will show the best of India to America!" They all stand silently waving good bye to him as he gets wheeled off to the tarmac with incense burning around his cage. Adnah, for the first time in her career as a professional animal handling agent, starts to cry as her husband sings a traditional song for Tommy.

And here he is again, alone in his crate, standing next to the jumbo jet that will take him to America. In the midst of all the commotion between the fuel tank passing and luggage handlers shouting and all the personnel running back and forth with their torches and walkie talkies he thinks back on the quietness of the sandy patch and Jimmy, and the mornings outside the Blue House when they used to wake up to Priya bringing water to them and the occasional person would walk by. Of how he stood outside his blonde human's room and she would open the door, half asleep, and let him in and he would jump on her bed and lie next to her, listening to her breathe. How easy life used to be.

The catering guys go up to him and say hi to the frightened little dog, and then the handlers load him unto the plane. He starts barking and scratches on the crate wanting to get out, to flee from all these scary noises all around him and the passengers in the terminal waiting to board the plane look down to see the dog crate being lifted into the plane and a few children wave at the dog inside. The co-pilot steps into the cargo area in the deepest and darkest part of the plane. Checks on the crate that has a frightened dog in it, talks to him to calm him down, and makes sure that there is enough water and food for the long flight ahead.

Then they lock the compartment and it all goes dark.

Engines start, rev up.

The pilot is in his cabin, receives some paperwork to sign as he prepares the plane for the long flight.

"And we have a dog. Did you check that he has water and food? Is the heating and ventilation on? It's gonna be a long trip"

The co-pilot nods "Yes sir, all clear."

"OK, let's get this baby going, it's time to go home"

The plane taxis out, Tommy is all alone in this big beast of a plane. The engines are on full power, deafening him, as it takes off.

As the plane flies over Mumbai, Adnah and her husband wave at him from their garden, but Tommy is feeling smaller and lonelier than ever.

He lies down and eventually falls asleep to the noise of the jet engines somewhere over the Arabian Sea while the pilot calls the Newark Airport Customs.

"Good Evening Sir, this is Captain Trevor Johnson on United 17 heading to Newark from Mumbai International.... Yes Sir, all clear and good. Beautiful night to be out, just flying over Dubai, can see the Palm island all lit up. Just to confirm we have all paperwork cleared, stamped and go for a Tango Oscar Mike Mike Yankee - as in Tommy, animal on board. Species Dog. Breed: Indian Mutt. He's fine sir, no need to keep the young lady waiting on arrival... . Yes, well, some people bring home t-shirts and illegal drugs, other folks bring dogs, what can I say. Personally I got myself a nasty Delhi belly yesterday. OK, yes, as far as I know he is young and healthy, so he should be alive and kicking on arrival. You have a good evening Sir, Over and out. Hon, can you get me another coffee and the newspaper? Everything fine in the cabin? And check on that Indian Mutt we have in the hold, will you?"

Tommy is so afraid, he has no window to look out from where he is, but along the way, his dog mother Sutara creates a star clad sky for his safe travels and is with him all the way across the Atlantic Sea. And as the plane reaches the shores of New Jersey, she tells her son that all that is coming will be good.

• • •

It's been a long and sleepless night. This is it, the moment of change.

It's six am and Lauren is at the animal desk at the airport with her paperwork.

She is holding Tommy's new collar and leash.

"They just landed, he will be here in a minute, Ma'am."

What if she fails? What if she can't do it? What if he will be unhappy, die and it will all be her fault again?

"Here he is!"

Lauren sees the crate being rolled in to the animal area and it is jumping and the little dog inside it is barking and whining.

An employee turns the cage around and she sees Tommy, all upset and scratching on the cage. He has had enough, after twenty-two hours in this cage he just wants to get out.

Lauren, stands there with the collar in her hand.

"Ma'am, is everything OK?"

He is here now, no turning back. Then she looks up and Sutara is there, giving the caretaker of her son a last breath of re-assuring hope. "You can do this. This is the only way you will find your freedom. Trust me. Don't be scared now, all will be fine."

Lauren takes one deep breath, and says "Yes. I am ready now."

She kneels down and opens the crate. Tommy is so excited and confused that he runs out, knocks Lauren over and then runs straight into the glass doors to the entrance of the airport and keeps running around and keeps wagging his tail.

"Can I take him now?"

"He's all yours, custom's cleared, guess he needs to pee badly."

Lauren manages to get the collar on and gets dragged out of the terminal by Tommy pulling the leash.

He stops at the first pole outside the terminal and does the longest pee in this airports history.

The pilot and crew from the flight walk out as Tommy has his leg lifted to the pole and they all stop and laugh at him, other passers-by stop and look as Tommy's peeing just won't stop.

"Sorry, it's been a long flight!"

"That's the Indian Mutt that was on our flight!"

"Thanks for taking good care of him"

"My pleasure, and you take good care of him! He's a fine looking canine! It was an honour to have him on board."

"I'll do my best!"

When Tommy finishes peeing the crowd applauds and then she manages to get him to a grass patch for more relief. He happily strolls around the airport with Lauren, totally un-fazed by the long journey. Tommy drags the leash to the right and left and is so happy to be out of the crate.

Lauren can barely steer him towards the car park with the crate on the cart dragging her in all directions as he runs up to people and wags his tail. Finally, she finds the car park, finds the car, finds the car keys and they get in the car. She tells Tommy to sit next to her on in the front seat.

Lauren sits down next to him and she takes a deep breath, looks at him and finally he takes a good look at her.

After all the commotion at the airport he takes her in, takes it all in. And then it sinks in. It's her, the blonde human he belongs to. She is with him. He throws himself over her with kisses and tail wagging.

He is where he needs to be, despite that scary journey, and in the passenger seat next to her, he looks at her again, with that look Lauren has never known another dog to possess.

"It is me! I told you we would be together! OK, let me drive, we're going to stay in a nice hotel tonight, with a garden and a pool. We'll get take-out pizza and go for a nice walk! And tomorrow we will have to fly just one more time and then that's it. Honestly, I am not sure what I am supposed to do. So you have to tell me, OK? Anything you want or need, you just tell me. Everything is different now, just so you know."

He puts his head on the arm rest and keeps looking at her as she drives out of the airport looking for signs and directions to the hotel.

He lets her put the leash on after she parks and follows her as they walk around the hotel grounds. He stays close to her and absorbs all the new smells and sounds.

He falls asleep in the afternoon on the bed, tucked in blankets and pillows under Lauren's watchful eye.

They watch TV and eat dinner together, a large pizza for her and roast chicken for him and as Lauren feels his warm body lying next to hers, she finally starts to believe that everything will be fine.

And Sutara looks at them from above. Her mission is finally accomplished; she guided her son safely to the human that will take care of him. She smiles as she watches Lauren stroke her son as he sleeps and whispers memories of India in his ears to make sure he never forgets where he comes from.

• • •

As Tommy is being loaded in the hold of yet another aircraft for the final leg to California and Lauren gets her seat she drops the envelope with all the paperwork for Tommy's journey.

Putting all the documents back in the document folder, she sees an envelope that says "to Lauren".

She opens it and it's a letter from Jerome. There are several photos of Tommy and a young Indian woman, an elderly man, a shabby street and of a porch with a sewing machine on. The last photo is of a little grass patch with flowers on. There is also a necklace with a Ganesh pendant.

It starts with "King Tommy".

On the tarmac the jet engines roar once again and the plane takes off towards Los Angeles while Tommy lies in the darkness in the hold wondering where he will be taken this time. Lauren reads Jerome's story of where Tommy grew up. How he was once called Raj and how this young beautiful Indian woman saved him and his mother. He still couldn't understand what made Tommy end up at the Blue House in Anjuna, but the older neighbour had something to do with it, he was sure. The young woman was so nice to him. "She gives you her blessing and says that Raj/Tommy has a special gift. That every time she was sad he would stand next to her and help her feel better. Have you noticed that? The necklace was Garati's and it is for Raj/Tommy. Wishing you safe travels and please take good care of our King for us."

She reads the letter over and over again, looking at the photos.

This is where it all started, and as the plane flies over the vast American continent it all starts to sink in. He is with me now, my King, she thinks as she asks the flight attendant one more time if the captain really did turn the heating on in the hold and if the captain really knows that there is a very important dog in there.

The flight attendant tells Lauren one more time that everything is fine; they do fly dogs all the time. But when she sees Laurens tears running down her cheeks she smiles patiently again and promises to double check that everything is under control.

● ● ●

It's close to midnight when the plane lands in Los Angeles and Scott is there to meet Lauren and Tommy. For the last time Lauren opens the crate and lets Tommy out, and he runs around the terminal happy to get out and away from yet another noisy aircraft. Scott kneels down to greet Tommy and he runs up to him. "So this is what has cost me all this money! Hey, you don't look like a dog that plays with stuffed toys! OK, let's get you guys home!"

They put the crate in the car, and Tommy jumps in the car and sits down on the driver's seat. Lauren puts Tommy on her lap as Scott drives out of the airport, back on the highway that will take them home.

"You know he should wear a seatbelt and be in the backseat. I read that in a dog magazine. "

"I'll buy one tomorrow, promise."

"This little guy seems pretty savvy about life. He just survived a forty-eight-hour journey and ten thousand miles of air travel! Look at him! He is checking everything out! OK, big guy, here's your first all American car chase!"

Behind them sirens scream and a car speeds past them with a police car chasing it behind them. Tommy barks at the sirens and the blue lights as the police cars drive by them.

"Hey Tommy! I like you! He's a real dude dog! Oh, by the way, Stuart called, he wants another painting. Can I borrow him when I go out on a date?"

WELCOME TO THE NEW WORLD

It's been a tough morning. Tommy wakes up Lauren early, he stands next to her while she is sleeping and breathes on her, until she stirs and turns around. He breathes on her again, until she opens her eyes and sees him smiling at her, with eyes full of expectation. When he is sure she is awake he stands by the door, scratching on it. It's time to go out! He has been awake on and off during the night. Again new smells and a new house. He has tried to walk down the stairs on his own, but couldn't figure out how, so steep and strange. He has never seen a staircase before. He has been wondering if they are going back to sandy patch soon or somewhere new. He has been wondering so many things in one single night. But he can sense the blonde human not being worried or planning new things, just sleeping deeply and dreaming. So maybe they will stay here for a while. But where is here, and what is waiting outside this house?

"Tommy it's only six am! Oh, Holy Lord Ganesha and all the Elephants in the world! Are you jet lagged?" She gets some clothes on and opens the door. Tommy runs to the neighbour's nice lawn and lifts his leg against a perfectly trimmed rose bush. He gets stung by the thorns and runs off to another lawn where he does a big poo in a bamboo bush. Lauren tries to figure out how to open the lavender scented bags but it's too late, the neighbour is awake and yells at her and this strange looking dog. She manages to get the leash on Tommy and then takes him to the park.

Tommy looks at her, excited. Everything is new and he is so happy to be walking and running around in this new world. She lets him run free and he smells his new environment, runs to shake off the stiffness in his legs after the long journey.

An hour later they return and as Tommy aims for another rose bush, Lauren says "No", and he gently steers away, aiming to lift his leg against Scott's car. Oh well, just this once....

Tommy doesn't eat any of the dog food Lauren serves him.

She sneaks into Scott's house and takes a piece of grilled chicken in his fridge. He eats all of it and Lauren can finally have her coffee in peace and quiet. She looks at the photos Jerome gave her again and holds the Ganesh necklace in her hand. She studies Garati's face and wonders about her life, how she lives and what she does. Garati smiling with Tommy, or Raj, her King. What made her call him Raj? She wants to know more about her and her life. But not now as she feels her feet being tickled by Tommy's paw.

• • •

Lauren walks in to the local pet store to return all the dog food not worthy of an Indian dog's palate. With Tommy in tow on a leash, she goes up to the cashier and asks to return the food.

As she asks for other types of food, Tommy is mesmerized by all the different smells in the large pet store. Aisle after aisle, smells of kibble, chewies and dog biscuits make him curious.

The shop assistant leads Lauren to a big freezer and shows her the raw meat diet, the buffalo bones, the frozen venison.

She picks out some samples for Lauren and as they turn to go back to the till, Lauren lifts up the leash only to find it has been chewed off and no Tommy standing next to her.

The store is large and Lauren walks aisle up and aisle down, calling his name.

She asks a lady with a big white poodle if she has seen a small dog with a chewed off leash walking around, and the lady answers "No" with a condescending tone.

As Lauren walks away the lady resumes her conversation with another woman.

"And when Gucci has passed all his tests, we will sign up for the Therapy Dog exam and then he will have accomplished everything!"

"Well, Dawn, Therapy Dogs are supposed to help people, you know, it's so that we can help the community with our dogs. It's an honour to be a Therapy Dog."

"I know, of course, but I just want to get on a plane with him"

"Dawn, you can't do that, Therapy Dogs are meant to give emotional support to other people, to help them feel better, not to bring them on a plane for free"

The white poodle lifts his leg and starts peeing on the dog toys.

Joyce quickly grabs the white poodle and drags him away from the toys.

"Now, Dawn, here; keep an eye on your dog! OK, I have to go now.... Honey, did you find your dog?"

Lauren is getting worried, he is gone. Then she sees it, a wagging curled up tail, by the grooming area.

He is standing next to an elderly man, who is sitting in the waiting area next to the grooming department. She sees how he stands next to the old man without moving, listening to the man who is talking to him, and giving him his full attention.

"You see, this is where we always used to come, the first Monday of the month, to have our Dolly groomed. She would bring Dolly here, and I would go and sit outside and smoke a cigar, thinking this was silly stuff, something that only ladies should do, you know, bring a dog to get groomed. And I would walk in through that door at four pm every Monday of the month, to pick them up, and she would look so happy when they brought Dolly out, all washed and pampered. And now they're both gone, you see. Married forty-five years, and she is gone, just like that."

Tommy looks deep into the old man's eyes as the man strokes his back.

Lauren walks up to them, the old man smiles at her, and she kneels down as Tommy is happy to see her, Lauren talks to the old man, holds his hand as he wipes his tears away with a tissue.

Joyce has been watching them, Lauren and the little dog with the gold coloured eyes as they say goodbye to the old man.

As Lauren pays for another leash and walks out of the store with the new dog food, Joyce calls her.

"You found your dog!"

"Yes, thank you!"

"Daniel comes in from time to time, his wife just passed away.

I wanted to ask you, what association are you with?"

"Did I do something wrong?"

"No, on the contrary, but what Therapy Dog association did you certify him with?"

"Therapy Dog?"

"I saw your dog with Daniel, he obviously has a lot experience."

"Oh, no, he just does that. He arrived from India last night. What is a Therapy Dog?"

"Well, I want to see him with our association. Here's my card.

A Therapy Dog goes to hospitals or other facilities and gives emotional support to people that are ill, in hospice or has special needs. It's a voluntary program; we also help people with Alzheimer or cancer. It's an amazing way to help the community, to help people with our dogs. Some older people are so lonely, and the contact they get to have with a Therapy Dog is really helping them with battling depression. I volunteer at a centre for adults with autism and we use my dog as a way to communicate with some of the patients. But they need to be special dogs like your one. Promise me you'll call. I wrote on the back the name of a good dog school where you can do all the training before you do the test.

It's a difficult test, not everyone passes it."

"A Therapy Dog?"

Lauren looks at the card, as Joyce walks away.

Helping lonely people? Sick people? Autism? Alzheimer's?

I was that person, she thinks, he was there when I needed him, he is always there when someone needs him. Heather was that person too, who needed someone who could see her.

THE LEARNING CURVE

"It's time for you to see what the ocean looks like on the other side of the world!"

As they walk down the beach and Tommy sees the long and wide California beach he gets excited. Finally, something that looks familiar! His happy place!

Lauren takes off the leash and he runs down to the sea, wades in the water and runs along the shore.

"Welcome to the Pacific Ocean, little man!"

Tommy starts chasing sea gulls and impresses the dog owners with his speed, his little body all streamlined and his tail standing right out for balance. He trots proudly back along the beach looking for Lauren.

She is running after him, calling him, but he's not hearing her, he is looking and starts getting worried, trotting in a confused zig-zag among all the people and dogs. Lauren keeps calling him, to no avail.

Another dog owner tells her to open her arms so he can see her, and kneel. "He won't know which one of all of the people is you otherwise, and call him as you wave at the same time."

She does as told and then Tommy sees Lauren.

He folds his ears back and runs towards her as fast as he can.

"Hi!" He almost runs into her and covers her with kisses.

They sit down on the beach, Tommy plays with the sand and lies down next to her.

"Welcome home!"

She gets the Ganesh necklace out of her pocket.

"Come." Tommy sits next to her.

"We are going to give thanks to all the people who helped us."

She puts the necklace around Tommy's neck and takes a few photos of him as he is sitting on the beach, with the Pacific Ocean in the background.

"Ok, now think about the important living beings in your life and say thank you to them. Just close your eyes and visualize them. Like this!"

Lauren sits in the lotus position and closes her eyes. Tommy looks at her and sits down on her foot.

When she doesn't react he licks her foot, tickling her. Lauren starts to laugh. "Ok, you made your point. We will say thank you your way. There!"

She points to a seagull and Tommy runs after it. He gangs up with a few other dogs and together they run along the beach. Lauren takes more photos and laughs at him.

Finally, she can relax. Tommy seems to be happy and can enjoy a bit of freedom. It will work. He will be fine. She takes a deep breath opens up her arms again so Tommy can see her. He turns his head towards her, as if smiling, and keeps running down the long wide beach with the other dogs racing with them.

Towards the evening, as Lauren sends the photos to Jerome and Adnah and Sky, Tommy falls asleep ten thousand miles away from the beaches of Goa in his new country where a lot of people look like his yellow haired human, where the streets were clean and no holy cows walked on the streets. Where dogs look and smell differently and all walk pulling a human on a leash.

As Tommy must be dreaming of hunting a big elephant, his legs shake in his sleep and a small whining noise follows the imaginary hunt, Lauren gets up and kisses him on the forehead. She takes off the necklace from Tommy's neck and puts it back in the envelope. Then she turns the light off, walks up to her bed and falls asleep, exhausted.

A few moments later she is awakened by hearing little paws walk up the steps to her loft and Tommy lying down next to her on the bed, by her feet.

. . .

Tara is sweeping up the basketball field at the back of the community college. She sighs and wonders what this new group will be like. With any luck half of them will make it to the end and then she has to be happy. Be happy, she thinks. I will be happy when my illustrations are published. All I want is for my illustrations to be published. She has spent most part of the day drawing a dragon, just like she has to present herself to her new students. The dragon and the mermaid. Fire and water, and in the middle a magic path of flowers leading the mermaid to the dragon's den. Beautiful, that's what it will be. The first participants arrive and she takes her seat on the bench, her illustrations will have to wait until she gets back home and all her children have fallen asleep.

It's the usual assortment of puppies and newly rescued dogs, the odd breed and of course, the usual blonde hippie wearing a t-shirt with some elephant on it and some way too loose colourful pants that will make her trip and fall.

"And what do we have here?"

"King Tommy"

"King?" And how old might this Royal Highness be?"

"I think he is a year and half or so. He's from India."

"An Indian from Indiana?"

"No, India."

Lauren looks at the tall, stern looking dog teacher with her long unbrushed dark hair and simple t-shirt that is way too big for her. Tara, that's her name. It's the first day of dog school, and Lauren is immediately terrified of her as Tara looks at her from top to toe and then stares at Tommy, wearing his most beautiful collar, flowers and diamonds.

"I can see that. Well, let's see what this Indian mutt can do."

Tara looks at the Indian dog follow the blonde woman. He is such a light mover, graceful, with his unusual curly tail and big ears.

"OK, y'all, let's get started before I lose my patience. Everyone, lets stand in a circle, NOW! Make sure that the dog is standing next to you, not in front, not behind, next to you."

Tommy stands next to Lauren, looking at her.

"Yes, like Mr Indiana there. Well done!"

Tara tells the group to start walking in a circle around her, and she studies every student and dog until she tells them to stop.

"So, walking heel, means having control. We walk with our dogs next to us, with a loose leash, and a smile."

She shows them how to teach their dogs to walk heel and looks at her group, wondering who will continue to train and who will end up giving their dog away, and for a moment she looks at the dog from Indiana and his eyes, and yes, her dragon will have gold coloured eyes. That would be a nice touch. Did she really say India? Who brings a dog from India? She must have heard wrong again. But he is doing well the little dog. She compliments the blonde hippie looking owner and tells the group to stand in a line in front of her. It's time to learn sit.

Tommy sits and holds up his paw, ready for a biscuit.

"Someone's been training! But you have to be clear when you ask him to do something, look!"

Tara takes the leash and leads Tommy, telling him to sit and then walk heel. He does it perfectly and Tara smiles at him.

"Homework for next week: Sit and heel, five minutes a day, so that they don't get bored! Thank you!"

As the class finished Tara sees how a man is applauding the blonde woman and the dog from Indiana. She smiles at them and hopes that they will come back for the next lesson. The dog definitely has talent.

Scott has been looking at the class and has been hiding laughing at the scene – unbelievable – Lauren really did it, signed up for dog school! He is proud of her, and Tommy recognises him from a distance and runs to him. Lauren takes off the leash and gives Scott a hug.

"Dinner on the beach?"

They drive to the dog beach and as Lauren and Tommy chase each other in the low tide Scott puts the take away dinner on three plates. Indian curry for three.

As the sun is setting they all eat their food. Not too spicy for Tommy, with lots of rice. He asks Lauren if she wants to go away next week for a few days.

"There is something you have to do. I took care of everything but this, only you can do it."

Lauren looks at him, and as he tells her, she says no, I won't. And Scott talks about closure, regardless of what one thinks, one needs to have closure.

"Anyway, it's what they would have wanted. The lake up in Big Bear at sunset."

And there it was, reality biting you right back.

"I really don't want to go there, to do it, to have anything to do with it."

"Think about it. Anyway, we're going. I booked a nice cabin and it will be good for us to get away."

• • •

"Hey, Indiana, don't turn around when you walk away from him!" The class at dog school is practising sit and stay. Tommy's ears are pointed straight up, waiting for something to happen while Lauren walks all the 20 feet away from him.

"Trust that he will do the right thing! OK, now turn around and count to five before you call him. Everyone, let's do it together!" Tommy runs straight to Lauren as the puppies run away from the owners and a pit bull refuses to move.

Tara sighs and thinks about her dragons and mermaids. She asks the class to do it again. This time they all have to do it right and it seems to help. You can feel everyone's concentration and as if on a magical cue, all the dogs run back to their owners on command. Tara looks at Lauren who is wearing a white shirt with stains in different colours. Great, fashion week seems to have come and gone without her noticing.

She thanks the group and gets ready to leave when Lauren walks up to her.

"Hey! Indiana!"

Tommy runs up to Tara, and she plays with him. Lauren shows Tara all the required courses and tests Tommy has to do before the Therapy Dog exam. Tara looks at the material and tells her the dates for the Good Canine Citizen test, and a vet clinic she can use for the check-up.

"He'll pass, just keep training and he'll be fine. You know, I did check up your dog on the internet, and I am not sure he is a mutt, you know. There are dogs in India that are called Indian Native dogs and he looks just like them. They are like Dingo's. The primitive dogs, that haven't been modified by man. You should look into it. Apparently it's a breed that's thousands of years old. They live free and in villages in rural India. This is the name of the lady that is doing all the research. You should write to her and tell her about the training you are doing with your INdog, as they're called."

"Really? A native dog? But they're everywhere in India."

"Yes, but not all are Native dogs. You see, his ears, his tail and legs, and his nose? That's the way dogs looked from the start. Quite interesting. He just has that look. When other breeds came into India with the English and the Portuguese, some of the dogs you see became mixed, or "mongrels" but the Indian Native dog is pure. He might be a bit mixed, as he is quite small, but he is a spitting image of those dogs."

"A real Indian then! That's quite amazing. I will write to this Indian lady, I promise. Thank you!"

"See you next week Indiana!"

And how did he end up in Mapusa then, she wonders. That's not exactly primitive. Well, his dog mother must have gotten lost, with all the new construction going on in Goa, she might even have gotten kicked out of her territory. Who knows. Origins, Lauren thinks, that's it. Stuart's new painting, about origins. She needs to work tonight again, all day she has been trying out new colours and nothing interesting came out of that except staining her new shirt.

Later on that night she gets it right, a hidden family tree, taking the colours to their rightful place. Scott is drinking wine on her patio and talks about his divorce and about his dating life. Like a big brother, she thinks, always the big brother she never had. She smiles at him, and he looks at her. "Am I boring you?"

"No, it's nice, this. Us together again, like this. It's good. Just like old days in Santa Barbara."

● ● ●

It's hot and the air is as dry as it gets at the top of the mountain in Southern California. It has been a beautiful drive, from the desert climbing up to the top of the mountain and where pine forests and green fields surround the lake.

A gentle breeze makes for a perfect day as Scott orders another glass of wine and Lauren lies next to him reading. They are lying by the pool at a nice resort by the lake and Tommy is hiding under her lounge chair, staying in the shade.

"What are you reading?"

"Start your own business for dummies. What about doing some things away from my art?"

"Love the "other things" – you sound focused!"

"I am! I could get an agent in the Caribbean and sell stuff there."

"Itchy feet?"

"A little bit. I miss the noise and the chaos. Everything is so square. Look, even the pool is square! I need round lines, that's what I need. I need to go out and party, I need street vendors, temples and incense!"

"Speaking of round lines, did you put on weight?"

She hits Scott on the head with her book and Scott retaliates by dragging her up from her lounge chair and throwing her in the pool with her clothes on. She manages to cling on to him and drags him into the pool as well.

At the same time, a flock of ducks fly over them, across the pool and the hotel. Tommy sees them, and runs after them, chasing them out to the street, onto the main road.

Lauren yells, gets out of the pool and runs down the road, after Tommy, who is happily running after the ducks, and then some cars, finally the loud noise from a police car makes him even more excited and off he runs after that one too.

"Oh God, oh NO. TOMMY STOP!!!!!"

The police car stops and Tommy stops running too, greets the police officer with a warm welcome as he steps out of his car.

Lauren, is gasping for air, running barefoot in her wet clothes shouting and waving her arms.

The police officer puts a leash around Tommy's neck and holds him tight.

"WAIT WAIT WAIT!!! I am sorry"

"Ma'am, there is a leash law in this state. We'll need to confiscate the dog and investigate this situation."

"Oh please, I am so sorry, it was an accident. We go to dog school, he is GREAT! "

"I don't think so, Ma'am. We're all going to the police station now".

"Oh please, Sir"

Scott arrives in his car, driving way too fast to please a small town police officer, and hits the brakes in front of the police car.

He gets out, his clothes soaking wet too, leaving puddles where he stands.

"Well Well Well, aren't we all having a blast in Big Bear?"

"This is my best friend, he can explain. He only just arrived from India and he doesn't really understand that things are different here"

"Do you speak English, Sir?"

"The dog."

"The dog needs to be on a leash. And this gentleman needs to learn how to drive. This isn't Indiana."

"India. The dog is from India. Not me."

He looks at Scott, Lauren, and Tommy.

"OK, you two, get a change of clothes. I will give you a warning for this time."

"Thank you, thank you thank you"

"If I see him again, running around, chasing ducks or cars, that's it, you're both off to the station and your friend is going back to Indiana faster than the Pony Express."

"Yes sir, we were just in the pool – "

"I can see that"

"He's a great dog, look: Tommy, sit!"

Tommy doesn't move.

"Sure. Ready for the nationals, I see."

Tommy has chewed off the leash. The police officer is holding the chewed off piece.

"I'll be damned!" The police officer tells Tommy to sit.

Tommy sits and gives him his paw.

"Have a nice evening now and enjoy Big Bear. You might want to try my cousin's restaurant, down by other side of the lake, it's called John's Kitchen. Tell'em Officer Joe sent you."

"Yes sir, we will. Thank you."

The police car drives off.

They burst out laughing.

"OK, don't say it. I'm buying dinner."

"You bet. "A trained dog!" Good luck with that!"

"OK, you are right, let's do it. Now, otherwise I'll change my mind."

"What, like this?"

"Yes."

"Are they in the car?"

"Like you said, left them in the trunk."

They drive along the lake looking for a suitable place for their mission. He parks across the bridge, and gets a bag out from the trunk. They start walking and follow a small path along the lake. As they walk they keep looking out for people, trying to find a quiet place.

They stop and Scott gets two boxes out. He hands one to Lauren. She holds it, and then wades out into the lake. Tommy stands next to Scott.

She opens the box and lets the ashes out on the lake. Slowly, gently, and touches the ashes as they lie on the lake, before they start sinking down into the mass of water.

Daughter and father. Past and present.

Maybe this is what happens when life is cruel to us. We just move on, aimlessly, trying to cope and trying to forget about the promises of youth. Do we get numb and stop trying to reason, to try, until it all catches up with us and then it's too late? The walking wounded, she thinks as she empties the last of the ashes in the lake. "I know how you felt, I do, and it's a horrible place to be." She whispers to her father.

Lauren looks at Tommy and then turns away from him and stands with the ashes and the sunset and says goodbye to her father.

Then they move to another place, and she takes the other box and walks out in the lake again.

Tommy follows her into the water, and stops when the water reaches his stomach. He stands there looking at her, as she hesitates, looking out across the lake, at the mountains.

It has been three years that I have lived in your world of darkness, and I can't do it anymore, I am sorry. For everything. I am sorry that I thought I could understand you, but I can't. I am sorry.

But I do know that darkness is a safe place to be in, but I don't want to be safe anymore. I love you and I am letting you go now, Heather, just like you wanted me to be, free.

Lauren finally opens the box with her sister's ashes and spreads them on the lake, she takes them in her hand, and says farewell.

They stand together and look at her, Scott and Tommy, and as she stands there in the lake she looks at Scott.

"We have to move. We can't stay here. Well, I can't and you shouldn't either. If not Santa Barbara, then somewhere else. I'm done now. And so are you, I know that."

Scott nods and holds out his hand to her to help her on dry land.
He holds her and closes his eyes. "I am so tired."
"I know."

• • •

"Do you miss India, Tommy?"
Tommy wags his tail, he runs off chasing seagulls, running along
the whole dog beach, then does his usual trot on the way back,
showing himself off to the world. He looks so happy, so at ease,
as if he had been here his whole life. It's only a week left to the
Therapy Dog exam and Lauren is confident he will pass. She has
already spoken to a facility in the neighbourhood and it will be a
good place to start. Different types of illnesses and situations, a
lot of lonely patients without families who went through painful
treatment. Perfect.
And in true Indian fashion, events need to be blessed and celebrated.
It's the Saint Francis day, where animals get blessed in the name
of the Saint and they drive off to the local church to attend this
not so Hindu celebration.
Dog treats are handed out by the priest and his assistants, they are
greeting all the new arrivals and a lot of people are there with their
pets. Dogs, cats, giant turtles, birds.
The priest invites everyone inside and soon enough the whole
church is full of pets and their owners. A giant turtle crawls around
on the floor and a parrot is sitting on the altar. Special prayers
have been written by the priests, they are about accepting the love
our animals provide, how they suffer because of us and how every
little living being should be given a dignified life.
And then the blessing begins and everyone lines up in front of the
priest.
It's Tommy's turn.
The priest is on his knees; Tommy walks up to him.
"What is his name?"
"Tommy"
"Tommy, in the name of our Lord you are blessed today "
And then the priest takes Tommy's head in his hands, holds him
and starts praying in silence to him. Tommy listens and looks at
the priest, listening to his prayers.
"Walk in peace, my friend, and may God bless you."

Tommy and Lauren walk back to their seat, and Tommy looks back at the priest, thinking back at the chapel on the field, next to the Blue House, and how he used to look into the small building with the big open doors, and wondered what all those humans did in that big room, singing and talking together.

He looks around the church, sitting on the bench next to his blonde human, and at all the other dogs in the church. He looks up to the ceiling, and the paintings above him. This is my new life, he thinks, and touches his blonde human to get her attention.

She puts her arm around him and together they sit in silence as the other pets get blessed.

Lauren looks at Tommy studying the church, and smiles at him. He always has to be so present and he demands complete presence. Her mind drifts in the silence of the church, and tries to remember the name of that guy she had met in Saint Martin. She wonders what happened to him, and if he is still in New York. That's it, his name was Adam. Adam what? Where did he work? What if I should write to him? To say what? I live with a dog?

Tommy touches her with his nose, again noticing when she day dreams, when her mind drifts to remote places. She takes photos of Tommy in the church, and the turtle, thinking it would be amusing for Garati to look at them. She has heard from Jerome, his studies are going great and apparently he can do his last year of school in America. Who would have thought, he finally will come here? She has told him she will help him, and can stay with her, but the school is in Chicago and it's still a few years away. He has also written that Garati is always happy to see photos of Tommy and doesn't stop talking, as if knowing that her puppy is safe makes her stronger and happier. Lauren smiles.

"You are making us proud, little man" she whispers to Tommy.

• • •

Dawn and Gucci, the white standard poodle, are waiting to cross the street on one of the busy intersections on the upper part of Huntington Beach. Gucci is all brushed and coiffured, looking very fancy and standing right next to Dawn. A friend walks towards them and Dawn does a very Mediterranean hello with kisses on the cheek and all.

Gucci stands next to her, his nose examining the crotch of her friend. "Oh yes, we are so ready for the test on Tuesday. He knows it all by heart now without a single treat! You see they're never allowed treats. I want Gucci to be a winner, it takes a special kind of dog to be a Therapy Dog! Look! Sit, Stand, Down, Heel!" Gucci sticks his long nose deep in between Dawn's friend's legs. "And then hygiene is very important, they all have to have their toe nails clipped…"

The noise of a Harley Davidson can be heard throughout the whole neighbourhood.

A big guy with a long beard, Hells Angels vest and cowboy boots decides to rev up the engine while waiting at the red light.

The poodle woman sees him and protects Gucci's ears.

Lauren is walking on the other side of the busy boulevard with Tommy in tow on her way to the ice cream place when her phone rings.

"Hello…. Adam!! You got my message? Hi…. I'm sorry I walked off…." Does he remember her? She asks shyly. The Red Piano, Saint Martin. He says he does and that he has been waiting for her to find him.

Lauren sees that woman with the white poodle at the traffic lights up the road. Where had she seen her? At the pet store?

"Are you still in New York? Seattle? Yes, I would like that…."

He wants to know if she wants to meet him.

As the lights turn to green, the Harley Davidson revs up the noise to an unbearable thunder and drives off at full speed past Lauren's traffic lights. Tommy growls and has a fit at the noise.

"Wait, I have to call you back."

Tommy's leash snaps and off he is chasing the Harley.

"NOOOOOOOOOOOOOOOOOOOO! STOOOOP! Not again!"

The Harley speeds down the big boulevard with four lanes in each direction in full blast, the exhaust popping and fuming, making wonderful sounds an Indian Dog loves to chase.

Tommy gets all his gears on and runs after the Harley.

Lauren is running after them, shouting and screaming for Tommy to stop.

She can hear that woman with the white poodle as she runs past her.

"Darlene, this is what I am talking about, feral, wild animals! I am calling Animal Control to have that criminal mutt put down right this minute!'

Gucci is pulling the leash, wanting to get a part of the action.

And one more time Lauren is running down the streets of California chasing her dog.

"STOOOOOOOP! I am sending you back to India right now, god damn it!"

She keeps running down the avenue, trying to see Tommy, still hearing the roaring of the Harley down the road.

Running up to a crossing, two cars have had an accident, Lauren is already crying. In her mind Tommy is hit by the car and dead but no blood, no Tommy, just someone who didn't hit the brakes on time when an elderly man didn't see the lights turn into red. The driver's shout at each other and as they get into a fight Lauren runs across the street in between cars.

She keeps running until she runs out of air, struggling to move forward.

By now Tommy has to be on Beach Avenue, run over by some truck and Lauren will go to jail and Tommy will be dead.

She stops by another red light, can't breathe, can't move, but has to. Then the roaring of the Harley starts getting closer, as if it's coming back her way instead of going towards the beach.

She sees the Harley, now it's honking and the Hells Angels guy is driving slower looking for something along the road.

And there it is, Lauren cannot believe what she is seeing.

Tommy is sitting on the Harley, his paws on the handle, happy as ever.

"Here HERE! TOMMY!"

The guy waves as her, Lauren start running after them, until they get to a halt.

"Tommy!!!!"

Lauren is so out of air and so upset she can't even speak.

The Hells Angels guy is playing with Tommy, who is still on the bike.

"Thank you, I don't know what to do anymore"

"Honey, it's OK, take a moment!"

"We have this test tomorrow; he will never pass it. Look at him, he will never be a Therapy Dog. It's FINSHED!"

"Hey, any dog that puts a smile on my face is a good Therapy Dog."

"What can I do to thank you?"

"Buy me a beer when you pass the test. This is a really cool dog! You know he runs as fast as my Harley? Tough little guy you have!"

"OK, thank you. I promise you. Owe you my life."

"You owe me a date, babe. Why don't I drive you guys home?"

Lauren is too tired to argue with the big man and gets on the Harley, behind him.

"I'm Hank."

They drive off, and Tommy is having the time of his life on the front, between Hank's arms. Lauren shows Hank how to get to their house, and as they drive up the street the noise from the Harley's engine makes the whole neighbourhood look out of their homes.

As Lauren gets off the bike and Tommy shows off jumping down to the ground, Hank gives her his card.

"If you ever need a dog sitter, I'd be happy to take him. I'll take him for a drive up the coast. "

He drives off as Scott comes out of his house.

"New date?"

"I'll tell you later. How far is Seattle?"

THE CROWNING OF A KING

No cats, no motorbikes, no squirrels, no ducks. We're in luck.
How did my life end up like this? Because of a dog? Because I
didn't know where else to go? Because I wanted to? Did I really
want it to? And how did I ever get the idea that I have a dog with
a unique talent? I should be painting right now, not following some
stupid idea that I have a dog that can change people's lives just
because he changed mine. Maybe we should just leave, now. I'll
tell them I won't do it.
I look at Tommy, he is the car, sitting next to me. I dig in my pocket
and find the necklace Garati gave him.
Carrying the heritage of India, of the Hindu's who helped him
when he was a puppy and the Catholic Indians who gave him a
sanctuary for a while, and everyone in between. All of all the people
whose lives have intertwined because of him. And then there is me,
whose life took a completely different turn because of you.
Ganesh, the Elephant God, who removes obstacles and protects
travellers. Who sometimes puts obstacles in your way so that you
can see what it is you really want, or need to know.
Ganesh, the Indian elephant. The God of beginnings.
I put the necklace around his neck and tell him that this is it, this
is all we have worked for and today, just for today, you have to be
the best you can be. You have always helped humans, but this is
like the Superbowl of helping humans.

Tommy looks at me with his usual serious look, reading my thoughts. My best friend, that's who you are, I tell him and I hold the Ganesha pendant and I tell him to close his eyes and let's pray together. And then I open the door and let King Tommy out. We are ready.

•   •   •

Lauren and Tommy get out of the car and walk towards the park, where a group of people and dogs are gathered.

As the people are filling out papers and getting to know each other, Dawn is holding her Gucci on a tight leash as she sprays him with hair spray and incessantly talking to the other participants about what an amazing dog he is. She tells a shy lady that she is sure her Gucci will get the highest points of all. Then she looks up and sees Lauren and Tommy walking towards the group. She instantly recognizes Tommy's proud walk and curly tail.

"Oh Lord, look what the cat dragged in. Joyce, let me tell you, this dog – "

Joyce, the judge, sees Tommy and smiles.

"Oh, it's the lovely dog from India! Welcome! How are you?!"

Tommy sees her and starts pulling his leash, running up to her to say hi.

"Now, don't we have high hopes for you?! Did you bring all the paperwork? I can't believe he remembers me!"

"Joyce, this dog, this is a very bad dog – yesterday he was chasing a motorcycle all the way down Brookhurst Avenue! And this.... this....person here did- "

Dawn is pointing at Tommy, pointing at Lauren.

"It was an accident – I promise – "

Joyce looks at Dawn.

"Dawn, your dog just soiled the test area."

Gucci has left a big smelly poop on the grass next to Dawn.

Dawn goes quiet and gets a bag out to pick it up. She holds the poop bag high as she points to Lauren.

"I was going to call Animal Control to have this mutt put down!"

"Dawn, Therapy Dogs are allowed to be lively and fun. Of course they are not allowed to chase cars down the road, but I am sure this is something that you can work on, Lauren?"

"Yes, of course, I just don't know how."

"I will help you with that, we will book you in for a few one on ones next week, OK? Now don't worry about that. Let's all get started! Remember that this is about the dog's ability to fit into a hospital environment, to be able to connect with patients, to handle stress in any situation. It's an honour to become a Therapy Dog, and if you pass, you will always have to be a role model. So let's get started and good luck!"

Lauren is almost in tears as Dawn sneers at her and struts past her with her poodle.

"Little Indian dog, why don't you start? Let's do some heel, sit, stay".

Lauren looks at Tommy, kisses him, makes up her mind about the past, and about the present.

"OK, Tommy, this is it! Come on, it's show time!"

Tommy looks at Lauren.

He feels the importance of the moment, he needs to make Lauren happy, she needs him now, and Joyce, the lady telling his human what to do is looking at him anxiously. Tommy trots happily along next to Lauren. He smiles at her, he had no idea he would end up in a crate and travel across the world, but he is here with her and that's all that matters. And she listens to him, to every single breath he takes and cares for him every day. Of course she can be absent minded and spend too much time throwing colours on those big white papers lying on the floor and dream herself away too much. And she left him, but she came back and took him away from the bad people.

Tommy looks at Lauren when she asks him to sit, lie down and stay and run to her.

He feels so much joy, because he can be with her and look at her when she sleeps. She doesn't know this, but most of the nights he usually stays awake to watch her, so that no harm will come to her.

He is always protecting his blonde human at night the same way she protects him during the day.

"OK, that was great. Now, have him stand here"

Tommy stands next to Lauren when an assistant rolls a wheel chair past him.

Then the assistant throws a metal tray on the floor, making a lot of noise, and Tommy keeps looking at Lauren and shows no surprise or reaction to the noise and strange chairs with small wheels squeaking next to him.

Then Tommy has to sit on a chair next to Joyce.

Joyce strokes him; Tommy gives her his full attention. She throws herself at him and hugs him. Tommy remains still. She gets a walker and walks with it next to Tommy, dragging it and trying to scare him.

Tommy just sits there patiently while all the tests are being done.

Joyce sits in the wheel chair, calls him, Tommy goes up to her, makes eye contact and stands right next to her by the wheel chair. She tries to pet him, pretending she can't reach, Lauren tells him to stand closer to the wheel chair, and Tommy walks up closer to Joyce, so that she can reach him.

He closes his eyes, and allows her to lift his paw, to touch his ears, to check his teeth.

"Very good! Guess he is used to all the commotion from India!"

"OK, wait over there. Now it's Gucci."

Dawn walks up with Gucci.

They do the obedience test, which works well; Gucci knows everything without even taking commands.

Then the wheel chair arrives and Joyce tries to get his attention, Gucci doesn't listen to Joyce and starts pulling the leash the other way.

Joyce calls him again and Gucci lies down on the grass, happy to roll himself in something dirty.

"OK, Gucci come back here, let's try something else. Here, have him sit next to me. Let's test his communication skills."

Joyce stands away from Gucci, with the stroller; she starts walking towards him and greets Gucci. The beautiful white standard poodle who only wants to be left alone and run with the other dogs on the beach, growls at Joyce.

"Dawn, you can join the others. Next!"

Joyce points to an area where there are treats lying on the ground.

"Walk past the treats, he is not allowed to sniff or eat."

Lauren and Tommy walk over the treats, Tommy stops, sniffs, "Tommy come!"

Tommy listens and walks past the treats.

Lauren sighs in relief, walks back to the group and waits for everyone to finish their test.

"All done! A Therapy Dog has an outstanding character and it

looks like we got ourselves a new Therapy Dog all the way from India! Congratulations! Your dog will become an excellent Therapy Dog!"
She shakes Lauren's hand and Tommy's paw. Next up is Gucci.
"Sorry Dawn, you didn't make it this time either. Maybe join us for the agility class on Tuesdays?"
Dawn walks away, dragging Gucci on the leash.
"And then we have Mary and Chilli, well done, you two, congratulations!"
Lauren picks up Tommy, hugs him, thanks the judge and walks away. She carries all of twenty-eight pounds of the first Indian Native dog to ever become an American Therapy Dog. The shift in Lauren's life is so apparent right now, everything has changed, and maybe it's enough like this. Maybe for a while it's OK to stay in one place and change the world one dog at the time.

• • •

"I got your favourite food".
The whole car smells of curry and Lauren is singing along some Indian tune on "Radio Krishna – the real voice of L.A."
She keeps looking at me and pats me on the head as she drives.
We head towards the dog beach, park and the bag that smells of curry and me get out of the car. As we reach the beach she takes the leash off and I run down to the sea. The tide is out and I run as fast as I can along the water, my paws love the sand just below the surface, it's so soft and the sand is compact enough to catch some speed and chase all the sea gulls away, way out to sea.
Some other dogs run along with me, but none are as fast as I am. I run and run, is there anything in this world that's as much fun as being on a beach? I slow down and feel hungry. It's been a long day and all those exercises I had to do left me tired.
I look for her, where is she? Did I lose her again? Then I see her, at distance kneeling down, opening her arms, it's our sign, so that I know how to recognise her.
I run towards her as fast as I can and she is calling me, laughing. I run into her and make her fall on the sand, run around her and tug at her hair. She starts chasing me and I run off again, until we find a place where she puts down a blanket, and gets the food out.

She makes one plate of curry for me, with my favourite chicken and rice, and one for her, with her boring vegetables that I don't like.

We eat and look at people and other dogs walk by.

I growl at them letting them know no one comes near my food and my human.

Then we lie next to each other and she keeps telling me what a good dog I am and how proud she is of me.

I close my eyes and think of what a lucky dog I am, because I have three mothers.

One is my Dog Mother; she is proud of me too. She was the most beautiful dog in all of Goa and she was free, and wanted me to be free too. But my life is so different from hers, I didn't grow up in the countryside and I never learnt to hunt frogs and mice. Her pain when she died will always stay with me, and her kindness to me has made me what I am today.

She still keeps an eye on me, some nights she wakes me up, and I look up to her, and in her silent world of dogs that are no longer with us, she whispers words of wisdom and makes sure that I will survive and be a good dog. She still nags at me about this and that, and then I growl, to let her know that I can manage very well, thank you. I am a big boy now. My second mother is Garati, the first human I met, and she was the one who taught me how to know what a good human is. The first thing I saw when I opened my eyes was her eyes, looking straight into mine, and then she was holding me against her neck. I remember her smell from when I was very small, when she used to hold me and sing to me. She used to let me chew on her dark hair that smelled of coconut. I remember everything about her, the horrible night my siblings died and her hands lifting me out of the mud when I was drowning. How sad she used to be and when she cried I would always try to tell her that things will change, will get better. And they did.

My third mother is the one lying next to me right now, and I always make sure that she will never leave me again. She has also been very sad and but now she is doing better. She talks to me and asks me questions. What do I want? I want to be everywhere, know everything and give love to people. And chase seagulls and motor bikes! But most of all I don't want anyone dying in front of me again.

I open my eyes again, and look at her. She strokes my forehead, kisses my eyes and says that she is truly blessed for having me in her life and that there is no one in the whole world as beautiful as me.

I close my eyes again and dream myself back to India, to my youth when I was free and trotted along the road all the way into Anjuna along the main road and would stop by the shop and wait for a biscuit from the shop owner, or chase a scooter all the way to Baga, and then run back in the middle of night, avoiding the other dogs and their territories, or humans throwing rocks at me.

I dream of one eyed Jimmy, he was my protector and best friend. How he taught me everything I needed to know and how he looked at me for comfort when he was dying. And Priya, and the treats she used to give me and how she got mad when that stupid son tried to hurt me. I dream of Zorro and the sadness humans can cause. I dream of Monsoon and the slow days of rain and the sandy patch where I grew up.

I reach for my blonde human's face with my paw, touch her chin and make a funny face.

She pinches my back and strokes my belly. The sun is setting and she covers me with a blanket. I love her, and with her I can be all that I am, a proud Indian dog named King Tommy.

She kisses my eyes again and asks me "What are you thinking about?"

"Chasing holy cows" I reply and she smiles.

King Tommy is eight years old now.

We left America and went to live in Europe in 2012, travelling and living in many places and countries.

King Tommy has impressed the world with his accomplishments.

He is a Therapy Dog in the USA and also in the UK.

He is an Obedience competition winner and a Rally-O winner.

He is an American Canine Good Citizen and a Canine Good Citizen in the UK.

He has done amazing work as a Therapy Dog in the USA, Italy, France and the UK, specializing in adults and children with autism that are afraid of dogs.

He has won the title Best Rescue Dog several times, won Best Cross breed and Most Handsome Dog. He is Best in Show.

In 2016 he qualified for Scruffts, the biggest Cross breed competition in the UK in the category Most Handsome Dog.

For the semi-finals we travelled to London with a journalist and with all my friends and a TV crew following us. King Tommy won again!

He is officially the Most Handsome Crossbreed dog in the UK 2016.

I was crying and picked up the King in my arms, ran around the whole show ring with him and cried again! What an amazing day for this small dog with a big heart.

At the time of printing we are anxiously waiting to go to the finals in March 2017 – King Tommy will battle it out with the other five finalists for the Scruffts Crossbreed Family Dog of the Year at Crufts.

It will be the first time a dog from India is invited to Crufts.

He is also featured in a documentary for Channel Four about Scruffts, airing March 2017.

King Tommy is the ambassador of the Indian Native Dogs and has been featured in magazines and newspapers in many countries encouraging people to help and adopt the beautiful but often neglected Indian dogs.

To me, he is a hero every day, giving love and still being the free spirit he was meant to be.

He is my best friend and it's a privilege to be a part of his life.

I wish him many more years to live and many more adventures to come.

Monique G Nerman